HEARTLAND

ANA SIMO

HEARTLAND

RESTLESS BOOKS
BROOKLYN, NEW YORK

First Restless Books paperback edition January 2018

Paperback ISBN: 9781632061508
Library of Congress Control Number: 2017944633

Cover design by Na Kim
Set in Garibaldi by Tetragon, London

Printed in Canada

1 3 5 7 9 10 8 6 4 2

Restless Books, Inc.
232 3rd Street, Suite A111
Brooklyn, NY 11215

www.restlessbooks.com
publisher@restlessbooks.com

HEARTLAND

1

Blue Ribbon

IT ALL BEGAN in the summer of 1976 when I won the Blue Ribbon at Elmira County's Junior Progymnasmata with "Benbassa," an inadvertently anti-Semitic fable. In the first of a long series of obfuscations about my person, I pretended to be fifteen to qualify for the contest, when I was just eleven years, seven months, three days and seventeen hours old. At the time I composed "Benbassa," I didn't know any Jews, unless one counted the sweltering Rafael Cohen, which no one did, including him. That didn't keep me from declaiming about The Jew: then, as now, I thought that ignorance about a subject is a rhetorician's ideal state, an inoculation against false certainties. These I confined to the quickly dispatched, clichéd tale: the miserly moneylender Benbassa is stabbed to death in a dark alley of Constantinople's Galata by one of his desperate debtors who steals his gold; the murderer, who does not know that the man he has killed is Benbassa, then rushes to the miser's home to repay his debt. (There was a great deal of gore and mistaken identities in my youthful stories.) The fable's heuristic meat, however, was Benbassa's duplicitous essence and his transcendent love of gold for gold's sake. Benbassa, the spiritual voluptuary, the absolute un-Elmiran alien, was me and I was him, as I scribbled on the kitchen table while my parents gurgled discreetly in their bedroom like oversexed carps in a stagnant pond.

Like Benbassa, I hoarded coins for spiritual pleasure and pretended obedience and ignorance in front of the adults, whom I secretly despised. I didn't doubt having been spawned by my parents—they and the Cohens were the only spics in Elmira County at the time of my birth—but I was convinced I was a superior mutant. My parents and the Cohens were valiant, yet imperfect prototypes. As for the native white Elmirans who lorded over us from their superior heights, eleven inches above our heads on average, they were rejects from the Creator's Divine Workshop. We feared and pitied the ugly, stupid, powerful giants. We humored them. They owned our bodies but not our minds. We kept this a secret. Thus, I knew my Benbassa inside out, like Dostoyevsky his Stavrogin, and Walt his ersatz Jew disguised as a Scottish duck. Benbassa was the Jew in me. His final punishment was also mine, a case of precocious fatalism disguised as morality: Truth will not set you free.

"Benbassa" was the first, and last, piece I enjoyed composing.

Writing made me want to puke. My mind festered with trivia, a writer's raw sewage, but I had nothing to say. I didn't find people or animals appetizing, so training on them a writer's carnivorous eyes did nothing but repulse me. Nevertheless, I dared not contradict my post-Blue Ribbon reputation as a budding rhetorician because I had nothing better to do with my life: I was just a girl, brown, short, ugly, and poor, and had vowed, at age seven, never to marry some hairy, simian male. Since a precocious Blue Ribbon goes a long way in a small, fastidiously self-important county seat like Elmira, my fate was sealed. For the next four decades, I went through daily, monthly, or bi-annual writing ablutions. If those hygienic exercises were too frequent, I'd gag and faint; if too infrequent, I'd lie sleepless at night, afraid to die if I shut my eyes, and slink about in the daytime, feeling bloated and wormy with words. Every few years, I'd manage to squeeze out a tiny turd.

Why didn't I quit when I still had time to become someone else—a gardener like my father, a maid like my mother, a janitor like Rafael Cohen's father, Ezequiel? I spent many a sleepless night peering in vain into the Blue Ribbon thicket, pondering the mysteries of my lifelong inertia. As I curl now in this dusty crack under someone else's deathbed, I can see it all clearly: I was born again that broiling August afternoon at the Elmira County Fair when the Blue Ribbon was pinned above my toilet-paper-stuffed bra, gluing writer skin onto birth skin amidst the award-winning cows so that any future attempt to peel it off would expose raw, pulsing flesh and result in a horrible death. A second rebirth was needed to escape the Curse. Yes, I see that now, in my inhuman clarity, but not when I still had bones, flesh, blood, hair—not even in my last fully human minutes.

So I drifted, clueless, in the arms of inertia and wishful thinking through early, middle, and late youth. For seventeen years in New York City, where I had arrived on foot in 1984, one of millions fleeing starvation in the heartland, I supported my writing curse with menial jobs (Resettlement Camp dishwasher, rat exterminator, public toilet cleaner, fetus disposal associate) and, after Reconstruction, with the greasy crumbs thrown once more to "minority rhetoricians." Small triumphs buoyed my life raft, providing an illusion of movement. In 1992, I published a eulogy of the forgotten zoological epic *Catomyomachia* in *The Seal*, the University of Laredo quarterly. In 1995, my most prolific year, I wrote two fables for the journal *Basileus*, one of which ended up in a homo-bestial anthology that was reviewed in *The New York Times*. That was my one flirtation with fame, although neither my story nor my name was mentioned in the review, given that my writing lacked sex, AIDS, and the compulsory people-of-color winks.

After a long drought, during which I got unfashionably addicted to Seconal, I hustled one of those spics-only-need-apply welfare stipends to write a biography of one Teodora Comenia del Castillo (1820–1877), reputedly the first Hispanic [sic] woman to write a novel in English. It was a laughable yarn and Teodora was a picayune prig, ever lamenting her hacienda and maids lost to the barbarians from the North, but the welfare money was irresistible. The best part was that I didn't have to write a word until I finished researching the subject, something that, given its obscurity, could take several centuries. Those were the happiest years of my life (2001–2011). I did nothing but eat, drink, fuck, sleep, fall deliriously in love, once (Oh Bebe, why?), and, in the glorious year 2001, cop some snowflakes for breakfast from the mounds that Zoë, my tranny Pre-Raphaelite roommate, left every night on the kitchen table, along with the business cards of her dazzled providers, corporat- ist America's most exalted retainers. Every morning, during this breakfast of champions, I dreamt of blackmail, but innate sloth and virtuous shock—The names I saw! The immaculate blond wives and children I imagined!—kept me from acting. I've kicked myself ever since for having lost the only opportunity I ever had to earn big bucks and still feel morally superior.

We both slept through 9/11, Zoë and I, after an early dawn snow binge. When we woke up, well past midnight, her cell phone was clogged with the cries and sobs of the haute corporatist dead and survivors. One man begged her as he died to rush to his midtown office before his wife got there and remove an Altoids can filled with smack from the top drawer of his desk. His secretary would help. Others, the dying and the survivors confounded, wanted to see her, touch her, smell her, fuck her, snow-dive with her. Right now. I escorted Zoë on her nocturnal mercy rounds from the Pierre to the St. Regis, and from the Waldorf to the Carlyle. On that Luciferian night, hotels were the last havens of civility in Manhattan. Only inside their well-ventilated bars could you unclog your nostrils of the stench of tire-collar death that permeated the island. Corporatist offices, where Zoë conducted much of her business, had turned into armed camps.

The next day I removed the Altoids can from the dead man's desk. Zoë was too frightened to go. His secretary tried to stop me until I threatened to tell the wife about her lunchtime quickies with the incinerated boss atop that very same desk. On my way out, she asked for a pinch of *dama blanca* and I gave her two out of pity for her anorexic ass and plastic ballooning boobs. Zoë soon moved to Constantinople with a Pentagon arms dealer, old both in age and in length of acquaintance, two handicaps more than offset by the size of his Lazard account. I haven't heard from her since, nor have I missed her. Like most people I have crossed, she belongs strictly to a time and place, and like most she had the courtesy to remain there, gracefully, thus allowing for fond memories. The rest of that year and into the next, I stapled on the back of Zoë's corporatist cards the edifying profiles of the 9/11 dead that were published in the *Times*. Like a still life's open-mouthed fish setting off plums, fowl, and skull on a large tray, the mellifluous, overflowing newsprint contrasted with Zoë's laconic verdict ("sdfa": "shrunken dick, fab apartment") and the dead man's engraved military-industrial power (GEN-CEO, ADM-COO, LTG-CFO). It would be fitting to have those corporatist vanitas with me now under this ultimate bed.

On January 6, 2012, the federal welfare bosses abruptly demanded to see the Teodora manuscript. Even if unfinished, even if just a draft of the first draft, even if just notes. Longhand is fine, too, exclaimed a Miss Sally Hume on the phone from Washington, D.C., sharpening her "fiiiine" into a curare-poisoned arrow. A lachrymose letter from the über-spic Executive Director followed. He was terrified that Hume's low opinion of me would tar all other Latinos [sic], including him. Like my mother, he yelped about my betrayal of him, thus shame to the race. That the honkie Hume was his subordinate only frightened him more.

I had no bone left to throw them. Cuntess Hume had specifically nixed any new progress reports of the kind I had masterly conjured for a decade. All payments were suspended. I was threatened with jail unless I returned the welfare money "in its entirety," or sent Hume the Teodora book. After my phone, gas, and electricity were cut off, and all I had left to eat were camping stove-cooked oatmeal and elbow macaroni, I was forced to sit down and write the first sentence, about Teodora's birth in a Laredo, Texas hacienda during a snowstorm. I was suspicious when my first writing day ended and I hadn't gagged or fainted, then creepingly hopeful when a second and third day—then a week, two weeks, a month!—went by without major incident. I was cured, I thought. Vera, my fuckbuddy at the time, mistook my giddiness for cheating and had me followed by a matrimonial P. I. She confessed to me after wasting $500 she didn't have. Thrilled with my cure, I postponed her punishment. I dumped her at the next New Year's Eve party. Her lack of faith deserved maximum pain.

That summer, fleeing Hume's nasty letters, I hid out in a pay-what-you-can arts camp in an obscure knuckle of the Finger Lakes. It was so obscure that it had escaped the locust-like destruction of the Great Hunger migration years, the Reconstruction's pharaonic zeal and now the attention of bloodthirsty, marauding gangs. Forest, lake, cottages, workshops, barns, main refectory, even the premonitory helicoidal evergreen labyrinth in the middle of an Italianate garden, were exactly as left by the Utopian commune that flourished there in the 1860s. Their sepia pictures—bearded men fanning themselves with their hats, stocky matrons in white perpetually sewing, knitting, and embroidering, golden-haired children, laughing at the enchanted future—looked at us reproachfully from the refectory walls. Everything went swimmingly at first, both at my writing desk in the morning and during my afternoon walks, which were timed to watch the local twelve-year-old girls, mysterious in their final days before their carnality overflowed, play polo by the nearby McDonald's.

One morning, as I was rewriting the section in chapter three in which young Teodora displays her fondness for Zebu cows, I discovered that I had left out all conjunctions. I checked everything that I had written so far, and found no conjunctions anywhere. Was it a computer glitch or . . . ? A shiver went down my spine, but I controlled myself. My equanimity was not grounded in character, but in my addiction to the little girls' knees sweating against the ponies' palpitating fur, which I was in danger of missing if I didn't get a move on.

The next morning, after getting lost in the labyrinth and then, suddenly, finding my way out, I decided to insert all the missing conjunctions. I couldn't. My hands shook, my fingers cramped, my eyes twitched, I was covered in cold sweat. I had to stop and lie down on my cottage's rough oak floor planks, fearing the onset of epilepsy, Parkinson's, or worse. That evening I tried again—my knees gave out and I fell to the ground, unable to move for several hours. At dawn I took the first armored milk truck back to the city. Lower Manhattan was a foul furnace teeming with rats even at noon. I was immediately sorry I had returned. Obviously, I had overreacted. At my corner's public laundry, I traded with a beggar two potatoes stolen from the art camp kitchen for a used Chinese battery-powered fan. Sitting in front of it, all windows shut to keep noise and rats out, I resumed my writing, sans the conjunctions. I imagined Miss Hume inserting conjunctions late into the night after the rest of the office had gone home. By the end of the week, this image had evolved into a delectable fantasy featuring Hume, whom I had never seen, naked from the waist down on all fours (rear view), typing each of my lost conjunctions with one finger. It was a singularly gratifying week. On the Monday after, however, I found I was also leaving out all prepositions.

This time I noticed it immediately. Since the conjunctions discovery, I was on the alert. An attempt to put back the prepositions ended with profuse vomiting and a bout of sciatica. I lost adverbs next. All of them ending in "ly" were the first to go, followed by those ending just in "y." Then all pronouns fled, except "it," which I still have. I tried writing simple sentences in French, Spanish, and Elmira High School's miserable Byzantine Greek, and there too I lost the ability to write conjunctions, then prepositions, then adverbs, and finally pronouns in those languages: each vanished simultaneously from the language loci in my brain. I had no trouble speaking, though. My lapses, or is it lacunae, were restricted to written language. An autopsy of my brain may hold some surprises for science, but the humanitarian whiff of brain donation led me to evade the Central Registry. Safe to say that not much brain matter is left in me now.

I abandoned the Teodora biography in the spring of 2014, thirteen years after I had officially taken up the project. Writing, always repulsive, had become such a ruinous business that no welfare handout or jail threat could put it in the black. My indecent Hume fantasies notwithstanding, I had to hire two dimwitted female NYU graduate students (a quadruple redundancy) to stick in what I left out. Every Friday night, I paid them in speed mixed with pink toilet-scouring powder. In exchange, they took my dictation of the missing words. Oh, they were efficient and vapidly deferential. They saw a spic lady who could be their mother and had no idea what I could do to them in my mind if I wanted to, which I didn't. I had to tolerate their clean, perky, blond and brunette presences in my midgetty, candlelit one-bedroom. One did have a way of slanting her eyes and touching her cheek with the fingers of her right hand that always gave me pause, but it was a prelude to nothing: an invisible windshield wiper would quickly wipe from her face any fleeting promise of lust. I had to lie to Perky and Clean: I told them that I was writing in a shorthand of my invention. Although obfuscation and delusion are second nature to me, outright lying is an intolerable strain, second only to writing. I disliked P. & C. for making me lie, and, aware that my dislike was unfair and irrational, I disliked them even more. In the end, I had to let them go because I was starving. I needed hard cash for my speed, not lost words. I tried to put back the diabolical conjunctions myself—prepositions, adverbs, and pronouns, one at a time, sitting in my own feces and vomit—but the effort must have broken my last intact synapses: one sunny Sunday morning, after an early spring snowstorm, I lost verbs, and, at dusk, I was unable to write nouns. I had sunk to the bottom of the swamp.

I sat in a corner for the next two days, pissing and shitting myself. On the third day, I accidentally stuck a wet finger into an outlet. It was inexplicably live. The shock slammed me against the wall. When I came to, my guts were in perfect working order and I was crackling with energy and determination. I scooped, disinfected, scrubbed, aired, showered, and finally called Miss Hume from a payphone impersonating my poor (dead) mother. My daughter had been aboard the ferry that was blown up this morning while crossing the Bosphorus at Eminönü, I croaked. She was now at a military field hospital on the European side of Constantinople with burns on 70 percent of her body. Hume was unimpressed. She demanded the Teodora bio or her money back, but I thickened my mother's Spanish accent and pretended not to understand, unctuously thanking her for wishing my charred daughter a speedy recovery. I then punched all the phone keys at once while yelling *"Oigo, oigo, oigo!"* and hung up on the bitch. Next, I methodically covered my tracks. To my landlord, and the world, I was leaving for Constantinople on a charity mission and subletting for three years to Dr. Petra Xin Hua Wu, a reclusive, retired Fujianese math professor. Dr. Wu put her name on my door, mailbox, and cell phone account, and returned Hume's undoubtedly irate letters with a bold "Addressee Unknown." By then, I had dumped my girlfriend du jour, an unemployed tax collector—she was getting fat and had acquired two hamsters in a city that didn't need any more rodents—and had bid goodbye to my few acquaintances (I had no friends).

Holed up in my apartment, I prayed that I would outlast Hume's vengeful interest in me. Only in the dead of night did I venture out, hunched under Dr. Wu's black wig, sepulchral makeup, and padded Fujianese overcoat. Now that all writing and related furniture and paraphernalia had been removed to the basement, the apartment felt airy, almost palatial. For a while, I felt light and soft—dare I say happy? I wish I could have held on to it. But always one to poke a rabid dog, I was soon back in my natural ruminative state, aggravated by New York City's traditional summer sewage floods, an onslaught of rats expertly swimming through the filth produced by twenty million eating and shitting souls.

I considered my predicament. Was a writer who could not write due to a mysterious brain disturbance still a writer, or was I finally off the diabolical hook? I had first wondered about this as an adolescent, puke dribbling, chin resting on the toilet bowl. Conscience smirked, not even bothering to voice its opinion of the shirking, cowardly creature that spent more time worshipping the porcelain god than at the writing table. Forty years of self-flaying had followed. The question, which now appeared before me written in fiery tongues, carried the added pathos of medical mystery; and with it, a promise of absolution. "My brain does not have the capacity to write," I murmured humbly. "Please, take back your poisoned chalice!" I pleaded, to no one in particular. The fiery tongues flickered and vanished. I knew what that meant. The door had been slammed shut in my face.

It was night when I woke up, sweaty and angry. I resolved to become my own master, or kill myself. I gave myself seven days. The first step was to find an exit strategy. I stayed up all night, but nothing came to mind and there was no one, or nothing, to ask— no books, computer, TV, cellphone, or radio. Dawn broke out in a rumble of sewage-pumping trucks. I crawled into bed. It was then that I saw an ancient Yellow Pages half hidden under the night table, where it had escaped the purge. I sat on the bed and opened it to the letter A, hoping that a word would jump out and point me toward freedom. I purred, chanted, and caressed the brittle pages from A to B to C, begging them to tell me what to do. By the time I got to J, I was tearing them out and flinging paper balls into a dark corner of the room to punish their muteness. My heart was in my mouth, a cliché courtesy of my grandmother, whose ashes (if they were indeed hers—no one knows what goes on in crematoria these days), in her Elmira grave, must have been rolling with laughter at my plight; she, who never doubted her own centenarian self for a second. My heart was in full gallop against my front teeth by the time I turned to K and something shot out like a comet's tail. It was the Word, shining, winged, barbaric: Kill. I knew immediately it wasn't me I was to kill, but someone else. Who? "Whoever made you waste your life," Grandma reverberated dustily from her grave.

The scales suddenly fell from my eyes. It wasn't my fault! Someone else was to blame. Killing that someone would liberate me. Who could it be? Both of my parents were dead. I had no pets or children. I scrupulously did not keep up with ex-girlfriends, all of whom I had dumped—if anything, they were the ones entitled to revenge. Still searching, I fell asleep. Knowing what I had to do, even if not yet to whom, made me feel serene.

At noon the next day, twelve hours after the Revelation of the Word, on the first day of my seven-day plan, I dared to walk in plain daylight to the corner mailbox to return Hume's latest ultimatum. As I was letting go of the mailbox slot, I saw Mercy McCabe lumbering toward me. She was grinning and waving, her fat ass tightly packed into those hideous Moschino leather pants favored by SoHo art merchants (in August!), her left hand clutching a congenitally ridiculous Hermès handbag, her mustardy hair, milky-freckled complexion, and pugnacious upturned nose buffed to a shiny finish under the sun. Did she know it was me under the Dr. Petra Xin Hua Wu accoutrements, or did she mistake me for one of her rich Oriental art collectors? "I got news for you," she whispered, lowering her hulking frame over my head. I was cornered. Her tiny blue eyes that locked on mine left no doubt that she knew that I was I. "Bebe and I just broke up," she said, gleefully watching my jaw freeze, and sweat and tears begin to stream down my Dr. Wu whiteface. As I fled from her, stumbling on trashcans, scraping my knees, and losing Dr. Wu's left slipper, I could hear her guffaw and yelp her contempt.

When I came to, late that afternoon, I was sprawled in my kitchen with Dr. Wu's robe stuck to my flayed, bloody knees. As I ripped it off, removing chunks of flesh, I yelled, "Not fair!" It wasn't fair that Bebe and Mercy McCabe had broken up after a decade together. It was monstrous. Ten years ago, Bebe had chosen Mercy McCabe over me, after a long and ferocious contest. As she disentangled her golden curls in front of a gilded, antique trifold vanity mirror—a McCabe gift, I later learned—Bebe, my unrequited child concubine, love of my loveless, licentious life, Bebe who sang every night in the filthiest male sex dive in town and reduced men to tears, Bebe, whose piercing, questioning, tactile gaze turned me inside out, Bebe explained her inconceivable choice to me by declaring, with the little-girl deadpan she reserved for such cruel occasions, that McCabe was permanent mate material, whereas I was not. Pressed by me to explain further, she stated that: A) I was poor and bound to get poorer, while McCabe was rich and getting richer; B) "I don't trust you." Point A plunged me into a metaphysical vertigo from which I never recovered: Why was I born with expensive tastes and no money? And, shouldn't civilization trump tasteless cash? McCabe couldn't even hold a fork in her paws! Point B was a great injustice. Me, not trustworthy? Me, the devoted, head-over-heels, adoring servant? The courageous, passionate, yet respectful, literate, and loyal best friend, denied even a private glimpse of Bebe's scrumptious body, but iron-willed enough to listen kindly, without batting a jealous eyelash, to her torturing account of how she allowed herself to be narcotized and lewdly pawed and sodomized by two dyke artistes the night before (when she had, by the way, stood me up) while posing in the nude for a bogus dyke fertility handbook?

I secretly raged and suffered for the next three years, while publicly indulging in non-stop dissipation and excess, before Bebe and McCabe's well-publicized conjugal harmony slowly began to heal the open wound. With every anniversary, the wisdom of Bebe's choice became clearer to me. It soothed me to picture the two of them dying of old age in each other's arms. Now, their break-up made a mockery of everything I had endured: rejection, suffering, forgiving (kind of), and, finally, forgetting. Bebe was back in my mind, more alluring and tyrannical than ever. And so was McCabe, once more a filthy swine after a decade's promotion to virtuous, bovine spouse. McCabe: my nemesis, my torturer. It was all her fault. I decided to kill her.

2

Prospecting

WE MET at her favorite Upper West Side brasserie, known for its brutal security guards and its chewy croissants reverently served amidst the vertiginous Gigi set décor. The head Janissary himself, stun baton in hand, escorted me to McCabe's table.

McCabe was hulking (six foot two, 260 pounds) and, this morning, sentimental. The malicious bully who had pinned me to the corner mailbox had metamorphosed into a maudlin lapdog. Bebe had finally gotten to her. When I arrived, McCabe was staring into her coffee, gripping the tiny cup with both enormous hands, in Hopperesque pathos, carefully contrived, no doubt, yet subverted by the cloying Belle Époque wallpaper. Her nose was red and tiny beads of water gathered around her nostrils, either from the coffee steam or from past tears. The mediocrity of her pain enraged me. Was that all the suffering she could offer Bebe? McCabe, the unworthy rival, the putrid usurper. "I think Bebe has made a big mistake," I said, patting her wurstish arm. "She'll be sorry the rest of her life." McCabe looked up slowly at me. Her face burned with supernatural hatred, an ecstatic Saint Jerome in reverse. I froze under my Dr. Wu mask: I've been found! She'll yell, *You hypocrite!* and smash my face. Instead, she said, "That is exactly how I feel," each word rolling icily off her tongue.

McCabe delicately put her empty coffee cup on the table. Two waiters scrambled to refill it, but she dismissed them with a tiny flick of her right index finger. Hatred made her skin glow. It slowed her movements and distilled her gestures. The voluble hog became a surgeon of souls. She explained to me with actuarial precision why Bebe would be the loser in the long run. Counting with her fingers, thumb first, jaw locked, until there were no fingers left, she demolished every imaginable reason Bebe could have had to leave her. Money, sex, fame, success, even love? Bebe had heaps of them, all of McCabean origin or instigation. Jealousy? Boredom? Spiritual awakening? Nah. Therefore Bebe had left for No Reason at All, and her senseless act would bring her eternal regret when she realized what she had done. "I'll suffer; but she'll repent," McCabe snarled. Then she put her forehead on the table and began to sob.

I staggered back home in a daze, on foot, oblivious to the dangers of fortified checkpoints and security corridors, and the even greater danger of stepping outside of them. My Fujianese habit must have protected me. (Aren't they the city's new royalty, after all?) I got home in one piece. The world, already upside down, had been tossed up again. Underneath McCabe's simplistic exterior there lay a viperous eighth stomach.

O dykes, o mores! It has been more than four decades since I tasted my first, and I cannot say I understand them, or myself, any better. Neither have those old questions, in any of their multifaceted aspects, ever been unequivocally answered: Who is she? What is she?

3

Execution

THAT NIGHT I DREAMT that Bebe and I were strolling through Round Hill, Elmira's tony neighborhood. I wanted to leave before someone called the watchmen on us—the occasional Round Hill sidewalk being just for show—but Bebe had to stop in front of every other mansion to comment on its size. She was barefooted, which further slowed our progress. She was scandalized that houses shrunk as you went up Round Hill, violating traditional real-estate dogma. "How come the smaller ones have the best views?" I explained that Round Hill had been built from the top down between 1916 and 1929 by Midwestern wheat and railroad millionaires. Each new house surpassed in size and magnificence the one above on the gently winding road. The last house to go up right before the Black Friday crash was a sixty-thousand-square-foot replica of the palace of Porphyrogenitus, wrapped around the lower rung of the hill. It was ten times bigger than Judge Wilkerson's amiable Prairie Style house, the first one built (by an early Wright disciple), which sat in a meadow at the top of the hill. "I think I could live here with you," Bebe said, embracing all of Round Hill with a sweep of her long, sinewy dancer's arms. She was wearing a sheer Nile-green sundress that uncovered her succulent shoulder blades. I felt salaciously warm inside. Money and (in her eyes) trustworthiness were beyond my grasp, but not Round Hill. I had deep, if vicarious, roots in Round Hill: my mother had been a maid, and my father a gardener at the architectural holiest of holies, Judge Wilkerson's house. I had practically grown up there. I didn't tell Bebe, though. Scoring a point in secret was sweeter: knowing I could satisfy at least one of her conditions if I wanted. In a retroactive, imaginary way, of course: but wasn't that the only way?

The next morning I couldn't get Judge Wilkerson's house out of my mind. There it was every time I closed my eyes. And there was Bebe too, luminescent in her green sundress, pointing at the chimney, the massive kitchen table, or the lion-claw tub, with a sly realtor grin. Bebe, who in real life, or what passes for it, had never even heard about this house. I tried to erase her from the picture, but she wouldn't budge. Her sharply curved talons had sunk into my brain, again. So, I gave in to her, as I always had when I was still her slave. I shut my eyes and let her take me through the house, from the formal parlor to the attic. It was a silent slide show, all sepia except for Bebe's green dress. It ended with Bebe dialing the Judge's black Bakelite phone.

I obeyed her inescapable command. After a dozen calls, I found out that the Judge, a childless widower, had died three months earlier. A gaggle of grandnephews had agreed to rent out the house while their lawyers fought over the carrion. I lit a candle to Bebe for pointing The Way. Later that day, I called McCabe at her eponymous SoHo gallery and asked her to travel with me to Elmira. It would be curative. Elmira was so deep in the barren heartland that Bebe's emanations would not reach her there. It took me two lachrymose breakfasts at Gigi's, avidly followed by the officially indifferent waitresses, to persuade McCabe that a retreat to Elmira was the only way she could avoid Bebe-induced mental collapse, and its concomitant financial ruin. (Had she not lost a multimillion Cy Twombly mosaic sale just yesterday by bursting into tears and calling the prospective buyer "a cheap hoodoo"?)

In the end, McCabe left her gallery in the hands of her able fag assistant and we flew to Elmira on a cloudless late August morning. Having shed Dr. Wu in the airport lavatory, I was now traveling as McCabe's spic maid. Before leaving on a lecture tour of China, the good doctor had bribed the super into returning Hume's menacing letters.

McCabe first wanted to rent "a palatial sixteen-room neo-Cappadocian villa carved on the rock at lower Round Hill, chock-full of extras, including Jacuzzi, sauna, indoor pool, home theater, billiards room, and a replica of the famous porphyry fountain that still graces the gardens of Emperor Theophilus's summer retreat." I counseled modesty, describing how Elmirans of old used to tar and feather—and occasionally torch alive—Yankee carpetbaggers. After much resistance, she broke down and reluctantly took the Judge's house.

Most of the old mansions on upper Round Hill were now empty, cared for by a discreet army of cleaners and watchmen. Their owners had fled during the Great Hunger and these days only returned for Fourth of July picnics and the occasional June wedding. But they still controlled the town and, with others like them, what remained of the countryside. However distant, their inbred disdain triggered old anxieties. That theirs or anyone else's disdain would have rolled off McCabe's thick back was an added indignity. So I decided to trot out the historical record to make an impression on her. Why I wanted the Judge's house I kept to myself: in my dreams, it always appeared as my childhood home. I knew every corner of the house from tagging along behind my mother as she waxed the floors, polished the Judge's oak furniture, and painstakingly dusted the locked glass cabinet that held the Baccarat punch set and the icon of the Annunciation. As I got older, I was allowed to approach the cabinet, but not to touch it. The fourteenth-century icon was brittle and resented the heat and humidity of the human body, the Judge had told my mother, giving her the only copy of the tiny cabinet key that he always wore on a chain around his neck. He taught her how to read the hydrometer inside the cabinet three times a day and to adjust the humidity-control device. And she taught me—theoretically, because I was to keep my hands in my pockets. The Virgin's terror at the muscular, winged female lunging at her knocked me out cold the first time I got close. After that I trained myself to resist her contaminating panic, focusing one month on her raised hand, then another month on the folds of her black mourning robe, until one day I felt strong enough to stare again at her terrified face. This time I managed to keep standing.

None of this I ever told McCabe, whom I distrusted not only on principle as my future victim, but because of certain revealing facts: in contrast to the fight she put up to rent the neo-Cappadocian villa, getting McCabe to agree that I'd officially be known as her maid was uncomfortably easy. "Groovy," was all she said, as she strode down West Broadway and I trotted behind, explaining to her deaf ears that the maid conceit would allow me to remain incognito from my meddlesome (nonexistent) Elmiran relatives.

The Judge's house was as I remembered it. McCabe took over the master bedroom that occupied the entire upper floor, while I settled in the Judge's study on the ground floor. I never went upstairs: I didn't want to encourage needless intimacy. Within days of our arrival, McCabe's existential pendulum began to swing back from maudlin sop to bully. She stopped wearing sunglasses at all times. The skin around her eyes looked less and less like macerated meat. She was still crying a little at night—her eyes looked puffy and pink in the mornings—but she was definitely on her way up. Her porcine blue eyes had begun to dart about the house and the garden, looking for something to do, or say. She even looked heftier. I kept out of her way. In recovery, McCabe was even less appetizing than in pain.

Downstairs was my empire: the Judge's study with its dark icon was the heart; the expansive dining room, the lungs; the ascetic parlor guarding the Wright chairs, the brains; the vestibule with the faience cane holder still harboring the Judge's boar-headed walking stick, the face, which one day would be unveiled to the world, when its features finally became clearer. Kitchen and pantry, with functioning dumbwaiter, were in the sub-basement, which had a separate entrance. I hired Petrona, newly arrived from Zacatecas, Mexico, with little English (an essential requisite) but glowing recommendations from an Anatolian expatriate family, to come every afternoon, Monday through Saturday, and cook a light lunch for McCabe and dinner for two, wash and iron McCabe's clothes, and clean upstairs—but not anywhere near McCabe's room. I took care of the ground floor and the garden as devoutly as my parents had before me. To Petrona, I was Señora Mirtila (not my real name), Señorita Maké's housekeeper. I spoke to her the barest minimum, always in soulless Voice of America Spanish, so that she could not place me geographically.

I ordered for Señora Mirtila the best cleaning, scouring, and polishing products from New York's Hammacher Schlemmer—the ones my mother longed for but never got from the penny-pinching Judge, the ones in the catalogues she rescued from the Judge's wastebasket and studied at night on our kitchen table. The gargantuan crate arrived, as planned, one afternoon while McCabe was out for her constitutional. I had the crate placed in the middle of the Judge's studio. Plunging my hands in the packing straw, pulling out the Dutch floor beeswax and the Belgian chamois, I felt like the Magi, who upon finding the unexpected plumpness in the manger, were voluptuously and insatiably hungry.

The days flowed agreeably. I would wake up at eight o'clock and work in the garden until noon, when McCabe began stirring in bed and Petrona would arrive. After giving Petrona the instructions for the day, I would abandon myself to the pleasures of cleaning and polishing the Judge's possessions until dinner. I developed a system. Mondays were for porcelain and faience; Tuesdays for furniture; Wednesdays for wooden floors, wainscoting and other woodwork details; Thursdays for clocks and assorted metal items like the Judge's penholders and letter openers; Fridays for silverware, and Saturdays for glass. Sundays, I plotted McCabe's death.

Three times a day I checked the hydrometer and adjusted the relative-humidity device, averting my eyes from the Annunciation icon. Now that I could, I dared not look at it directly, even less touch it. I wore around my neck the Judge's key, discovered in his desk drawer. My mother's key, which she had returned to the Judge before dying, was nowhere to be found.

I saw McCabe only at dinner, which Petrona served at six o'clock, before leaving. Bebe was never mentioned. It had been my therapeutic suggestion, but McCabe's obedient silence should have been a warning to me. McCabe had recovered her natural volubility. She did not converse: she harangued. Her only subject was her own forcefulness, even when she was seemingly talking about something else. News items were her favorite self-launching pads. Half of her sentences began with a rhetorical, "Did you read about . . . " It didn't matter if I had, or not. She would paraphrase the entire article, adding her own explanations and footnotes. At first I'd interrupt her with a sharp, "Yes, I read that," even if I hadn't. "What about this other . . . ?" she'd volley back. Soon I pretended ignorance about the first item proposed, to save us time. McCabe had an unnatural memory for facts, figures, and quotes, and a passionate enthusiasm for regurgitating them at dinnertime. She knew the rules and lore of all sports, including obscure ones like Zorbing. Money, celebrity gossip, horse racing, science, and security trivia were at her fingertips. But it was all about her. Paradoxically, she never talked shop. She warned me early on that her own line of work was off-limits, at the dinner table or at any other place or time. It wasn't necessary, since art galleries, hers in particular, had on me the same vomitive effect as the defunct Macy's fitting rooms. McCabe's only conversational originality was her footnotes, always irrelevant to the issue, as when she linked Inuit whale hunting to America's military decay. However dull her dinner blather, McCabe had started so low in my estimation that just finding out that she read the *Times* and the *Journal* every day from cover to cover (at least in her enforced Elmiran idleness) impressed me against my will. I realize it only now, under this dusty bed, as I try to breathe with what remains of my nose. At the time, her vitality exhausted me.

McCabe was not just fleshy. She was a sweaty, breathing, walking, talking chunk of meat. A big flank steak, reputedly honest and nutritious, but capable of harboring the stringy and the coriaceous. What had Bebe fallen for? Without the discipline of mind to sublimate, explain, and abstract, images from my decade-old cabinet of horrors flashed back whenever my gaze inadvertently wandered to McCabe's flesh: Bebe licking McCabe's drippy cunt in 3D, for example. This happened at the table, when McCabe's statistics and animal vitality had put my brain to sleep, and my unfocused eyes caught a glimpse of her fat thighs as she suddenly stood up to rescue

25

a fork that had flown out of her enthusiastic hand. I always lowered my eyes to my plate while McCabe came to table, or engaged in her cutlery gymnastics, but she was often faster than my reflexes. Bebe and McCabe's blissful matrimony had sealed the repulsive cabinet. I did not want it reopened now. Killing McCabe had to be on pure and moral grounds. Not from herbivorous repulsion. Thus, I struggled with McCabe's flesh at dinnertime as a pious lover would. But not to love better: to hate better, as Justice does, in her rational and calculated way. Besides, McCabe had her subtleties, like all good cuts of meat. Only Justice could do justice to them.

One day, for example, I heard the sound of a mandolin upstairs. Someone was playing "McKinley's March" at finger-breaking speed, either live or recorded. At dinner McCabe asked if the noise bothered me. I said I had not heard anything and waited for more musical information, but she changed the subject. Another day, at dusk, I looked out my window and saw a figure in the distance, by the far hedge, doing triple somersaults. It seemed smaller and more limber than McCabe, but who else could it have been? By the time I returned with the Judge's binoculars, the figure was gone. But all that happened much later, that Fall.

A week after our arrival, I took McCabe on a Sunday stroll through Elmira's derelict Main Street. Reconstruction had been a smashing success in Elmira. All the old shops were boarded up. Scraps of plywood and moldy particleboard had been slapped on by panicky owners who'd been first ravaged by strip malls, then had to flee a barbarian invasion. Only a Chinese takeout remained. A Wal-Mart thirty miles away had sucked dry the last holdouts, the Cantonese cook told us, and was now crushing the one half of Elmira's female population it employed (the other half waiting at home until the Beast called them).

It was a miracle that the town was still hanging on by its grimy fingernails. Except for our state capital, site of the metastasizing National Penal Colony, all other towns in the heartland had been bulldozed years ago to deny shelter and food to the homicidal marauding gangs. An inspired decision: the gangs had migrated west and the countryside was pleasantly empty and pacified.

On the edge of town, I showed McCabe the ruins of the candy store where I got my first lesson in economics: quick butt squeeze, fully clothed = two gummy bears; longer squeeze half-clothed (pants off, but panties on) = four gummy bears; and letting stinky Dwayne slip his hairy hand inside my panties and rub my butt = one Milky Way bar. I didn't tell McCabe anything about Glorita. Not even her name. I'm positive. Glorita got two Milky Way bars for letting Dwayne put his finger flat inside her butt crack. He offered her a bubble soap bottle to let him stick his pinky just a little inside her asshole, but she got scared of his big hands and ran away. Next day I saw Glorita blowing bubbles from her porch. She told me her godmother had bought it for her. I knew she was lying. This was the first time I felt a weight on my forehead and eyelids that made me lower my eyes, which I later discovered was shame. The dictionary, from which I got my sentimental education, told me that shame combined feelings of dishonor, unworthiness, and embarrassment. My shame at Glorita's first lie was purely the shame of dishonor. I neither felt unworthy, nor embarrassed. Like Tirant lo Blanc, I would have killed a ferocious dog with my bare hands to cleanse my honor. But Glorita did not own a dog. Condemned to dishonor, I was freed to sink even lower: I began to watch Glorita from our attic window with a pair of toy binoculars I had stolen from Woolworth's when my grandmother wasn't looking. I kept a log of Glorita's after-school and weekend comings and goings. Soon, there wasn't much

I didn't know about her. It wasn't hard: she lived next door, we were in fourth grade together, and took the same school bus every day.

Glorita had long legs ending in a tight little butt, and a small torso with tiny hard nipples that already showed under her tee shirts. Her skin was the color of light tea with milk, and as soft as my red velvet dress. Everybody always said that she had a very pretty face, a term I despised, perhaps because it was never applied to me (or to any boy, Rafael Cohen once sympathetically pointed out). I thought then that Glorita was ugly, with her big mouth that tasted like plum, slanted hazel eyes, strong nose and frizzy reddish-brown hair. Being near her always made my stomach a little queasy (I didn't know the real meaning of "dangerous" then). Through my toy binoculars, she was at once repellent and fascinating, like the shellacked bees Ezequiel Cohen pinned into his insect collection with color-coded pins: purple for the queen, royal blue for the male consorts, forest green for the workers.

One night I was woken up by a faint squeak coming from next door. By then, I had developed a refined ear: I could tell whether Glorita was trying to sneak in or out of her godmother's house through the kitchen screen door, her bedroom window, the garage, or even the front door. I ran to my window. Glorita was walking through our backyard, shoes in hand. She was wearing her old blue dress from third grade, now too short and too tight for her. "Are you nuts or what?" I whispered, softly so she wouldn't hear. I climbed out of my window and followed her. She headed straight to the road that led to town. Fool! Scumbag Dwayne is going to kidnap and torture you. I'll have to kill him. I'll rescue you. Glorita looks me in the eyes, her soft arms locked around my neck, her lips quivering close to mine . . . . Half an hour later, Elmira's broken sidewalks suddenly sprang up on either side of the road, now renamed Main

Street. I immediately tripped on a crack and took a dive. Glorita walked past Dwayne's candy store. She was walking fast now, running, and I had trouble keeping up with her. She was just a silly girl, but she sure could run.

When I caught up with her, she was approaching the back door of our school. Someone opened the door and Glorita slid in. I went around the building a hundred times that night, clockwise, and when I got dizzy, counterclockwise, sniffing at the bottom of the doors, hoping to catch Glorita's scent, trying all the windows with my drug-terrier paws to see if any would give and I could jump in and carry her out on my back to safety. And licking the back doorknob, which she may or may not have touched. There wasn't a sound, smell, or sight all night, except for my breathing and sweat, and my pee trickling over all four corners of the school building. I ran home at the first sign of light in the sky, afraid of my mother's wrath. Ashy and exhausted, I pretended a stomachache that morning, but pity was a luxury my three-job parents couldn't afford. On the sidewalk, waiting for the school bus, was Glorita, fresh as a morning gladiolus.

McCabe and I reached my old school. "It looks like a fucking prison!" her contralto boomed. I realized that she had not said a word during our walk. She stared directly into my eyes. I looked away, afraid she might be trying to read my mind (I don't believe in mind reading, I'm a rationalist, a rabid Darwinian, I worship at the altar of logic, but one is most afraid of what one doesn't believe in.) "Whatever happened to Glorita?" McCabe asked.

4

How and Why
(a Philosophical Pause)

I HAD LURED MCCABE to Elmira to kill her. Picturing her death in Manhattan had felt fake. Shifting the scene to Elmira made it instantly true. Moved by such vigorous realism, I had picked up the phone, figurative tears still in my eyes, and asked McCabe to meet me at the brasserie. Soon we were flying to Elmira.

Pulling weeds in the Judge's garden a few weeks later, I asked myself, Why here in Elmira? The question made me dizzy. Like looking at millions of stars in a black night above the Elmira cow fields, or coloring the picture of the Dove, the Eye inside the triangle, and the Rising Jesus.

To keep my head from cracking, I shifted from the bottomless "why here" to the modest "how," as I attacked the dandelion roots with a sharp garden fork. I did not want to kill McCabe in her sleep, or from behind, or while she was looking the other way, or by surprise, not even if frontally. I wanted her to be aware of who was killing her and why. Even more: I wanted her to realize what monstrous harm she had done me, and to agree that her death could not even begin to repay her debt to me and to the natural order. In short, I wanted McCabe to judge herself, pronounce herself guilty, sentence herself to death, and beg me to carry out her execution. After much feigned hesitation, I would consent to this. It would be a big favor, a sacrifice on my part to commit a cold-blooded crime to improve her moral standing, even at the risk of lowering mine. That'd be the icing on her guilt cake: a new crime on her long list of crimes against my humanity to be atoned for by her, pre-mortem.

No dry, unilateral killing this one. No bilateral killer and killed, executioner and executed. This was to be an affair of universal truth and justice, our own private Nuremberg trial. Furthermore, McCabe had to fully agree to, even propose, all the steps that I must take to hide her corpse and escape the imperfect justice of men.

I sat on the damp soil to catch my breath. Under the garden glove, my right index finger hurt from clutching the weeding fork. Some dandelions I had pulled a few days before were showing again. Had I missed them or did they normally sprout back so quickly? Tonight I would look that up in the Judge's "Useful and Noxious Weeds of North America." To get McCabe to sit in majestic judgment of herself would take time. Weeks, maybe months. We had arrived in Elmira at the end of August. It was now mid-September. I wanted to wrap it all up by Christmas.

Remembering that Indian summer day, now that frost has begun to cover my outer shell and I have lost all feeling in what used to be my right hand, I regret having given so much thought to the form of McCabe's death, and so little to the substance. With reflection, I may have realized that I had two irreconcilable desires, each opening a distinct path: one, to get McCabe to acquiesce to her death; the other, to give Elmira the fresh blood it was thirsting for, so it would finally let go of me. The first path could be taken only by someone born without the Elmiran blood curse (like McCabe herself, but then, McCabe would not have despised me if I had been a McCabe, nor Bebe rejected me—a paradox I did not grasp that balmy afternoon while struggling with the weeds); the second path of indiscriminate bloodshed was open to anyone capable of decisive action, whether human or mutt. I thought myself free—by choice, if not birth—but indecisive. So I took the first path thinking that it would lead to the second, like those streets that change names without one having to turn a corner. It didn't. In the end, my Nuremberg followed its languid course in the Judge's old house, while Elmira tired of waiting with gaping jaws for the fresh meat promised to her. Oh, unforgiving, wrathful Elmira.

5

Baking

MCCABE SPENT MOST AFTERNOONS in the kitchen, of all places, sunglasses atop her head, Dolce Vita style, sausage frame encased in D&G one day and Missoni the next. Unafraid to burn or stain her rich rags, she baked and baked. Her signature creation, her only creation, in fact, was a bourbon prune cake. She baked large quantities for the Church of Saint Glykeria, Martyr at the bottom of the Hill, which Petrona delivered every Friday evening on her way home in a fancy basket covered by a red-checkered napkin. Mrs. Crandall, the appetizing head church lady, returned the empty basket on Sunday afternoons. McCabe opened the kitchen door for her the first time to bask in her gratitude, but did not invite her in. Mrs. Crandall left dazzled and thirsty for another glimpse of the celebrated SoHo art merchant. By the time she got home and reported back to her crone troops in lengthy phone calls, her gratitude had turned into abject adoration. Reports of the reports reached me the next morning via Petrona, who had heard the increasingly fantastic accounts, in Spanish, from the spic delivery boys who brought in our food from the state capital's only fancy grocery store. Their pit stops at the kitchens of the town's petty notables provided them with a rich source of gossip. At my request, we did not patronize the local Wal-Mart, the only other source of food outside the state capital: I'm a picky eater and McCabe, who couldn't care less where her food came from, was nevertheless swayed by my warning that her standing in Elmira would suffer if she was thought to eat from the same trough as the hoi polloi.

McCabe was so thrilled with my English translation of Petrona's Spanish version of the white gentry's phone follies, that she made me retell it over and over until my voice got hoarse. Each time, she demanded more details. These I offered, not from Petrona's account, but from the bottomless pit of my intimate and anthropological memory of the Elmira massas. McCabe laughed at my stories the way people laughed when they knew how to laugh, and writers knew how to write them laughing: so hard that tears streamed down her cheeks, so hard that her belly rolls, arm rolls, and jowls gleefully shook, with a laughter so stentorian that it rattled the Judge's window panes. I can still hear her laugh. Accurately, now that my ears have fallen off, like my nose and all other bodily protuberances, and my memory is cleansed of self-pity. McCabe wasn't laughing at Elmira's rulers; she was laughing at me still laughing at them.

From that moment on, as Señora Mirtila, the housekeeper, I was charged with opening the door for Mrs. Crandall, retrieving the basket, and offering a different excuse for McCabe's absence in thickly accented English each week, so it would whet her appetite. One week McCabe would be in bed with a migraine, the next she'd be en route to Antarctica, the next she'd just been called to the White House (this one, which I repeated occasionally, always made Mrs. Crandall gasp).

Mrs. Crandall was also the head librarian in Elmira's public library, the only one still standing in the state. It always embarrassed me to see her behind the main desk, with her curvaceous body badly tamed by dresses whose soft, clingy fabric belied their severe cut. She should have worn tailored suits, preferably pant-suits with longish jackets, to hide her provocative flesh. It would not have been a solution, just an improvement on the current, intolerably voluptuous situation. A black burka would have only increased Mrs. Crandall's carnality: it was as bad as that. When the Caliphate finally reaches Elmira—sooner than we think—she will be the first to be stoned to death. I could see their viewpoint, while naturally abhorring it. Her presence among the books was a provocation. I dared not think of her at Saint Glykeria, Martyr, although Byzantine churches have always felt like boudoirs to me. Was Mrs. Crandall unaware of the power of her flesh? Were the other librarians? The church people? Mrs. Crandall's rectitude was so unimpeachable that no one dared acknowledge the copulating elephant in the middle of the room, which was her flesh. However, the men at the faded polo club bar must have exchanged at least subliminal messages as she walked by, no words, but maybe a raised eyebrow, a batted eyelash, given that Mr. Crandall was old Elmira, and, as such, chairman of the club's board, and bank president with life or death power over their mortgages. It must have been a trial for Elmira's white rulers to live with this unmentionable thing, Mrs. Crandall's carnality. They're not easy, the lives of our rulers, even in their present, shrunken conditions. On the other hand, I bet the town's spics, female and male alike, talked freely about Mrs. Crandall's bountifulness. We're that crass and uneducated. Our lack of discretion and boundaries will either hasten the triumph of the Caliphate (the backlash theory), or altogether prevent it (the sensual overflow theory). I take no sides since both sides abhor me, the homo vermin. I'm as embarrassed by us spics as by Mrs. Crandall, but the white townspeople's code of silence repulses and frightens me. It courses underground, so no one knows what foulness it carries. Spic sex babble, equally repulsive, is at least out in the open for all to see.

Even now that I was back—thirty years older, wiser, richer (in strings to pull and big words to use, if not cash)—white Elmirans, rich or poor, still scared me. I couldn't get into their skins, guts, or brains. Uncomfortably, like someone trying on a coat that's too small or too big in an overheated store, I nevertheless managed to penetrate most of Spicdom, and on certain, narrow wavelengths, even most of your blacks and Orientals. Around white Elmirans I felt gaseous while they seemed solid and tri-dimensional, or vice-versa. Physically different, as in Law of Physics, not flesh.

Against my will, then, I was often forced to be near to Mrs. Crandall's disturbing buttocks. It would have been out of character for Señora Mirtila to want to read Turgenev's complete works in English, as I did. So I cleverly pulled out the yellowing library index cards for all of Turgenev's novels, shuffled them by order of desire from top to bottom, and took the deck to a horrified, but bravely collected Mrs. Crandall. Señorita Maké wants me to bring her two of these each time, I said in laborious Mirtila English. Mrs. Crandall tried not to stare at the flowery peasant scarf on my head, but its visual pull was irresistible. She stood up, shaking her head to regain control, then took me to the library's humid cellar where all the old books no one read anymore had been relocated after a flood. Only the new ones everyone craved (the Harlotquins, the astrology and demonology self-help manuals, and the Nostradamuses) were displayed on the safer main floor. Below, we stood silently before the hand-carved oak shelves holding exquisite nineteenth-century editions of the canon of our dying civilization: *The Alexiade* and *Tirant lo Blanc* and the complete Hawthorne, Justinian, Dostoyevsky, Saint Theresa, Melville,

Prodromos, Balzac, Cervantes, Akindynos, and so on, awaiting the next flood to destroy them. "Here," Mrs. Crandall said in a soothing, nightingale voice, pointing at the Turgenevs. "We will come here every time to find the books Miss McCabe wants," she added, enunciating each word carefully. She then smiled the pained smile with which white Elmirans, who are very good-hearted, show compassion for the less fortunate.

6

Scratching

A SCRATCHING NOISE woke me up in the middle of the night on our third week in Elmira. I jumped out of bed, drenched in sweat, imagining it was Glorita's front door. It took me a few seconds with my eyes open in the vibrating darkness to realize that it was now thirty years later and Glorita no longer existed. Someone by that name might live somewhere, perhaps even on the other side of town, in the muddy lowlands across from the river where the spics had moved, but my Glorita was no more. Glorita, who, I could now see, announced Bebe. Even if Bebe had never reminded me of Glorita. Why could I now glide in the dark from Glorita to Bebe, cause and effect, but still not backward? This was not normal. I listened to my ears in case there was a tiny palpitation, a sure sign, I had recently read, of an aneurysm. A lesion to the left or right lobe of my brain might explain why I could go forward, but not backward in this memory, and a lesion to the hippocampus or the middle temporal lobe why I had never thought about Bebe and Glorita in the same breath, as obvious as it now seemed. I was blinded by appearances. Bebe's milk-white, peachy-creamy boobies (her words) and Glorita's tanned, assertive earlobes with the old-fashioned half-moon golden earrings decorated with peacocks. So contrary in substance and flesh, yet so close to each other in my heart of hearts. I sat on the bed

38

in the dark, in a Buddha pose, holding in my mind Glorita's right earlobe and Bebe's left nipple. Floating over the bed in ecstasy and revelation: *elle est plongée dans un oubli étrange.*

A grating sound brought me back to earth. I got up and looked out the window. McCabe was walking on the gravel path toward the front gate. A dark blue sedan pulled over silently. She slid inside. The car took off as noiselessly as it had arrived. Where was she going on a Tuesday at three in the morning, in a town that shut down the moment the sun set behind Round Hill? When I woke up the next morning, I thought I had dreamt it all. Until I got outside the gate and noticed the fresh tire marks.

At dinner, McCabe was uncharacteristically dry. Her soliloquy lasted no more than two minutes and covered only one subject: the severe cognitive disorder which had suddenly struck first-generation "new humans" on the eve of their fifth birthday; pending tests, they'd been isolated from their one- to four-year-old cohorts in the secret facility outside America where they were being raised. That was all. I pricked up my ears. She had not quoted her sources, as was her custom. "Where did you get all that?" I asked. "Everybody knows it," she growled, baring her teeth. I knew she was lying. There was no word of this in the *Times* or the *Journal*. Was it fantasy, gossip, perhaps truth? But where did it come from? I had persuaded McCabe not to bring a cell phone or a tablet. After all, this was to be a period of healing. And Elmira was blessedly disconnected. McCabe didn't receive any mail. Anything requiring her signature was FedExed to her overnight by her assistant, along with the daily *Times* and *Journal*, and returned by her immediately. There was no TV set in the house (the Judge hated them). Other than the two papers, the kitchen radio, locked on the Elmira station, was our only source of information. There was a phone in the kitchen and another one in the Judge's study, but none in her upstairs room. Besides, the story that McCabe had just regurgitated sounded like a written report, not phone gossip. Could she have gotten it from the blue sedan driver, or from someone they had met? After that day, I began to listen carefully to McCabe's dinnertime monologues. She was up to something and, stupid as it might be, I should know about it. Crime and punishment is a fragile mechanism that can be upset by even a microscopically unaligned event. Like Monsieur de la Trouille's famous automaton, the one that was supposed to release a miniature guillotine over the neck of an equally tiny curé figure but, due to a .000001-mm misalignment on the guillotine's dented wheel, instead sliced off the tip of Monsieur de la Trouille's index finger, eventually provoking his death of septicemia at the Hôtel-Dieu. I read this in an antique clock magazine that my mother fished out of Judge Wilkerson's garbage one rainy afternoon and put in my hands with the warning, "Don't let the Judge see you reading this." I must have been six or seven. "Why?" I asked. "I don't want him to know I'm taking his magazines home," she said, polishing the Judge's desk with the kind of cheap wax that always has a slightly rancid smell, even when new. "But he threw them in the garbage," I said. "Precisely," my mother said, turning her back to me to signal that the matter was forever closed.

A few days later, when McCabe and I were eating stuffed Cornish hen, she suddenly burst into tears. Fat, abundant tears fell on her plate and began to liquefy the bird's grease. I kept a sympathetic expression on my face while I observed the interaction between the warm, salty water emanating from her beady blue eyes and the slowly de-congealing grease of the hen. "I did not love," she hiccupped. "Not deeply, I mean, not really, not the way I should have loved." I controlled a tickle in my throat, a tremor in my stomach, afraid my own half-digested hen would shoot out of my mouth and hit the pervert on her reddening nose. Was she referring to Bebe? I dared not ask. I hoped she wouldn't tell. I did not want to kill her in a rage. Besides, there was nothing on the table to kill her with. You don't put out a carving knife for Cornish hen.

She was a brute, McCabe, particularly when she drank, and she had already polished off a bottle of the cheap red wine I got for her (given that she couldn't tell the difference, was unwilling to learn, and mocked me when I tried to teach her, I reserved the good bottles for solitary consumption in my room, and drank water at table while she contentedly guzzled crap). Once before, drunk on the day after our arrival, McCabe had socked me in the nose after I broke the rule and mentioned Bebe. I lost consciousness. When I came to, McCabe wasn't there. She had locked herself in her bedroom—her suite, really, because it occupied the entire upper floor of the house. The Judge's only folly, as Monsieur de la Trouille would say, in an entire life of sobriety and civic uprightness, was to have knocked down all the partition walls on the upstairs floor shortly after his wife's death, turning a warren of dark tiny rooms into a stupendous open space. I saw it briefly the day McCabe and I arrived, after which I forbade myself to go up the stairs to her landing, much less to knock on her door. Only once did I feel any desire to break this rule: when I got back on my feet the night she knocked me out cold. I almost banged on her door and kicked in her ugly teeth. I did not do anything of the sort, but only added another line to her indictment. Next day, her first on the job, Petrona came down from McCabe's room holding in front of her, sleepwalker style, a bundle of vomit-soaked sheets.

7

Elmira

THE LITTLE OHIO RIVER, which is not a branch of the Ohio River, but of the muddier and narrower Wanetka, slices through Elmira in a fairly straight line. The east bank rises steeply for about half a mile in a succession of hills and meadows culminating in the one where Judge Wilkerson's house sits. Geographically, this highest point is Round Hill, but Elmirans call the entire area by that name. It is here that the town's masters used to live before the Great Hunger and where they still occasionally return. The successful doctors, lawyers and orthodontists (no dentists) near the river, the more serious money higher up, say, for instance, the CEO of the now defunct Krimble Dairy Industries, the biggest in the state, or the owner of the equally defunct ARCO Engineering Corp., who had a lock on all highway work in these parts. There was also a former state Governor or two, magically able to afford Round Hill after leaving office. Even higher up was whatever was left of the old money, entrenched in their hereditary estates, people like Judge Wilkerson and his wife, Myrna, whose family house this was, and whose great-grandfather built railways as far away as Chicago and Biloxi. The Judge and Mrs. Wilkerson used to visit New York once a year around Christmas, to meet with their portfolio manager and shop at Bergdorf's and Paul Stuart's, moderately, for they were not showy.

Downtown Elmira is on the west bank flatlands, directly across from Round Hill and linked to it by a short bridge. Main Street, with its graceful nineteenth-century brick buildings that still house the inept county bureaucracy, ran decorously along the river for about half a mile before it dissolved into a decrepit shopping center, two white-trash trailer parks and several car dumps masquerading as garages.

Beyond the grisly Royal Tire and Brake, where car, dog, and perhaps human carcasses intermingled, began a swampy area that stretched all the way to the county line. It was there that a local man, after bribing the proper authorities, slapped in an illegal sewer line draining into the river, built a two-way road above it, and began selling lots on either side. He called it Shangri-La.

For fifteen years there were no takers. Then one day, some Negroes who worked at Elmira's poultry factory were spotted building a small cinder-block house in the lot nearest the main road (the degenerate continuation of Elmira's Main Street). Soon, others followed, working nights and weekends to build their little grey houses. By the time I, the first spic baby, was born, all the lots on either side of the original Shangri-La road were built, down to the cheapest ones by the river edge, where we lived, and which periodically flooded. Afterward, five more roads sprouted parallel to the original one, with lots snapped up by the Mexicans who replaced the Negroes in Elmira County's remaining poultry factory. But that happened long after I left.

When I was little, there were only two spic families in Shangri-La, Rafael Cohen's and ours. Neither was Mexican nor worked with poultry. Rafael's father was a janitor in our grade school until he retired. He never learned English. Not a word in forty years, beyond *gumornin, guafernún, zenquiu, gubái, no spic inglich*. According to my mother, the good and the bad thing about Ezequiel was that he was content with his fate. My mother and Ezequiel had grown up as next-door neighbors in La Esperanza, a dusty-red sugar mill town in the old Cuban province of Santa Clara, and gone to grade school together. Ezequiel had ended up marrying my mother's cousin, Genoveva, a few months after my parents' own wedding. The two couples had left La Esperanza together in 1958, looking for jobs up North. Ezequiel had left reluctantly. My mother's mother, recently widowed, soon followed them. Somehow (I never got a satisfactory answer why) they had ended up in Elmira's Shangri-La, where Rafael and I were born in 1964, two days apart: he on the twenty-fifth of December, I on the twenty-third.

Now our four parents were buried side by side in Shangri-La's small cemetery. They braved the Great Hunger, refusing evacuation to protect their homes, and survived on potatoes, wild roots, and questionable fish for seven years. Then, they all died of natural causes statistically much sooner than the national median in both their native and their adopted countries: phlebitis (Ezequiel), lung cancer (Genoveva), heart attack (my father), diabetes and renal failure (my mother). Genoveva and my father would have died any- where anyway, but Ezequiel and my mother were killed by the Elmira General Hospital, which sent the first one home to die unattended and grossly mismanaged the second's treatment. If only I could graft McCabe to Elmira, so Elmira dies with her: two vultures with one stone. Now there are only two little founding spics left: Rafael and I. He is in besieged Constantinople today on a surprise national security mission, the radio says. And I am looking at Shangri-La from the top of Round Hill, a brownish spot on the river bend, barely visible in the early morning mist. I should weep: it's the appropriate thing to do. I try but I can't.

8

Fasting

MCCABE DID NOT COME DOWN for dinner on the evening of September 14. The precise date is carved in my ears, where the braying from Saint Glykeria, Martyr reverberated all day—it was the Feast of the Exaltation of the Cross, and one hundred frenzied Kyrie Eleisons were sung every time the bearded one lifted the cross. When cotton balls failed, I plugged my ears with melted wax, burning my fingertips and the outer rim of the ear canal, and the thunderous braying became a mere muffled sawmill screech. Deprived of hearing and, oddly, olfaction for the day, I suspected something was afoot only when I saw Petrona leaving a tray by McCabe's door. The tray held a silver bell cover, a bottle of Perrier-Jouët, and a vase with a yellow rose freshly cut from the garden. The dinner table was set only for me.

Petrona was pureblood Aztec, thus inscrutable. Today there was an additional shroud drawn over her face. She had done three things she was absolutely forbidden to do, which would have allowed me to rip her heart from her chest had I been one of her ancestors: gone up the stairs to McCabe's door, cut a rose (had she used a kitchen knife, or had she broken into my gardening shed?), and brought a champagne bottle up from the cellar (had she picked the lock or stolen my key?). Worse, she had not consulted me, the housekeeper.

I, and only I, was Petrona's interlocutor in the household. She was allowed to speak only to me. Never to McCabe. I had made this threateningly clear to Petrona from the moment I hired her. Was she now taking her instructions directly from McCabe? I put on my own zombie mask, so that my Popocatepetlian rage would not erupt over Petrona's head. It was a delicate situation. If Petrona realized that I had noticed, I would be forced to question her. This would be a sign of weakness, proof that I did not know what was going on. Would Petrona dare do all of this without McCabe's approval? Doubtful. But if McCabe had broken our contract and ordered around Petrona behind my back, it was McCabe I had to dress down, so that she, not I, could set matters straight with Petrona the next day. After which, I would have a stern talk with Petrona and reluctantly forgive her, just this time, because Señorita Maké had been confused for a moment about the lines of domestic command.

I chewed on my odorless tofu stew while rehearsing these disciplinary scenarios. The back door fluttered, signaling Petrona's exit. Lord, have mercy, I said, unplugging my ears. There was absolute silence. I stayed in the darkening dining room for a long time, listening, but not a sound came out of McCabe's room. When I glanced up the stairs, the tray was gone.

The cellar key was in its place, in the top drawer of the Judge's desk, which I kept locked at all times. The brass key that opened the drawer was in my pocket, on a key ring that included the house and gardening-shed keys. I checked the drawer lock with a flashlight and the tiny magnifying glass that I used when tightening the screws on my reading glasses. The drawer did not seem to have been forced, but a professional would know how to pick a lock without leaving any trace. I could not imagine Petrona having that skill. (But, for all I knew, she could have been Raffles, the silk-handed thief. My lack

46

of imagination about her was purely racial.) The gardening shed appeared equally free from human disturbance, although there were animal footprints on the dusty floor, something small and clawed, a field mouse or perhaps a weasel. The only window hung unevenly from rusty hinges, closed but not locked. Animals are stronger and smarter than we think, even mice. They could have broken in and left without a trace. I nailed the window shut. It was beginning to drizzle when I shone the flashlight on the yellow rosebush. There were twenty-seven roses, including three unopened buds. I memorized their position: it was too wet to make a diagram. From now on, I'd be able to tell if one was missing. As it turned out, I never could. The yellow roses continued to appear on McCabe's daily tray, and my nightly rose count yielded numbers so disparate that they signified nothing: fifty-three roses and seven buds on the second night, thirteen roses and seventeen buds on the third, and so on. But that first night under the drizzle, I went back in with a feeling of accomplishment and quickly fell asleep.

The morning after, the empty tray was outside McCabe's door, with the champagne bottle upside down in the bucket. I decided to say nothing to McCabe or Petrona. Perhaps McCabe was having a painful menstrual period or had lost a bundle of money and was depressed. I was afraid to think the obvious, that Bebe may have been the cause of McCabe's sudden disappearance. That it was a relapse. I did not want Bebe inside McCabe's mind, particularly not as she had long been in mine, as a torturous, unattainable ideal. Cruel Bebe, the eternal fourteen-year-old wood nymph, was my exclusive property.

Bebe as she had been at the very beginning, when I first saw her, alone on the outer edge of the male fuck circle, across from me, in the penumbra of sweaty male bodies, her eyes lazily caressing them, almost tactile yet indifferent. A slight young girl in a long, dirty fur coat, unafraid of the men, rats, and sewer effluvia under the last bridge still spanning the East River. We were the only two female watchers. The slow, silent male sexual field separated and consoled us, protective and dangerous, like the river's black velvety bottom.

It was the night Zoë fled to Constantinople and the splendors of her elderly arms dealer. The night in October, exactly a month after 9/11, when refugee hordes broke out of their resettlement camp in the mainland and tried to enter the island (mixed in with a few marauding cannibals, some say). The Citizen's Militia repelled them upstream and the river turned red with blood. "There's not enough rat meat for everyone," the girl said, as we walked the dark streets. She had just arrived from Nebraska, where things were much worse. "No one's left there," she said. "I've always been hungry." She was white but wanted to be black. "Why?" I asked. "I want to sing like a black woman." She said she was fourteen, but looked twelve and sounded as old as the hills.

That night, she slept on my dingy kitchen floor. I did not offer her my bed. That's how insignificant she seemed. The next morning, she was gone. But every day she was absent, her presence grew. The details of her body, voice, and gestures became denser and stronger. I craved to see her in the flesh. I looked for her everywhere. One night, when I was beginning to forget her, she knocked on my door, and I was hooked. The electric charge between us was as potent as that in the male fuck circle. Except that we never touched. She refused, once. And I don't ask twice. But we both kept seducing each other. What fun. All that inexplicable pleasure and grief! All that extreme passion unrelieved by the flesh! Two and a half incandescent years. Then McCabe showed up.

McCabe did not come down to dinner on Wednesday, or any other evening that week, or the next. I could no longer play the ostrich. It was a relapse. McCabe's mind had to be cleansed of Bebe, emptied of her, and filled with me: with my suffering and humiliation and McCabe's guilt. I realized that this was not going to happen spontaneously as in a Turgenev novel, because I did not have his lightness of touch. From now on, I would have to tear myself away from the daily joys of cleaning, polishing, and contemplating Shangri-La from the heights of Round Hill, and get to work on McCabe's coarse brain. Every day. With discipline.

Those two long weeks with no one but Petrona to talk to, I mapped in detail McCabe's re-education, the necessary condition for her righteous execution. I wrote it in my mind, the only place where I could write without any loss of words. I wrote it in the past tense, to thwart any potential mind reader, civilian or military, human or mechanical.

I have forgotten all but one section of the brain-cleansing method I created for McCabe. Entitled "Humility," I composed it during my daily searches of Petrona's car, looking for signs that she was actually taking home the food that McCabe was supposed to have eaten. (What if McCabe was not inside her bedroom and Petrona was her accomplice, secreting the uneaten food in her car?) My searches were thorough, if futile and quick. In the three and a half minutes Petrona spent in the service bathroom shedding her maid uniform and putting on her sad brown dress, I'd scan the interior of the car with a penlight, but mostly I sniffed. My sense of smell was highly developed, closer to a hound's than a human's. All gone now, along with my nose. "Humility" remains imprinted in what's left of my brain because it was born, a line at a time, in the restricted space of Petrona's dank car, at the same hour each day, with the same smells, light, and shadows. The words come back attached to the seats and the brake, the steering wheel and the filthy mat: "Humility is the ointment that heals all wounds."

9

Fishing

TWO WEEKS LATER, a tall, emaciated figure glided silently into the dining room. Darkened eyes sunk in bony eye sockets; high, rounded forehead; forceful nose with delicate nostrils; thin lips; closely cropped black hair that revealed a small, well-drawn skull. The carving knife was two inches away from my right hand, but I dared not grab it. The intruder hesitated for a second, then brutally pulled back a chair and sat on it, spreading her knees.

It was McCabe. It had to be. She, a convention from this point on because she was more than that, and also less, had not yet mastered her new body. Every time she jerked her skinny frame about, as if it was still a hundred pounds heavier, I concentrated on my plate, afraid to show any awareness of her change, or her unexplained absence. Fear was the first and most enduring feeling the new McCabe provoked in me. At the time, I thought that it was compassion, fear of breaking the frail reed, the pitiful sack of bones topped by the incongruous half-mute pinhead. Now I see that it was fear not for, but of her, of what she could do to me. Had I recognized it earlier I might not be dying now under this moldy bed. It was, at the beginning, like being confronted with a body snatcher. I even felt sentimental about the old pig McCabe, whom I might never see again. I wished I had gotten to know her better.

The new McCabe ate voraciously and silently, unlike her logorrheic predecessor who forever pecked at her plate. I hardly heard her voice, beyond her short but courteous greeting at the beginning and end of each meal. It was old McCabe's voice and it wasn't: equally deep but stripped of its boom and reverberation, perhaps because it was filtered through a thinner frame. The burden of conversation was now entirely on me. None of old McCabe's hobby horses resonated with her. She smiled tentatively across the table and once put her fork and knife down for a few seconds to indicate that she was listening. But her darkening eyes were pulled back irresistibly to the half-eaten steak on her plate. Conversation was made insubstantial by the intensity of her hunger. "Burning desire" became not a figure of speech at our dinner table, but a physical fact. I often expected her gaze to turn to ashes the meat on her plate, the tablecloth, even my hands, if I left them on the table. She ate noiselessly, so if I didn't say a word, absolute silence would set in. In that silence I stared at her hands as she cut her steak and held my breath as she lifted each piece to her mouth. I always expected the piece of meat to fall back on the plate because she never stuck the fork in deep enough, but it never did.

She never mentioned her absence or her metamorphosis. Neither did I. We both pretended that nothing had changed. Or perhaps it was just me who pretended. I have no proof that she was aware of her transformation, although I tested her indirectly many times. Once I asked her if she still liked her deerskin moccasins. (Old McCabe had worn them every day. She owned half a dozen pairs, specially handmade for her at the Reservation Penitentiary in what used to be Arizona.) She furrowed her brow and tightened her lips in cartoonish concentration. "I'm not sure," she finally said. The next day she wore moccasins for the first and only time. They fit her narrow, elongated feet perfectly, as if they had been made for them and not for old McCabe's E-wide hooves. Her clothes also fit her new frame. They were not unlike fat McCabe's clothes (I spotted Moschino leather pants and Dolce and Gabbana sweaters), but they looked worn. It was impossible to tell if they were the same clothes, only altered, or altogether different ones. I doubted she would own an identical set several sizes smaller. Unless she had bought them, planning to lose weight in Elmira. This seemed the only logical explanation. That was a favorite word of mine, "logical," constantly abused to mask my intellectual laziness and moral cowardice, and in this case, pure fear.

It occurred to me that this McCabe might like the outdoors more than her heavier predecessor, who had huffed and puffed on our excursion on foot through Elmira. I organized an elaborate fishing trip on the Wanetka River, which would culminate in a picnic by Wanetka Falls. McCabe nodded in what I interpreted as acceptance, and one morning we drove out at sunrise to a point about twenty miles upstream, with the Judge's old canoe on top of McCabe's leased armored Land Rover and a food basket Petrona had prepared the day before.

With her bony frame slumped on the passenger seat and her eyes half-closed, McCabe seemed at ease for the first time since her return, maybe even modestly content. We drove in silence as the cratered pavement turned into gravel, then packed dirt, then rutted tracks, and back to pavement, only to resume the cycle in typical post-Reconstruction county-road fashion. Stealing road funds had always been an Elmiran passion, even when I was five, and this road felt buttery-smooth (until it disintegrated in winter, thus requiring spring re-buttering). Reconstruction was a frenzy of thievery, here more than anywhere else. With road monies now a quaint memory, it was every man for his own patch: gravel for the rich and absent (all of Round Hill), packed dirt for the local gentry still clinging to their revivalist dreams, mud and disintegration for all others, according to their means. Only downtown Elmira had two blocks paved with stolen federal military-grade pavement. I swerved right to avoid a boulder. McCabe gasped. "Look," she said, pointing at a flock of birds flying in a V formation ahead of us. I shot her an open-mouthed glance. "Green-winged teals," she added, clearly amazed that I didn't know. "Going to winter on the Gulf Coast." It was the first full sentence that had escaped her lips. She talked about the migration of gadwalls and teals for the rest of the trip in a deliberate way, often pausing to find the right word, or correcting herself whenever she felt she had been inaccurate.

In another era, McCabe's sudden eloquence would have been considered a miracle. Now it almost landed us in a ditch, when I lost control of the car, stunned by the unexpected, if tentative, flow of words. I had concluded by then that McCabe had become autistic. My awe soon turned into suspicion. I slowed down to a crawl for the rest of the trip, so I could record in my mind every single word she said, to analyze it later in my room, sitting at the Judge's desk. Was McCabe's past muteness and sudden interest in ornithology a deliberate front, a diversionary maneuver to cover whatever she was up to? (I did not think yet to add: or whoever she had become—or, worse, whoever she may have always been under the head-to-toe Moschino leather.) Or was it an outpouring of forgotten memories, unguarded by her now emaciated body and crumbling willpower?

"The Biloxi Marsh is their promised land," she said with sudden emotion. "Men never conquered it." I glanced at her and thought I saw tears in her eyes, but it was such a fleeting image that I cannot be sure. We were on a dusty stretch of the road with less than perfect visibility. Her voice was calmer now, almost dreamy, like someone reminiscing about their childhood. "On Christmas Day, 1624," she said, "Pedro de Horta built a settlement at the southern tip of the marshes and left there a garrison of eighty men. When he returned from New Spain, what we call Mexico, a year later, he found only a man—a blacksmith named Álvaro Ejido—and a dog. Both were dying, curled up in a cot inside the soldiers' mess room, a round mud-walled shack with dry grass roofing. Ejido pointed to where his seventy-nine companions had been buried, first in neat rows marked by wooden crosses, then in trenches for six or eight, and finally in a deep pit, layer upon layer of corpses, separated by thin layers of mud. The last two had died within hours of each other, about a week before Pedro de Horta's arrival. By then, Ejido was too weak to bury them. Their rotting bodies still lay on their cots, in the larger, rectangular mud-and-grass shack that was the soldiers' barracks. Pedro de Horta was afraid the men had died of the plague, so he ordered the entire compound to be burnt down, along with Ejido and the dog, now both dead, and the two rotting soldiers. Pedro de Horta chose two *marranos*—not pigs, but insincerely converted Jews—to carry out his order, because he was not going to risk the life of a born Christian. The marranos, always eager to please so that their original sin and subsequent duplicity might be overlooked in the New World, or at least not passed on to their children, covered their noses and mouths with their shirts and piled enough grass on top of the four corpses (counting the dog) to set a good fire . . . . "

I interrupted, to show her that I was attentive to her story: "Like a Hittite funeral pyre." She glanced at me. It was an imperceptible glance, but I caught it on the edge of the rearview mirror. There was that same little smile on her lips I had noticed when I invited her to go fishing, but in her eyes I saw (or imagined I saw) a flash of indulgence, as when we forgive a small child for committing an imperfect crime, like stealing a cookie and forgetting to brush the crumbs off her face.

"They set them on fire," she continued, looking out the window and ignoring my interruption, "but when the grass was consumed the bodies underneath were only half-charred. The two marranos had to repeat the operation seven times (pile up the grass, set the fire, wait until the fire died, root with long tree branches into the smoldering grass to uncover what was left of the bodies, repeat). In the meantime, Pedro de Horta and the rest of his (Christian) men waited for them aboard their ship. Around the time of the fifth torching, the men threatened mutiny if they did not sail immediately. De Horta later wrote in his diary that he considered abandoning the two marranos in the marshes, but that the faces of the would-be mutineers, contorted by fear into the shape of wolves, made him change his mind. He held off his men, with whippings and prayers, through two more torchings, until the marranos came back on board. They were isolated in the bowels of the ship until they arrived in San Cristóbal de La Habana, a week later, but neither of them got sick, De Horta reported in his diary. The two marranos asked his permission to stay in the city and he granted it, since they were now old and had served him well for many years. This was the first and only time men tried to colonize the marshes." McCabe closed her eyes and seemed to doze. We were reaching the river. "What did the men die of?" I asked. "Does it matter?" she said, her eyes still closed.

10

Sea of Tranquility

WE SAT IN THE CANOE in silence, transfixed by our fishing rods and the dark green water, avoiding each other's gaze. It became scorching hot. We did not catch any fish. McCabe insisted on carrying the picnic basket alone all the way to Wanetka Falls, about two miles up on foot and then down a steep, rocky path. She swayed under the basket's weight and, a few times, staggered and almost lost her footing, but she cut me off with a sharp "No, thanks," when I offered to help. I walked a few steps behind her, so I don't know if her face showed tiredness or any emotion. When we finally sat under a weeping willow overlooking the Falls, she looked perfectly fresh.

I told McCabe how I used to picnic under this willow every Sunday in August with my parents and grandmother. I left out the Cohens, who always came along. It must have been my instinctive prudence. Call it paranoiac reflex, if you wish. While I almost never lied, I always suppressed some facts, the reasons opaque even to myself, more like unformed forebodings bubbling up from some subconscious cesspool of fear than reasons in the strictest sense, that is, reasons as a product of the brain's actuary function, which also churns out shopping lists and tax returns. Seldom did I tell a story about myself that had not been cleansed of certain details that I feared could be used against me. Ninety percent of them were completely trivial. However, I felt safe only if I had taken something out of a story and hidden it in a mental lockbox. How did I get to be so secretive? Being a spic in Elmira and a homo to boot? Or did it have a genetic basis? Survival of the secretivest. Not a bad thing in spite of its ugly hiss.

By the time I was done reminiscing, McCabe had devoured all of her food and was eyeing mine. I told her she could take as much as she wanted, because I was not hungry. She ate nine chicken wings, a pound of potato salad, and half a strawberry-rhubarb pie, licking her fingers between each course, and then dozed off. I had never seen McCabe asleep. Old McCabe's pink, fat self had repulsed me so thoroughly that I usually focused on her left earlobe when politeness forced me to look at her. I always kept a good deal of physical space between us. This new McCabe did not make me gag reflexively. There was a peculiar serenity about her, as if a plump blood sausage had been emptied out, the skin tightened and scraped with an abrasive substance, and then filled with an odorless, colorless essence. Her serenity allowed me to examine her now, with an entomologist's cold precision.

She was wearing old jeans tucked inside half boots, and a man's red plaid jacket over a brown turtleneck. It was the first time I had seen her not encased in leather. Her breasts had shrunk to the size of grapefruits. The freckles on her face were smaller and less close to each other, or maybe bigger and so close to each other that they gave her a new complexion, ivory replacing ruddy and blotchy. Perhaps it was just an optical illusion, now that her face was less round and the skin pulled back over her bones.

Since her reappearance, she had eaten twice as much without gaining an ounce. Heaping plates of steamed potatoes and pig knuckles, tureens of tripe and oxtail soups, goat stews, mounds of fat sausages of all colors and origins—among which I could identify only the boudin blanc from having seen its picture in a magazine (not being a sausage lover myself)—scrambled eggs with calf brains, and a variety of stewed animal entrails all began appearing on the dinner table from the first day McCabe returned, as if Petrona again had received instructions behind my back. There were now two distinct dinners served: mine, faithful to the master menu of the month I had given Petrona; and McCabe's, increasingly visceral and gargantuan. Only good wines were served now—the ones I kept under lock and key—different ones every day, cannily chosen. Every day, I checked my key and the wine cellar lock, still spying on Petrona, hoping to catch her stealing my wine or ordering the meats that McCabe now ate, which were delivered daily and in vast quantities.

Petrona was her usual hieratic self. She was the only one in the household who had not changed: surrounded by unexplained phenomena, I acquired for a while a nervous twitch on the left corner of my mouth that made me look as if I were smiling even when distressed. On arrival, Petrona always greeted me with a *Buenos días, señora* in her obsequious pre-Columbian lilt, quickly glancing at the tip of my nose, never my eyes, and then lowering her eyes back to half-mast, which is where she kept them when she was around me (in her own home I was sure that she was a straight-gazed, unblinking John P. Wayne). Her departure was identical, gesture for gesture, the only difference being a subtly textured *Buenas noches, señora,* evoking each night a different shade of contempt. In between, on the rare occasions on which I spoke to her, she stuck to her meretricious script with Noh-theatre discipline. Petrona behaved as if she were immortal, connected every minute to all the Petronas that had existed before her and would exist ever after. I felt vertigo one day looking at Petrona's impassible face, which suddenly became the face of millions. Was that what Mrs. Wilkerson felt when she looked at my mother's own guarded face? Spying on Petrona yielded only one curious fact: she liked to eat sugar cubes. I never found out how any of the household's new food and wine transactions were accomplished, and I dared not ask. After all, everything in this house—the food, the wine, even Petrona—belonged to McCabe. I was a guest.

I removed McCabe's boots and socks so I could examine her feet. She stirred but did not wake up. Her feet, which had seemed elongated, were in fact still beefy and pink, and covered with freckles. So were her hands. They were the only parts of her body that had not changed, as far as I could tell (I had never seen McCabe naked or even at the beach). Hands and feet now looked incongruous, a graft performed by a surgeon devoid of aesthetic sense. She opened her eyes just as I finished putting back on her socks and boots. That night I replayed this scene in my room. Hadn't she opened her eyes just a beat before I had withdrawn my hands from her left foot, like an actor stepping on another actor's cue, a microscopic step that neither the audience nor the other actor can see, but both can sense, or at least suspect?

11

October

KILLING A PIG IS EASY. Pigs are like fat babies. Hot-blooded, squirmy, squealing, sly, and utterly useless unless you like their meat. Feeding them both to sharks, as the sublime Montevidean advised two centuries ago, would have raised humanity a tiny bit closer to the angels. It's physically harder to kill a pig or a gargantuan baby than to twist the neck of a goose, but it's morally easier. Cuteness will not stop you if, like me, you do not confuse sentimentality with morality. You will put on your butcher's apron and get to work.

McCabe used to be an easy kill. Not anymore. She was now closer to a bird than a mammal, except for her wolf-like appetite. She was still gaunt despite the prodigious amounts of meat she ate, but a thin, steely layer of muscle and tendons now covered her bones. You wouldn't notice it unless you touched her, as I had while she slept under the willow tree. It was now mid-October. The cool air had chased away the gnats and the mosquitoes. Dust had vanished from the streets of Elmira, resplendent in the lingering Indian summer. The townspeople had begun wearing bright red jackets and hats, so that hunters would not mistake them for deer.

After her passionate account of the migrating birds, McCabe had become silent and elusive again. Not unfriendly, though. She smiled at me the few times we crossed paths in the garden, a tentative, embarrassed little smile. She seemed to spend her days pacing the property line, deliberately, like a prospector counting her footsteps, with her eyes always fixed on the ground. I did not have an uninterrupted view of her journey, even with the Judge's binoculars. McCabe would disappear behind a copse and reappear an hour or two later half a mile to the left. She could have gone to town and back. Yet I was sure that she hadn't. It was a deduction grounded on an objective fact. I observed that every day McCabe would begin her walk at one cardinal point and that every two hours on the dot she would appear at the next. The entry point and the walk itself would proceed clockwise for four days, and counterclockwise for another four. Someone sneaking to town wouldn't trap herself in such ironclad routine.

The re-education and killing scenarios I had imagined for her predecessor did not quite fit this peculiar automaton either physically, logistically, or, worst of all, morally. Justification and execution procedure alike had to be retooled. I resented the bony creature for making me redo my homework, and tried to whip up resentment into murderous motivation, but that was too ridiculous, even for me. I began to take long baths before going to bed, seeking illumination in the water. Watching the hypnotic filling of the tub, I wondered if it would be painless to take sleeping pills and drown.

In that state of mind, I stood one day at dusk on the edge of the Judge's property, overlooking the river one hundred feet below. I stood there every day to watch the sun set beyond Shangri-La. I do not care for sunsets, but I liked staring at Shangri-La, which at that hour looked like a bunch of tea leaves at the bottom of a dirty teacup. I had a feeling someone was watching me. When I turned around, McCabe was there. I had not heard her approach, even though the ground was already thick with crunchy red and yellow leaves.

"They tried to kill him," she said, flatly. "Who?" I said, turning back toward the river and Shangri-La to hide my face from her. She did not immediately answer, but I already knew. Out of the corner of my eye I noticed her lips moving in silence, as if trying to find the right words. "The National Security Advisor," she finally said, one slow word at a time. My mouth dried out. I could not speak. "A car bomb. Crossing the Bosphorus," she said; and then, mistaking my horror at her intrusion for concern: "But he's unharmed." We were now facing each other. I had trouble breathing. My knees gave out. On the ground, I covered up by pretending to examine a weed. How had she found out that I knew him? Was she spying on me? At least she had used his official title, instead of his more intimate name. I had nothing to do with Rafael Cohen. Since I left Elmira, thirty years ago, aboard the last refugee bus to make it out of the starving heartland, I had hardly thought about him. I was already erasing Elmira as the bus took off, and I waved back to my parents, grandmother, and godparents Genoveva and Ezequiel Cohen, all of whom preferred starvation at home to begging in the city. Rafael always sent me Christmas cards, but we had met again only twice, at my parents' funerals. The last time I had seen him was seven years ago, at my mother's wake, right before he published the essay that would propel him from academia to the West Wing. He did not seem to resent that I did not reciprocate with his burials: when his mother and then his father had died I just sent Hallmark condolences. Still, Rafael Cohen belonged to me, to my most secret memories, not to McCabe.

"I heard it on the radio," McCabe said, as if reading my mind. It was as simple as that. No spying, no mental eavesdropping, no conspiracy: just a regurgitation of the radio news. Like old McCabe used to do. How she would have riffed on this one, from appetizer through dessert. I suddenly missed old McCabe, missed her bombastic speeches, her heft, her booming voice, her unshakeable certainty that she was always right, and so rich she could always get her way. My eyes moistened, I had lost my good, old McCabe, my pal in reverse, the one who had been with me all these years, the one that I personally had to kill. Someone else had beaten me to it. I suddenly hated the new McCabe I had in front of me, shifting instantly from neutral to two-hundred and fifty miles per hour of murderous hatred. The McCabe before my eyes, the gaunt impostor, the body snatcher, the miserable mutant, must have noticed, because she said, "I'm sorry if I upset you. It's a slaughterhouse out there," and she gestured vaguely toward the flaming horizon. I stood up, wanting to hit her. She looked at me with curiosity. My white-knuckled fists seemed to hold a particular fascination for her. She knew, and she was going to let me do it. I had what I wanted, the Nuremberg trial, from beginning to end, in just one second, not through any elaborate plan on my part, but nonetheless happening right here, and now. I could push her off the edge. I should have. For what old McCabe and Elmira had done to me. And for something that now seemed even more monstrous, for what she had done to old McCabe. We were frozen for a few seconds, silent-movie style: me with my fist raised, and her looking at me sweetly, like the girl in *Broken Blossoms* gazes at the Chinaman who has just saved her. Then I turned and ran away.

12

Father and Sons

WHEN PEDRO ANDÚJAR and Jacinto Benavides left the Buena Esperanza, each with a gold *onza* sewn inside the seam of a shoe, they decided to part ways. It was easier, they reasoned, for one marrano to pass unnoticed in the chaotic port, than for two. Jacinto Benavides went off into the free Negro quarter to find a woman and drink himself to death. He had time for the first, but not for the second. A month later, he was knifed by his woman's common-law husband who, in jail for murdering another Negro, was let out unexpectedly because the Spanish *alguacil* needed room to accommodate some tobacco smugglers who tried to skimp on their bribes. The murderer and the woman—in reality, a fifteen-year-old mulatto girl who, unbeknownst to her, was carrying Jacinto Benavides' daughter—dumped his body in the bay after removing all his clothes. They knew that Jacinto Benavides had been circumcised and might be a marrano. This, they felt, was none of their business, since it was a squabble among Spaniards, a marrano being just another kind, adept at some witchcraft that worked only in Spain, and not the island. Just in case, they cleansed the mulatto girl's hut, where the murder had taken place, using herbs and chants that she had learned from her African mother. The clothes and shoes were sold to a street peddler, who may or may not have found the gold onza inside the shoe.

Someone at some point must have, because poor people never threw away shoes or clothes, but used them until they disintegrated upon their bodies, at which point the gold onza must have fallen on the ground and made someone very rich and very happy.

Pedro Andújar walked away from the port as soon as he found a quieter street. In San Cristóbal de La Habana, on the first days of the year 1625, a quieter street was one where the sweaty, screaming mass of soldiers, pigs, prostitutes, beggars, half-naked urchins, criminals, dogs, and street vendors with their greasy, smoky braziers frying pork, plantains, and cassava began to thin out, replaced by the tiny shacks of the mulatto cobblers, leather workers, cabinet makers, tailors, mercers. A hurricane had struck two months earlier, opening gaps in the fortified wall built to protect the city against flooding and attacks by the English, French, and Dutch. Most of the artisans' shacks were now missing something, but their owners continued to work inside them as if the roof, or door, or walls were still there, like the actors in *Fuenteovejuna*, sitting inside their painted cardboard shops pretending they were real. Pedro had seen the play performed by an itinerant troupe in Cádiz, right before he first sailed for the New World. He had been in San Cristóbal de La Habana three times before, the last time two years earlier, but he had never been separated from Jacinto Benavides, and had never left the port area, where Jacinto said a man could find all he needed to recover from the brutal months at sea: drink, food, and women, in order of importance. On his earlier visits, he had been a glutton for all of these, particularly nísperos and mulatto women, both of which were abundant here and became one in his mind. He had never seen either before. He drank to please Jacinto, who loved drink more than anything else in the world, even if it made him cry and speak in broken Ladino, which could have gotten them both burnt at the stake. Pedro and Jacinto had been inseparable for ten years, from the Canary Islands, where they had both enlisted in the Buena Esperanza at the age of fifteen, to Cádiz; from there to Veracruz; and then back a year later by way of San Cristóbal de La Habana. They were inseparable, but only on land, when no one was watching them. On board the Buena Esperanza, each pretended the other did not exist. If forced to speak to each other in public on the boat, they would do so with distant courtesy. Neither wanted to be a marrano for the rest of his life.

Pedro had never uttered that word, marrano. Growing up in Santa Cruz de Tenerife, he was terrified that if he did, the word would stick to him forever, give him bad luck, make him grow a curly tail and stiff hairs that would stick out of his nose. He no longer checked the base of his spine every morning when he woke up, as he had done ever since a playmate had called him marrano. That was the first time he had heard it. However, he was now doubly repulsed by the word, because he had become thoroughly Christian in culture, while still deeply Hebrew in temperament, neither of which he knew yet, and pigs are loathsome to both from different angles. Jacinto, though, had no allegiance to anything outside his physical appetites, or so he claimed, though Pedro remembered Jacinto's drunken tears and pseudo-Ladino babble, his ostentatious way of stuffing himself with pork at every opportunity. Jacinto laughed at the word marrano and, when they were alone, to see Pedro squirm, he liked to sing softly in his ear an obscene ditty he had composed, rhyming marrano with *ano* (anus), and *ojo del amo* (eye of the master) with *ojo del ano* (asshole). Sometimes Jacinto would just mouth his rhyme at Pedro, snorting and wiggling his nose like a pig, shaking his big frame and the curly blond locks that San Cristóbal de La Habana's mulatto girls fought with each other to touch, so that Jacinto never paid for sex.

Perhaps because they were so different, while being alike from birth, the happiest time on board for Pedro was the one night a month that he and Jacinto stood guard together. They were alone for eight hours and could talk without witnesses. Unlike on land, Jacinto was always sober here. Captain de Horta, so lenient in other ways, ruthlessly punished any sailor who got drunk while on night watch: the first time, fifty lashes and ten days in the brig with only stale bread and water. If repeated, the man was left at the first port without a penny, and with a bad word whispered in the ear of the local alguacil, which in their case would be, or include, the troublesome marrano.

On their last watch together, the night before they reached the Biloxi Marsh, which the Spaniards called "*Marasmo*," Pedro had gone over the story of how he and Jacinto would jump ship in Veracruz, their last stop. They would bribe a public scrivener to get themselves new Christian identities and blend into the population. Pedro had been planning every detail for over a year, forcing Jacinto to save, so he, too, would have a gold onza when the time came. It gave Pedro great pleasure to tell Jacinto the story of their future together while they stood on lookout at night, half-whispering so he wouldn't be heard by anyone else (Pedro had noticed, watching *Fuenteovejuna* on that makeshift stage ten years earlier, that the line prompter hiding under a cardboard half shell did not whisper as much as he half-whispered, so that only whoever was sitting on the first row might catch a word or two. The one time the prompter was forced to whisper a line again because the actor had not heard it the first time, his whisper carried all the way to the back of the courtyard theater and the audience jeered and threw chicken bones. Pedro never whispered after that.)

In Pedro's story, after getting their new names, he and Jacinto would buy a mule and two horses, and make their way to the northern reaches of the New Spain, where one could get land for free. "You're standing all crooked," Jacinto said, when Pedro had them already in their haciendas, married to two Indian princesses in whose father's land Eldorado was located (at Jacinto's insistence, this had been added to the story a few months earlier). "You still look crooked to me." Pedro straightened himself again. "You look like an old man," Jacinto said, with unexpected bitterness, which he then tried to hide by grunting softly and wiggling his nose, pig-like. Pedro did not say anything else the rest of that night. He was startled by Jacinto's sourness. He did not understand it then, and he did not understand it forty-seven years later when, on his deathbed, he asked Jacinto, who had died long ago, "But what about Tenerife?" No one around him knew who Jacinto was, and what had happened in Tenerife, or even what or where Tenerife was. It is doubtful that Jacinto himself, had he been sitting next to the seventy-two-year-old Pedro, would have known specifically what it was about Tenerife that Pedro had in mind, although Jacinto, who had an excellent memory, would have remembered all about it, or at least those parts that were important to him, and either way would have been satisfactory for him and the dying man.

On his deathbed, what Pedro remembered was the day Jacinto had revealed to him the word marrano. They were eight-year-olds, battling with tree-branch swords in front of their parents' shacks, on the dirt road that led to the better parts of Tenerife. Jacinto, golden locks flowing, was as usual Tirant lo Blanc, and Pedro, the Sultan Mehmet. "*Portez comme un joug le Croissant!*" cried the fearsome Sultan. "*Groin de cochon! Nourri d'immondice et de fange. Nous n'irons pas à tes sabbats*, you filthy marrano," cried back Tirant, cutting off the Sultan's head and saving Constantinople. On his deathbed Pedro was asking Jacinto how he could have abandoned him, when the two should have been bound together forever, after Jacinto taught him that terrible word on a dusty Tenerife afternoon. The old man had forgotten by then that it had been he who had decided on that last night at the crow's nest to leave Jacinto. Unless he now meant not leaving in a physical sense, but abandoning love, which is what he thought Jacinto had done that night when he said to him, "You look like an old man." Those were the last words spoken that night. After that, they were both distracted until dawn by the smells of the approaching Biloxi Marsh.

Pedro had a crude map of San Cristóbal de La Habana in his hands. He was going to the church of Espíritu Santo, whose parish priest was said to be kind to those who had sincerely converted and become good Christians. He helped them start new lives free of the stigma of their origins, after satisfying himself that they were not opportunistic marranos. The church was on one side of a muddy plaza. The entire city seemed to be built on mud. The lower parts of the façades, even the palaces, were thickly caked. Streets dissolved in mud only to reappear again, even now in December, when it had not rained for a month. All the wealth of the city was indoors. Outdoors, pigs and garbage ruled, worse than in Tenerife's poor marrano neighborhood. When Pedro had a palace like the one across from the church of Espíritu Santo, he would pave the surrounding streets and order that they be kept free of pigs and garbage.

Father Leandro was in his vegetable garden when Pedro arrived. Pedro introduced himself and tried to show him his baptismal certificate, which stated that he was baptized in the Church of the Conception in Tenerife at thirteen months of age, when in truth he'd already been thirteen years old. His father had sold his only mule to bribe the sacristan, on whose penmanship and gambling habits the town's dwindling marrano population depended. Pedro's father and mother had pushed him to leave as soon as he was old enough to board a ship. There was little to eat in Tenerife and even real Christians were starving and setting sail for America or Constantinople. More importantly, in those windswept islands off the coast of Africa, a small and inbred world, it was impossible to hide or pass: a marrano would always be menaced. His three sisters had stayed behind. What else could they do?

Father Leandro did not take the paper from Pedro's hands. He did not even notice Pedro was holding it in front of his eyes. The priest was examining a sickly-looking turnip. "I can't make them grow in this heat," he said, through clenched teeth, reminding Pedro of Jacinto that last night at the watchtower, even if Jacinto's teeth were white and strong while Father Leandro's were crooked and yel-lowish. Pedro felt like running away. He had never seen icy-white anger before. He thought all anger was red, hot, and meaty. He was twenty-five years old, but he did not know much about the world outside the Buena Esperanza and the port whorehouses. "Take this to the kitchen," Father Leandro said, giving him the turnip. "I will hear your confession tomorrow."

Pedro worked in Father Leandro's vegetable garden every day from dawn until the morning mass was over. Then he cleaned the church and the sacristy, carried water and wood to the kitchen, and spent the rest of the day doing errands. For this he was given bread when he woke up, a good, hot meal at noon, and more bread before going to bed. He ate well here, compared to the Buena Esperanza, and put on some weight. He slept in the kitchen, on top of the massive stone cookstove when it was cold and rainy, and on the floor away from it on sweltering nights. He had been lucky. The seventeen-year-old Negro boy whom he replaced had disappeared a

71

few weeks before his arrival. Father Leandro refused to hire another Negro boy, not because he loathed Negroes as he now loudly proclaimed, but because he was heartbroken and afraid that the new one would remind him of the one who had left without a word, after Father Leandro had raised him from the age of five. "Almost like a son," he would tell himself in the privacy of his room, looking at his sagging face in the mirror. At the time, refusing to hire a Negro servant in San Cristóbal de La Habana was tantamount to renouncing servants. It was a miracle that Pedro had appeared at the church when he did, in the opinion of the cook, a vast mulatto woman who paid no attention to Father Leandro's rants about the ingratitude of Negroes, which she found self-evident and not in need of reiteration. "He spoiled that boy," she told Pedro. "I always said it'd end badly." Pedro agreed with everything she said, and was rewarded with extra bread. He was guarded, though, with her and everyone else. His first confession with Father Leandro was very satisfactory. Pedro knew his catechism inside out and gave all the right answers. He did not lie to the priest, but kept certain things to himself. These were things that he could not peel off himself any more than he could peel off his own skin. He reasoned that they must not be acquired habits or sensibilities, let alone sins, but rather traits he was born with. God had made him that way. He would shed his marrano skin, gladly, and become a Christian, but he would not toss away the self that God had created, the self that Jesus had died on the cross to redeem. Pedro would have been appalled to realize that he was being duplicitous, throwing his marrano skin to the Christian wolves so that he could keep his inner Jew safe, in some secret box. But he never did because he never told anyone those "certain things." Not Father Leandro. Not even his wife and children. Only sometimes did he tell Jacinto in his dreams. Little by little, those "certain things," as he himself called them, lost their names and any connection to other people, places, or history and became just who he was. When he died, he did not know he was dying as a Jew, but he did know that he was dying as himself.

13

Dry Blossoms

FROM ACROSS THE RIVER I could see the tiny stick figure high up against the darkening sky. McCabe was still standing on the edge of the ravine, where I had left her. Was she waiting for me to return and push her to her death? My elaborate plan for justice had not accounted for meekness. Oh, what meekness on the face of a criminal can do to the judge and executioner. Meekness, which carries no understanding of the crime, whether factual or moral, because it is an essential trait, like the wings of angels, that precedes any action or thought, even birth.

I sat on a fallen tree trunk to catch my breath. I had fled down Round Hill and across the bridge, then followed the trail by the water, toward the sunset and the remaining light. The shadows from the east were nipping at my heels as I rushed down the trail, trying to keep my feet dry. That is how Turgenev would have written it, and that is exactly how I remember it. The trail was getting soft, announcing the beginning of the marshes. By the time I collapsed on the tree trunk, the shadows had overtaken me. I did not have a flashlight, but I did not need one. I had taken the trail for years as a kid to sneak into town.

I stood up and began to walk toward Shangri-La. I do not know why. My feet just took me. I looked back up at the Judge's land before the river turned. It was now too dark to tell if the tiny stick figure was still there.

Shangri-La did not appear before me all at once. It crept in, lazily, as always. First came big chunks of brush in between the little cinder-block houses. Then, the brush became smaller, and larger the number of mangy dogs and barefooted children staring at me in malignant silence from their tiny backyards.

In the white neighborhoods to the east, decks, gardens, terraces, and picture windows overlooked the river. Shangri-La, on the other hand, turned its back to the water, which it saw as the enemy. Windowless rear walls fortified her against it. Her first lines of defense were the slivers of mud enclosed by rusty chicken wire that were grandiosely called backyards. You could not sit inside a Shangri-La house or stand in any backyard and look at the river. Nor would you want to if you were in your right mind. The river did not flow by Shangri-La: it stagnated there, foul and ugly, breeding mosquitoes long before sewers were installed and began disgorging fecal matter into the waters. Once or twice a year, without warning, the river swelled and flooded the backyards. Chicken, pigs, and children were then corralled on front porches, while flood ditches were dug in back.

Shangri-La preferred to face its inner roads, once a symbol of progress and civilization when they were new and sidewalks had been promised. Now crumbling, they were an indifferent sight to the current inhabitants. The few old-timers who did remember sat on porches with their backs to the road, enclosed in thickets of morning glories and potato vines that kept their disappointment out of sight.

I climbed the low riverbank behind my parents' house, holding on to roots with my hands while my feet slipped in the mud. After my mother's death, seven years ago, I had sold the house for $15,000 to a Mexican who worked at the remaining poultry-processing factory. That money was long gone. I reached the chicken-wire fence and crawled under it into our pathetic backyard. The house had disappeared. Only charred ruins were left, covered by a forest of thick, oversized brambles with killer thorns.

I was nailed to the ground. Not by shock, but by egocentric predicament. The house was not there, yet it was still there. As long as I stood there, it would remain there. I had been happy in this house. I had a happy childhood. Even my sometimes unhappy adolescence was happy. I was loved here. An only child, I was my parents' pride and hope, my grandmother's joy, Ezequiel and Genoveva's indulged goddaughter, standing in for the little girl they kept trying for in vain, and Rafael's brother, pal, fraternal twin. The burden of past happiness became unbearable. Charred ruins were the ointment that healed.

Night had fallen. My limbs regained movement. In the dim reflection of the corner streetlight, I stepped into the land that had held my old bedroom, trying not to get flayed by the thorny brambles. They were impossible to avoid. Soon, my left hand was scratched and bleeding. I kept my right hand in my pocket for protection.

The ground was higher where the house had stood. Its charred remains had created a thick layer of blackened chunks of concrete and wood. It was in that rich fire loam that the unusually robust brambles had grown. If they spread throughout Shangri-La, life would become hell for men. Every summer and fall my father and Ezequiel spent entire weekends with machetes in their hands, hacking away at the old brambles, pygmies by comparison to these, and burning them to the ground. Just so that Rafael and I could play in our contiguous backyards.

Had the house burned down accidentally, or was it arson? Nothing remotely useful had been left in the charred debris—no copper pipes, bolts, electrical wire, or roof tiles, but plenty of mosaic shards. We had green and gold Byzantine mosaic floors in every room just like they had in La Esperanza, even if they were expensive here, and impractical in the cold, humid winter months. My parents had installed them by themselves, working nights and weekends. I carried them from their boxes on the porch to the room where, crawling on their hands and knees, they placed them down. It took them two years to finish the whole house.

The Cohen house, next door, kept its original cement floors. Years later, when cement floors became fashionable among the very rich, Ezequiel bragged that he had seen it coming. My parents never contradicted him, although I once caught my mother rolling her eyes. They loved Ezequiel and indulged him despite his lack of ambition, which, my mother explained to me one night, was his only fault, but not his fault. I understood then that people are born with a certain moral temperament that they cannot change and should not be blamed for. At school I was taught the opposite. Every first Friday of the month, the principal made us yell in unison, pumping the air with our little right fists: "Yes, I can!" "Yes, I can!" "Yes, I can, and I will!" The future National Security Advisor loathed those Inspirational Fridays as much as I loved them. He just mouthed the words until the day he was caught and severely caned on his bare buttocks in the principal's office. After that, he screamed like everybody else, which was for him an unbearable humiliation.

I picked up a gold mosaic shard from our living room and put it in my pocket. The Cohen home was still there, on my right, packed now with destitute Mexicans, judging from the rotting lean-to shacks filling its backyard and the blaring *norteño* cacophony. I wondered if the house was rented, sold, or squatted in. Standing in the midst of the bramble forest that used to be our kitchen, I could not see Glorita's house on the left, but I heard its soft hum. "Every house has a distinctive breath, and every room within every house," Bebe had once said, showing me her room-tone calibrator.

It was snowing when Glorita moved in next door with her godmother, Altagracia, a cook in the white people's retirement home on the other side of town. Glorita was five years old, like me. Our carnal liaison began that same day, rolling on the snow in her new backyard, warm tongues licking each other's frozen lips, and lasted until the day I boarded that refugee bus. We were nineteen then. I never heard from her after that.

A father was never mentioned. Glorita's mother, who had died in childbirth, was complicatedly related to the godmother. So Altagracia was doubly bound to raise Glorita. A godmother raising an orphan was better than an ordinary parent. Altagracia was somebody in Shangri-La. She'd had a choice and done the right thing. I envied Glorita her godmother. Altagracia was wide, and regal, with copper skin the color of Glorita's hair, and a native south-Texas drawl that got stronger every year. No one ever ratted on Glorita, kid or adult, because they were afraid to break Altagracia's heart.

I could have gone down to the riverbank and climbed back up to Glorita's house. Instead, I chose to walk through the brambles to reach the road, a half-hour Via Dolorosa through our phantom kitchen, living room, porch, and front yard that bloodied my arms, hands, and face.

The corner streetlight blinked, then went off. Blind, on the pitch-black road, I walked the short distance to Glorita's house guided only by its hum, which became polyphonic as I approached, a weaving of room tones, as Bebe had explained to me, presciently, that day years ago. The house was shuttered and intact. There was no name on the gate. My eyes had gotten accustomed to the dark. I looked around to see if anyone was watching. Earlier, there would have been a dozen eyes behind the window shades, but this was dinner and telenovela time. The norteño racket had given way to women's bravura crying and fighting, punctuated by flashes of alarming symphonic music. The front yard and the porch were clean and empty: no furniture, no sign that anyone lived there. I circled the house trying to listen, but my footsteps were the only sound. A car came down the road. I hid behind the house, not wanting to be seen. The car did not stop. Abruptly tired and hungry, I longed to be back in the Judge's house, which now felt unreachable in space and time. I sat in the dirt, leaning against the back wall, facing the chicken-wire fence and, beyond, the invisible river. I must have fallen asleep.

When I woke up, the quarter moon was out, and Shangri-La was perfectly silent. By the position of the moon, I calculated that it was just after midnight. I circled Glorita's house again, leaning my shoulder against doors and windows and pushing hard. The kitchen door gave in with a groan. Like all kitchen doors in Shangri-La, it was on the right side of the house, toward the back. I stepped in and closed it carefully behind me. The hinges made the same scratchy sound as when Glorita sneaked out at night. The house was scrubbed clean and smelled disconcertingly fresh. There was a new fridge in the kitchen and a big, new TV set in the living room. The rest was old and faded, as if it had always been there. At first, it felt unfamiliar, except for a few items that I immediately recognized: the two rocking chairs that Glorita and I used to bring out onto the porch, unless it was raining (they were her godmother's two good pieces of furniture, left to her by her mother); Glorita's little-girl bed with the hand-painted flower buds on the headboard, which I always looked at while we kissed; her matching dressing-table; her bedroom wallpaper of tiny roses braided with gold.

After a while, however, the entire house seemed to be as I remembered it. Every single item was true. Even the new fridge and TV set now appeared in my mental snapshot if I closed my eyes. The present was becoming memory, implanting itself more vividly in my mind every minute I spent in that house, while my true memories dried out and turned to dust. Sitting on the rocking chair where Glorita always sat, her naked leg slung over the arm, I fought back against the power of the house. I tried to hold on to what remained of my memories, those brittle, wispy, shreds, to prevent what I was seeing now from supplanting them, but it was a lost battle. I could not tell whether I was holding on to the old, or the invading new. Like the woman giving in to the sweetness of the conquering pod, I meekly let the house enter my mind.

14

Reckoning

GLORITA AND BEBE are like Saint Theresa's two candles, so close that they produce a single flame. Yet, they can be separated, and each will subsist. Distinct, but one. First there was Glorita, then Bebe. Each announced the other. Forward and backward. Yes, my timid epiphany: Glorita announced Bebe, but Bebe also announced Glorita. I see it clearly now.

When I had a well-fed brain, it was too enslaved by Bebe's flesh to understand. Even after she became Mrs. McCabe and I declared myself cured of her, the longing to touch her, lick her, smell her armpits, swim up and down inside her persisted—locked in a cage, in some shameful corner, but alive. Unrequited lust is eternal, as long as there is flesh to support it. I never even stole a kiss from Bebe, unlike with Glorita, whose every delicious corner I poked and squeezed for years. Glorita, who denied me nothing, except perhaps her love, I forgot until I came back here. I did not even keep her in a cage. She was erased. Or so I thought. And McCabe? Was she one, or two? What was she? These are mysteries I would like to live long enough to understand.

Now that all the flesh I have left is in one tenuous brainstem, philosophy comes naturally to me. I have no trouble understanding abstractions that used to elude me when I was a short, stocky, female biped. Infinity and immortality are as simple to see, hear, smell, taste, and touch as boiling coffee. Losing my sensory organs has sharpened my memory of the past. Of the present, all I can perceive is how dry, brittle, and powdery I am becoming. I cannot imagine my last shred of flesh surviving for long in this sub-zero temperature. I won't suffer. I do not, I cannot, feel cold. I can keep time, though, so I know that today is January 31, and that Rafael Cohen has been dead for thirty-seven days.

15

The New World

IT WAS DAWN AND SNOWING when I stepped back onto the river trail.

Snow in October is not unknown in Elmira, even if the natives feign dismay and disbelief each time it appears. I find this particular local affectation endearing. Elmira has thousands of sharp instruments to gauge who belongs and who doesn't, yet only this painless social glue. Anyone, even if she plucks chicken feathers all day and lives in Shangri-La, can join Mrs. Crandall in the certainty that snow has never before fallen in October. It's a little fib that costs no money and very little loss of dignity. It doesn't even rate as a venial sin. You can go back to Shangri-La holding your head high, become one with the massas every October until the brackish sewer waste posturing as a river freezes over. At which point, you can see the rats trapped under the surface ice, trying to claw their way out, in vain.

Round Hill emerged abruptly beyond the river bend, its top swimming in a swirl of snow and low clouds. If McCabe were still standing there, she would be as invisible to me as I to her. I wished that she had stayed out all night, and that she was now frozen, delivering both of us from what would come next. I had returned with her to Elmira in complete confidence, a surgeon with a steady hand and a precise diagnosis. Now the malignancy had metastasized. McCabe was not who she used to be. Or was she? Glorita was back. Bebe, where was Bebe? I prayed for the Tongues of Fire to appear again and cleanse my mind, calling aloud as the snowfall turned into a blizzard, slowing and finally stopping my progress.

Somewhere near the bridge I curled inside a hollowed tree trunk. I pulled my sweater over my head, and kept my hands in my pockets, remembering that most body heat is lost through the hands, feet, and head. It was not the first time in my life that I had been caught in a blizzard midway between Shangri-La and Round Hill. Glorita and I had spent a tasty hour and a half huddled inside a similar tree one night when we were fifteen. I could feel her warm body next to mine now. "How come you never told me about Glorita?" Bebe said, wedging herself between my left arm and the tree side, her arms crossed over her chest. She was wearing her Sandra Dee sweater, a pink angora confection found at the Salvation Army shop on Fifth Avenue. "I had forgotten about her," I said, truthfully. Bebe opened her blue eyes a little wider, held them like that for a beat, and then allowed them to slowly retrieve their natural shape. This was her highly skeptical glance, tiny enough to be deniable. I respected the convention. There was a soupçon of cynicism in that glance, signaling to the world that Bebe was awfully smart. She was, but not as much as she, and I, once thought. I reacted to her glance with rearguard petulance as usual: "I don't mean 'forgotten' in the legal sense. If the FBI questioned me, I would have to confess to having known Glorita, and having been born here. But we can't conduct our lives like a courtroom drama. We have to allow room for forgetfulness." Bebe stared at me with her normal eyes, a long time, unblinking. "Are you trying to hypnotize me?" I said with forced cheerfulness, shutting my eyes.

When I opened them, I was in bed, in the Judge's studio, under many blankets. I heard whispers. Someone took my right wrist. I felt a sharp pain. Everything went black again.

I came back up in sharp jolts, like an archaic sponge diver. Bleeding from every orifice, vomiting, defecating. Each hole trying to outdo the others in grotesque display. "Is she dying?" someone whispered. "A cloaca," someone else whispered. When I opened my eyes again, sunshine filled the room. The trees outside were green. Through the half-opened window came a soft breeze smelling of apples and molasses. I was on dry land. A rustle made me turn my head to the right. McCabe was sitting next to the bed in my favorite chair, a small red leather notebook on her bony knees. She was wearing the same jeans and plaid red jacket she had worn on our fishing trip. I shut my eyes again, hoping she would tire and leave. Skeletal McCabe, unlike her chubby predecessor, was so quiet I wondered if she actually breathed. I kept my eyes shut until the soles of my feet hurt as if I were walking on burning coals. It was dusk outside. The room was in shadows. She was still there.

"It's Thursday, November 1," McCabe said, as if reading my mind. I had been away from this world for a week and a day.

McCabe refused to give me a painkiller. Instead, she brought me a vegetable broth and a sliver of bread pudding with a touch of molasses. I drank the broth by myself, shakily holding the hot bowl to my lips. She spoon-fed me the pudding, gently, without even asking. I couldn't have held the spoon, or found my own mouth.

While she was gone with the empty tray, I tried to sit up. I couldn't. My upper-body muscles shook with the effort. My legs wouldn't move. Had they been amputated? I fell back on the pillows, covered in sweat. McCabe was suddenly standing by the bed. I hadn't heard her return. She pulled down the starched white sheets that covered me from the chin down. My feet were wrapped in padded bandages snaking up to mid-calf. "Frostbite," she said. "It will heal." I did not believe her. Anything can be wrapped to resemble feet. McCabe bent and produced a bedpan from under the bed. She handed it to me, along with a hospital buzzer that must have been installed while I was sleeping. She then left the room, walking noiselessly on her hiking boots, still caked with Wanetka River mud.

McCabe had pronounced "frostbite" and "heal" crisply, and fluently, with no trace of her earlier hesitations, or of the raffish Brooklyn accent that Old McCabe affected to better peddle her overpriced gallery merchandise. In McCabe's newly smaller mouth (how can a mouth shrink?), which dominated her face in ways Old McCabe's big mouth never did, the inanimate now became intimate, without ceasing to be inanimate. This is how it must have been between Dr. Mengele and his patients. Or the Tribunal of Faith and the falsely accused true converts.

I never asked, and McCabe never told me, how I had gone from the tree trunk in the blizzard to the sickbed. I was grateful for her silence, because I did not want to be grateful to her for my life.

I was now a doll for McCabe's Mary Magdalene to play with, tearing my limbs in subtly different ways each day. Every morning, when McCabe emptied my urine and feces and changed my pre-gangrenous bandages, she would put me on the rack, torn between reason and humiliation, with its black-bile corollary: *ressentiment*. I did not know then that I was experiencing an overflow of gratitude.

Ressentiment is indispensable for the criminal palette, but only in small, controlled doses. This sudden excess, imposed and not chosen, was rotting my insides. I could no longer see myself as a Lizzy Borden. So, each time McCabe left the room, I tried to cleanse myself of the rot. Each time I failed. Sleep helped, once. I prayed for amnesia, McCabe amnesia. I actually said a prayer aloud, both truthful and insincere: "Oh, Lord, I am an unbeliever . . . " it began. Like sleep, the prayer only worked the first time.

It was bad enough for my criminal project that a doctor had already seen me four times. He was bald, petulant, and always wore an orange hunter's jacket with a white fur collar. The first time, I was unconscious. The second time was the day after I woke up, when he congratulated McCabe for her dexterity with bandages, declaring that she would have made an excellent nurse. The third was a week later, on the seventh day of my dismemberment on the rack. The fourth, a week after that, on November 16, my fourteenth day of agony, when ressentiment had sucked me dry, and the doctor, sensing I was more compliant, found me much better.

"Explain to her," he told McCabe across my sickbed, as if I weren't there (and I wasn't: I was wearing my invisibility headscarf—the infidel had seen me dangerously bareheaded the day I was being de-frozen), "that she must not walk until I authorize it. I still don't like the look of those toes. We're not out of the woods yet."

His last phrase hung in the air for the rest of the day. McCabe felt it, and so did I. She broke down first. "We're going into the woods, not coming out of them. Don't you think?" she said, glancing out of the window. This was the first time McCabe, Old or New, had asked my opinion about anything in the ten years we had been acquainted. "Depends on which woods," I croaked, throat tight, uncertain. McCabe was thinking so hard that her face became even paler, her lips bluish, and her eyes bloodshot. She was facing me now, trying to dig out sense from a remote hole, using the philistine brain that she was wearing, courtesy of Old Pig McCabe. Stop! I ordered her with my mind, but Reason prevented me from getting that merciful word out of my mouth, hoping that McCabe would keep her teeth clenched until all oxygen to her brain was cut off and she would drop dead in front of my invalid bed. "The woods of chance," McCabe finally said, fixing her eyes on mine. "You mean fate, McCabe," I said, distracted by Reason's incongruous butcher's apron. "No, I mean chance," she said, with a frosty firmness. "The right word is 'chance'. The woods of chance." She then did something she had never done before: she sat on the side of my bed. Prudently, midway between my head and my feet. Startled, I let her. I even welcomed her (this I admit to myself only now that I am breathing my own dust to dust). For an instant, ressentiment and reason flew from my mind, taking the Magdalene with them. I was seeing the New McCabe as if for the first time. She had won the right to sit on my bed. She had forced the mind of a hog to think in a direction other than satiation. Even if Kant's bones did not lie there, even if the phrase "woods of chance" was infelicitous and un-euphonic, to utter it was a victory for the human spirit.

McCabe suddenly looked livelier than she had since our drive to Wanetka Falls, when the sight of the migrating birds had given her the kiss of life, and the eloquence to tell a story that I, in bed now with my feet beginning to throb and burn, had almost forgotten. "The woods of chance," she repeated, savoring each syllable. Hearing it a third time, slowly spiraling out of her mouth, sent an electric shock up my chilled spine. Was McCabe threatening me? Did she know what I was up to? If she did, she could easily strangle me with her big hands or asphyxiate me with the pillow. I still couldn't move. I looked at the side of her face. Was she stupid but lucky, as I had always thought, or very clever? Innocent she couldn't be. No one could. Innocence was Bebe's kingdom, as imaginary as the one down in Florida. McCabe must have left the room while I choked with fear. She was back now, with her nurse's tray. She put on a pair of clean latex gloves and began undoing the bandages on my feet.

16

Migration of the Soul

THE END OF NOVEMBER was so balmy that the Judge's yellow rosebush flowered again, and trees clung to their ochre and scarlet leaves. The *Gazette* warned Elmirans that their town was below the level of the Little Ohio River, and when polar ice caps fully melted, it would become a new Atlantis, just like Bangladesh and Fiji. Elmirans reacted to the news with local pride concealed under a curmudgeonly shell. At the library, the two world atlases that Mrs. Crandall kept on a shelf near her desk were in such high demand that she decided to leave them out permanently. They were put on a table, far enough from her so that people would not be embarrassed to be caught looking for submerged Fiji and Bangladesh, but in her direct line of vision, so that no one would rip out a page or walk off with the expensive volumes. Not that Elmirans had ever vandalized their public library, but certain people, who had moved to Elmira from other, coarser places, would have done it a thousand times already had it not been for Mrs. Crandall's vigilance.

A week after the woods of chance incident, and following a fifth visit by the doctor, McCabe rolled up the carpet and vacuumed and scrubbed the naked floorboards. "That's where it belongs," she said when I finally asked her why she was moving the Judge's Biedermeier console from one corner of my room to another. It was not an opinion, but a fact, she said when I prodded her further: she had no opinions. McCabe's accounts of herself were always too objective and materialistic to be truthful.

For the most part, however, I was left with no explanation of her whereabouts or behavior, such as the night when she came in, breathless and sweaty, two hours late to change my bandages, or the afternoon when she opened my door several times and glanced at me from the threshold without a word.

If McCabe was a random cipher outside her Magdalene duties, it was not because she was rude. On the contrary, she treated me with what is usually referred to as "great care." Coming from her it was not insulting. McCabe seemed new to the world in this, and so many other ways. Her abruptness was innocent. She just did not believe in the healing power of explanations, as she herself would tell me later in her own, sharper words, which I cannot now recall.

When she was done drying the floorboards, McCabe brought in a shiny, new wheelchair, and put it by my bed. Then she sat across the room, to watch me go from bed to wheelchair. All this without a word.

A nurse, a home attendant, a friend, a neighbor, a lover, a co-worker—a normal person, in short—would have helped me go from bed to wheelchair, at least this first time, and would have made sure I knew how to, or else taught me. Not McCabe, whose blank face was unreadable: sadistic voyeur, sink-or-swimmer, or worse, squeamish about touching me? She had never offered to bathe me. I would have refused, of course, but it bothered me that she had not asked. She made sure my night table was well stocked with antiseptic hand wipes and lotions, and every morning she left fresh underwear and pajamas on my bed. My feet were the only part of my body that she had ever touched, always with surgical gloves.

Shame made me want to wait until McCabe was gone to try the wheelchair, but fear of falling and breaking a bone prevailed. So, I did my trick in front of her, putting the required brave smile on my face after every false start (there were four). When I finally managed to sit on the wheelchair, I almost clapped and barked for my fish.

I spent the rest of November mostly sitting by the window in my wheelchair. The Judge's studio was on the west side of the house, so I had a view of his rose garden and the rolling meadow that ended abruptly in a one-hundred-foot drop down to the river. If I had pushed McCabe off that edge a remote month ago, I would now be walking the New York City streets, free at last. She would not have put up a fight. None of my flesh, hair, or buttons under her nails or in her stiff, rigor mortised fist, no suspicious scratches or lesions on either one of us. Clean. Perfect. An inexplicably lost opportunity.

I couldn't remember what had made me run away. So I rewound the scene in my mind, analyzing it frame by frame. Was it McCabe's usurping the name "Rafael Cohen"? Her snatching Old McCabe from my claws? Both had pushed me to kill, not flee. They now seemed insignificant slights, and my surge of hatred against McCabe a petulant reaction. I found the microscopic trigger on the last frame the twentieth or thirtieth time I scrutinized it. Lillian Gish in *Broken Blossoms* was Bebe at fourteen, when we first met. Same blonde locks, blue eyes evoked by the black and white emulsion, little English-girl face incongruously attached to a coltish American body (tiny breasts, unformed hips, round, high, tight little ass emerging). Lillian Gish had Bebe's body, but not an ounce of her soul. Bebe was not naturally sweet, pure, and innocent, though she trafficked in all three qualities, a great comedian reprising a classical role. Bebe never would have looked sweetly at the Chinaman. But McCabe did.

17

Domesticity

ONE MORNING IN LATE NOVEMBER, the bulky bandages on my feet were replaced by a lighter set. That evening McCabe told me, "You will soon be allowed to walk." She was sitting next to me by the window, gazing at the sunset sky through the Judge's binoculars. I asked her what she was looking for, since it was too late in the season for migrating birds. She was looking for laggards, she said, small flocks delayed for whatever reason, perhaps confused by the warm weather. They were rare, but not unheard of. She pulled out her red leather notebook and a pen from her shirt pocket, and wrote something on it. Seen upside down, it appeared to be some kind of shorthand. The Judge's blooming yellow roses attracted a constant swarm of butterflies. I pointed them out to McCabe. She was afraid of butterflies, she said. I laughed unguardedly, which I regretted immediately. Luckily, she didn't seem to notice. "Not live ones," she said. "Dead ones." Dead butterflies inside the house brought bad luck, she explained. Superstition did not fit in the picture I had been composing of the New McCabe. She didn't seem to be the type, but then, neither are most serial killers, if you believe what their neighbors say on TV. Old McCabe liked to bellow, "Knock on wood!" and slam the nearest surface at the least provocation. It seemed an assertion of her larger-than-life status more than a superstition, but who knows? I never asked her. Now that I was immobilized, able to study this McCabe from up close, and desperately needing to understand her if I was to carry out the mission that brought us here, I realized how little I knew about Old McCabe. I didn't regret it that day, watching the butterflies swarm over the yellow roses, and I don't regret it today. I knew Old McCabe's broad strokes. She was solid, bursting with life. She was my rival. She got Bebe. What else was there to know? New McCabe, on the other hand, was like a charcoal smudge with a flinty core. I could not imagine her with Bebe, or anyone else.

The array of multicolored pills and syrups I had to swallow each day was cut by one third, and then by a half. I asked to be taken off the ones that made me drowsy. McCabe called the doctor, but he insisted that nothing should be changed. Or so she said: I never saw him after that. I began to keep some of the pills in my mouth, while pretending to swallow them. Then, when McCabe had left the room, I'd spit them out and hide them inside my pillow. I was soon able to identify the narcoleptics. A clearer brain was worth the slightly increased pain.

Now that I could wheel myself to the toilet, McCabe spent less time with me. I could see her walking around the garden in the early morning, even under the drizzle, until the FedEx man drove in with a packet of her overnight letters from New York. He would return at noon to pick up the load she was sending back. This was the busiest time of the year for art merchants, she said, when I asked about the increased activity. She always answered my questions in a clear, concise way. I would even say truthful if I were a jury member, although she rarely initiated a conversation. At first, I was careful not to ask her too many questions, even rhetorical ones, to launch a conversation, because questions are far more revealing than answers. Boredom made me relax my rule, but only after she had pronounced the words "the woods of chance," and began to shed her Magdalene habit, of which only her nightly bandaging of my feet remained. Any day, I expected her to tell me that she had to go back to New York City. My only hope was to be on my feet at least two days before her (our?) return. I couldn't think of a way to kill her from a wheelchair.

I felt no ressentiment. McCabe had snuffed it out when she put her finger on chance. Blindly. By chance. I forgave her on that day for anything she may have done (she, personally, distinctly, and through her, the first McCabe, the one whose execution I still thought would set me free). I had forgiven her, even as my overfilled bedpans allowed her to play the Magdalene a while longer. Her presence did not bother me. It actually put me into a comfortably neutral gear, equidistant between happiness and sadness, boredom and excitement, vigil and sleep. She was now cutting some yellow roses from the top of the bush, which she could reach with her long arms. Those were not my secateurs in her hands. That is, the Judge's secateurs, which I kept under lock and key in the gardening shed. She was moving her lips. Singing? I put down the binoculars. Perhaps this was not meant to be a crime of pure reason.

18

Pilgrims

MCCABE AND PETRONA spent the entire day before Thanksgiving in the kitchen. Mrs. Crandall joined them at noon. I saw her zoom up the driveway in her husband's black Lincoln Continental, halt in a gravel-scattering screech, and run into the house carrying in her arms something bulky and heavy in a blanket. All day long I heard the three of them laughing among the clash of pots and pans. That is, I identified Petrona's and Mrs. Crandall's laughs, which I had heard before (Petrona's at the kitchen phone, when she thought she was alone; Mrs. Crandall's at the public library, all the time, shamelessly), and I assumed the third one must have been McCabe's. It was the laughter of a crystalline soprano. As different from old McCabe's ample contralto guffaws as a coyote's howl from the twelve bells of St. Mary le Bow.

Mrs. Crandall was the last person I expected to see in the house. This was a puzzling and unwelcome development. Had McCabe invited her? Why? When? Was this the first time she had been allowed inside the house, or had she been here before? I had not heard her voice inside it, or the voice of any other stranger except the doctor. There had been whispers during the first days after I had regained consciousness, but I could not tell dream from reality then.

At noon I heard Petrona leaving the lunch basket outside my room, as usual. I instantly wheeled myself to the door, hoping to cross-examine her, but I was too late. When McCabe had brought me my breakfast at nine o'clock, as usual, she asked me how I'd spent the night, as she always did, and we said something about the weather. Not a word about Mrs. Crandall or the upcoming kitchen activities. I would now have to wait until the evening to ask her. Directly, or deviously? I had not confronted this dilemma since we had settled into our dispassionate domestic routine. I felt rusty.

Evening was when McCabe and I spent some time together. She would sit next to me by the window, scanning the sky with the Judge's binoculars and jotting remarks in the small notebook she always carried. When it rained, we would play Chinese checkers. That soon began to bore me. The only unknown was the speed with which my blacks would slaughter McCabe's reds. "Don't you feel sorry for them?" I asked her, after one notably swift carnage. "Someone has to win," she answered indifferently. I found a dusty Scrabble set that the Judge had wedged between Toynbee's *A Study of History* and Carlyle's *The French Revolution*. Scrabble would expand McCabe's vocabulary. I would have to let her win now and then to keep her interested. Fear proved stronger than boredom in the end. I couldn't even bring myself to touch the letters. Was it just a reading game, or could it be considered a form of writing? I had not tested my illness since that Sunday evening in New York when I lost nouns, the last words I could still write.

After birdwatching or Chinese checkers, we would have dinner on the Judge's desk, from a cart Petrona would leave outside the door before going home. She was surpassing herself in the cooler days of November. We ate pozole, choucroute, boeuf bourguignon, an airy arroz con pollo, polenta with mushrooms. I decided to give her a Christmas bonus out of my own pocket. To reward her improved cooking, and also to get her on my side for when the time came. The wines were cannily chosen, too. Was it Petrona, or McCabe who picked them? Both were wine illiterates. I never asked. I didn't even care anymore how they could get into the wine cellar while I was still holding the only key. The endgame was approaching. Besides, I confess that I enjoyed my nightly oenological surprises.

After dinner, I would choose music for McCabe. Easy things at first, like Chopin's mazurkas. She would sit in a straight-backed chair, her long legs stretched before her, crossed at the ankles. If asked, she would say this one was very nice, and that one she did not understand, and that other one she liked less than the one she had heard a week earlier. Since I had already forgotten which was which, and she could not remember titles or composers, she would whistle the music for me. She was an accomplished, pitch-perfect whistler. She spoke using two hundred words at most, but had the instinct of a good hunting dog if dogs hunted music, not ducks.

On Thanksgiving Eve, when it got too dark for McCabe to scan the sky for laggard flocks, we dined on a pumpkin velouté soup (a Mexican standard reinterpreted with a delicate French technique. Petrona astounded me—I did not think McCabe, much less Mrs. Crandall, could have pulled this off), braised quail and jasmine rice, and leeks au gratin. The wine was a Cahors Clos Triguedina 1998. Two bottles. Dessert was an upside-down pineapple cake. "Is this our Thanksgiving dinner?" I asked in my most inoffensive voice, fishing for information about Mrs. Crandall's presence and the unusual kitchen activity, which the size and art of this dinner alone could not explain, since Petrona had been gradually exceeding herself on both counts for the past month. "It's only Thanksgiving Eve," said McCabe firmly. Was she dumb, or just a bad liar? Unable to tell, I uncorked the Cahors, tasted it, and declared it extraordinary. She smiled indulgently, as she often did, lately.

There was a prodigious amount of food on the table that evening. Dinner lasted more than three hours. "All we're missing now is the flying hog," I quipped when the wine went to my head. McCabe's face suddenly became so pale and translucent that when she drank wine to hide her perturbation I could see it swirling inside her mouth. I showed her the Judge's translation of Rabelais' *Quart Livre*, one of the few works of fiction on his bookshelves. The skin on her face slowly recovered its normal opacity and hue. Her hands were greasy from the quail, she said, so she did not want to touch the book. I opened it to an illustration of the monstrous, bejeweled hog flying over the andouille army opposing that of Pantagruel. The andouille warriors were depicted throwing off their weapons and falling on their knees, their hands joined together in silent adoration of the winged hog, on whose golden collar the Ionic inscription ΥΣ ΑΘΗΝΑΝ ("a hog teaching Minerva") could be read. McCabe examined the illustration for a long time, while chewing on the tiny quail bones. She asked me to tell her the story, because she would never be able to read a book as old and valuable as this. "Put it back on the shelf. I'm afraid of an accident," she said, her voice raspy from all the eating and drinking. I obeyed and she relaxed on her seat, attacking another portion of quail.

I told her about the battle between the scholarly giant and the tripe sausages, halted by the grizzly hog flying from the north, making up half of it: my forgetfulness matching McCabe's ignorance. When she asked for more, I narrated young Gargantua's culinary excesses, which I envied and remembered better. Soon I was also eating the quail with my fingers. We were not piggish, McCabe and I, even if we used our fingers to separate the flesh from the bird's dainty skeleton. Forks and knives were still used for the rice and the leeks; dessert spoons, for the cake. McCabe followed the story as avidly as she was eating the bird. She was starved, not just for food, but for words.

We ate and drank everything on our table—and on Gargantua's—to the last crumb and drop: our bird flesh and bones, caramelized fruit, flaming soup, the thick and velvety Cahors, and his sausages, boars, hams, eels, cheeses, and barrels of cheap wine. The table was a battlefield littered with bones, the white tablecloth soaked in Cahors blood. I wished McCabe were the size of a quail, so I could snap her neck, dismember her body with my own hands, eat her meager flesh, and hide her skeleton in this miniature Antietam. The perfect, effortless crime. But McCabe was a giant when measured against the average quail, and even compared to me, slowly shrinking in my wheelchair as my inactive muscles and bones atrophied.

My eyelids felt heavy. When I woke up, my forehead was encrusted with quail bone shards. I must have dropped it on the table with a loud thump, like a reverse wax seal. McCabe was standing next to me with a glass of water. I drank it. After thanking her for the pleasant evening and wishing her a good night's sleep, I wheeled myself into the bathroom to empty my painfully full bladder and pick the bone shards off my forehead. When I emerged, ten minutes later, all signs of our banquet were gone. The dining table was, once more, the Judge's desk. All lights were off, except for a table lamp at the far corner. I was alone. As I was wheeling myself to the bedroom, I heard a rustle. McCabe was sitting in the dark, in her music-listening chair. It was past one in the morning. I was exhausted. I should have refused to choose music for her that night.

We ended up listening to César Franck's *Symphony in D minor*. I had been tempted to play it for her before, but always held back at the last minute. She was not ready for it, I thought. The first time was precious. Unrepeatable. What if she just heard a jumble of sounds, but not music? Worse, what if she tried to make sense of it with the only building blocks she had (implanted in her brain via countless elevator, movie, TV, Top 40 and airplane exposures) and re-composed Franck's wrenchingly sublime cry into a cheap, weepy soundtrack? I could not risk that. This was music I had listened to hundreds of times since I first found it at the Elmira public library, at the age of fifteen, long before Mrs. Crandall dreamt of marrying Mr. Crandall and moving here from . . . where? I had sensed, obscurely, from the first time I saw her, that Mrs. Crandall was not an Elmiran by birth. Only now, while fingering the archaic Franck CD, did my mind gel around the fact of Mrs. Crandall's questionable origins. Questionable not because she was from somewhere else, but because she was insufficiently so.

While pretending not to be impressed, Elmira secretly embraced with pride those it considered the true foreigners in their midst—from Chicago, New York, Boston, and, when it existed, St. Louis—all wealthy, white, and inaccessible. That's how Elmira dealt with the truly foreign, whether human or meteorological (such as the news that Elmira would become a new Atlantis). Spics, niggers, Chinks, wogs, etc., were not foreign, but alien. They need not be discussed here.

But beyond the truly foreign and the alien lay the disdained: the small towns on the far edges of the county whose inhabitants Elmira classified in two distinct categories: the unwashed and semiliterate who liked it there (and which Elmira, while avoiding them in person, endowed from a distance with all manner of folkloric virtues), and those who dreamt of becoming Elmirans. Mrs. Crandall pertained to this last category, as revealed by her rebellious buttocks. Her rise to more or less full Elmiran-hood must have been arduous and dangerous. She began acquiring an Amazonian grandeur in my mind at that moment, a new Liberty Leading the People. Transfixed by the image of Mrs. Crandall, splendidly barefoot and bare-breasted, charging forward over a barricade and a pile of heroic corpses, I recklessly put the Franck CD in the player.

The first chords brought me back to the room. McCabe was staring at me, but quickly looked away. I must ask her what Mrs. Crandall was doing in our kitchen, I thought as I let the moment slip away. Then the music swept into the room, dwarfing us, taking control. *Free will is a joke, little human quail*, it said. Before surrendering, I managed to position my wheelchair across from McCabe. Those were our usual seats, at opposite angles, separated by a red oriental rug and a low table where I kept the books I was reading, now all from the Judge's bookshelves (I had not asked McCabe to get me books from the public library, wanting to keep her out of the public eye). The books between us were old and opulently bound, books I would never have read on my own, or even held in my hands, such as the account of Caesar's conquest of Gaul, and Thucydides' history of the Peloponnesian War.

When the music stopped, McCabe's eyes were closed. I could not tell if she was awake or sleeping. "What do you think?" I said, and then, when she did not answer: "Did you like it?" She opened her eyes. She looked tired, or sick. I offered her a glass of water. She declined it. In all my preparations to get rid of her, it had never crossed my mind that McCabe could get sick, could die a natural death in a hospital. "It's too intimate," she finally said. I saw the intimacy of her naked, lifeless body under the hospital sheets, with only her hands and face uncovered. "That music," her voice echoed, as if I were waking up from anesthesia. "It's too intimate."

Shame does make your face burn. Mine did. I had been caught crossing a line I had not seen. I apologized repeatedly until McCabe's calm gaze stopped me. Then I apologized for apologizing. I did not tell her the one thing that might explain my faux pas, and at the same time render it more intolerable: César Franck's symphony had been my secret soundtrack for Bebe, as it had been, earlier, for Glorita. Telling her would have been "too intimate," nauseatingly icky, and turned me into a creep—which I am not, in spite of everything I have confessed so far. More importantly, it would have discredited me in her eyes. Turning this sublime monument of the Western musical canon into a private, jerk-off soundtrack was bad taste of the worst order, the kind that makes white people laugh, and spics cry, and thus confirms the subhuman nature of the latter along with their propensity to confuse emotional bulimia with culture.

There was one last, dishonorable reason for not having told McCabe all about César Franck's *musica interrupta*: I was afraid she would beat me up. Old McCabe could still be lurking somewhere inside this pale creature. The bridge of my nose had thickened permanently after Old McCabe had punched me, the day after our arrival. It was a subtle change, probably invisible to all but me, for whom it was (and still is, even in my terminally disembodied state) a disfigurement. Every day I checked my nose in the mirror a dozen times, repulsed at the new Hottentot bone with its tiny incongruous bump, until little by little, I forgot the bridge of my original nose, narrow, straight, perfect. A Madison Avenue plastic surgeon I consulted under an alias, by phone, said that to restore my nose to its original shape he needed a clear picture of it, in profile. I did not have one. The second-best option was to find my birth nose among the three hundred and forty-seven in a catalogue he sent. Not only

I did not find it, but hours of studying hundreds of similar noses destroyed the memory of mine.

Underneath every shameful secret there always lies another. While César Franck's *Symphony* was my secret soundtrack, there was another behind that, even more secret, one that I had denied all my life. It was an old song that my grandmother first heard as a child in La Esperanza, a syrupy, heart-wrenching bolero. I listened to it as much as to the Franck piece, and for much the same reason, though at the time, I never allowed myself to think of Glorita, or Bebe, or anyone or anything else while I did. I emptied my heart and my mind first, as they say you must do when listening to Bach's partitas, to better appreciate their architecture.

I was not ashamed of using Franck's music for my own tawdry ends. Only of being found out by the Big White Eye, whether Cyclopean (attached to the flesh and blood of individuals) or diffusely societal. However, my ultra-secret bolero triggered such shame and fear that I did not even want myself to know that I was listening to it. Decoupling sense and consciousness was a Shangri-La specialty: we were all born with that gift, although Rafael and I excelled at it. This little song had to be decoupled for security reasons: it unveiled my spic soul. If the knowledge that you listened to it—or even knew that it existed—fell into the wrong hands, you could be squashed. I kept the bolero recording hidden under a loose floorboard at the bottom of my closet, not even trusting my parents, or my grandmother, or the Cohens with my secret. It would have given them the same intimate knowledge of me that I had of them. They used to listen to that bolero when I was little, but then they stopped, because it made the men sad, and the women smile at them indulgently to hide their even deeper sadness.

If I could have told McCabe about the bolero that evening, confessed that there was something even more shameful and inappropriate than the Franck symphony. If I had played it for her then, would she still have found the symphony "too intimate," and would that have changed anything because removing even a tiny cog alters the flow of events, as Hollywood has been warning us for two centuries? I did not have the choice that night, because I had forgotten the bolero. It just came back to me a moment ago in this cold, dusty landscape in which the underside of a mattress is my last sky. I am listening to it in my mind right now.

19

Burnt Feet

THE HOUSE WAS SILENT the next afternoon when I woke up. There was no lunch basket by my door; no one came when I rang my hospital bell or yelled. And the phone by my bed was dead. Outside a storm was raging, a typical Elmiran Thanksgiving storm—a North Atlantic gale with its black skies, brutal galley winds, and forty-foot waves, which central casting had successfully adapted to the heartland.

"A Thanksgiving message from *El Jefe*," Ezequiel Cohen bellowed every year in Spanish, pointing upward with his drippy, buttery corn on the cob, and waiting the required three beats before the punch line: "You're all in the same boat!" Then, a theatrical aside in broken English: "'Cept dat soma yous travel firs class!" Everyone, even Genoveva who never laughed at her husband's jokes, would crack when Ezequiel said "yous" in what he called his Little Sambo accent. Our Negro neighbors down the road couldn't get enough of it. Ezequiel was asked to do the Sambo in their front yard at least once a week.

In my first year and only year in college I found out that all this was wrong. I lectured my parents, both of whom agreed it was awful while shuffling their feet and avoiding my gaze. I slammed the kitchen door on their Stepin Fetchit noses. When I tried to force my mother to talk to Ezequiel, she stared at me as if I were a slimy, green creature from outer space, the first such stare in a line of thousands that would stretch onward for the next two decades, until she died, well before her time. I considered approaching Rafael. He must have heard an even harsher judgment at his college about his father's hobby. After all, he was not going to backward Elmira County Community College like I was, but to—gasp!—Harvard. On a full scholarship, complemented by assorted little grants which he kicked back to his endemically hand-to-mouth parents.

I did not envy Rafael, then or now. He was a genius. He would have been Mozart if he had been born with musical genes. More importantly: he was a good son, and remained so to the end. That was his biggest accomplishment. He made us proud. His triumphs were ours. He deserved the very best in life. That was the prevailing wisdom in both our families, to which I subscribe to this day. I never spoke to Rafael about his father's Little Sambo deviationism, afraid to upset the delicate mechanism of genius and ruin our only future claim to fame. There was nothing delicate about squat, dark, meaty, wide-chested Rafael, who never missed a class, or a chance to stuff himself. His body was just the physical envelope. His mind, able to grasp advanced math while mine could not even understand a simple equation, seemed like the mechanism of Monsieur de la Trouille's automaton, frail under the weight of complexity.

The last time I saw Rafael's father alive, he was about to perform Little Sambo for three Negro generations in their front yard. The grandmothers and mothers sitting in their rocking chairs, the men leaning against the porch pillars in small knots, elegant and sullen, the children perching on the steps, all wearing their Sunday best, including shiny new shoes, because they had just returned from church. Ezequiel opened his mouth. The men doubled up with laughter. The women held their shaking bellies or clutched their hearts, fanning themselves faster and whispering in each other's ears, each whisper triggering a fresh wave of laughter across the porch. The children shrieked, clapped, and pointed at Ezequiel in his frayed, but immaculately clean and starched school janitor's uniform, which he always wore in civilian life. Ezequiel, whose only intelligible words in English were Little Sambo's. Puppet or puppeteer? He sure made them laugh.

Lightning struck so close that a monstrous boom shook the Judge's house and the sky lit almost simultaneously. The lights blinked. The boom echoed for several more seconds with the power and malice of an earthquake aftershock. I wheeled myself away from the window. I had once seen a windowpane shatter in our house during a storm like this. In the intense light, I saw McCabe's leased Land Rover, our only vehicle, parked on the driveway.

The Judge's studio, which I occupied, was slightly elevated above the rest of the ground floor. To reach the living room, the kitchen, the staircase leading to McCabe's rooms, and the front and back doors, I had to go down three wide steps. I'd never make it in the wheelchair. I would have to walk. I considered keeping the bandages to cushion my feet. The image of bloody pulp oozing from inside them made me change my mind. I peeled them off slowly, afraid of what I would find. I had not yet seen my frostbitten feet. When McCabe or the doctor tinkered with them I always looked away. My feet were whiter than the rest of my body, an unnatural white with a pinkish hue like white baby buttocks in a diaper ad. They also seemed smaller, though my toes were still painfully swollen. I would have to walk on the balls of my feet, lifting each up and down, clubfoot-style, careful not to roll them forward. I grabbed the Judge's letter opener, the only weapon in the room, and wheeled myself to the edge of the first step. McCabe could be unconscious, or dead, from natural or unnatural causes. Petrona could have been caught in the storm and forced to go back home. Or a burglar could have killed them both. I did not want to believe McCabe could have left. Wasn't the Land Rover still in the driveway?

I pushed myself up on the wheelchair armrests, set the balls of my feet down, and then released my arms. The pain was blinding. When I came to, I was at the bottom of the steps. I must have collapsed and rolled down. My arms were bruised, but my nose was intact. Another blow to it and I would be exhibited as a descendant of the australopithecine. When I recovered, I fell on my knees, not to thank God, but to crawl on them. Luckily, crawling comes naturally to spics. Didn't it win José Ferrer an Oscar last century? I wished I had had his Lautrec kneepads. I left bloody strips of knee skin on the floor. I think of José Lautrec now, but that day my model was not him, but Saint Lazarus and the thousands who walked on their knees to the old leprosy colony at El Rincón, in my parent's native island, where he has a sanctuary. My grandmother was a dyed-in-the-wool, absolutist Deist. She hated priests, nuns, pastors, *santeros*, and all other intermediaries as fervently as she believed that there was Something Big Up There. I don't believe in miracles, she said, and most of those saints and miracles we hear about are frauds. However, God is great and he does sometimes grant especially good people the power to work miracles, not thousands or hundreds of miracles, but one here or there. Saint Lazarus was one of these. But not all cures attributed to him are true. Ten percent, maybe—the other "cured" are lying or under the power of suggestion. People like to fool themselves. That is why the power of suggestion is so dangerous, she warned me.

My pilgrimage on my knees around the Judge's house did not end in a miracle. I found no dead or unconscious bodies. The kitchen was as clean as an operating room, with no traces of the cooking of the day before, not even a faint smell. The garbage cans must have been washed and disinfected before new bags were put in. The refrigerator, gleaming and freshly defrosted, contained a modest amount of new, strategically chosen staples (eggs, milk, butter, my tofu, hot dogs, tomatoes, lettuce). No cooked food. The freezer was packed with the meats McCabe consumed. Judging from the even layer of frost on the top, it had not been disturbed recently. Whatever McCabe, Petrona, and Mrs. Crandall had cooked the day before (and I was sure it was not last night's Rabelaisian dinner, which bore Petrona's lone imprint) had disappeared, and no forensic analysis could reconstruct it. They had literally erased their fingerprints from every surface. The bulky shape wrapped in Mrs. Crandall's blanket could have been a very large turkey, or a small pig, although the latter was doubtful even as speculation, given that Mrs. Crandall was not, even remotely, a spic. The living room was equally spotless.

At the end of the pilgrimage, after walking two, ten, twenty miles on their knees, the devotees of Saint Lazarus must climb the steep staircase leading to his shrine, still on their knees. It is only if and when they reach it that supplicants may beg the saint for a miracle. The gray stone steps have turned pink and shiny from the blood of a hundred thousand ulcerated knees. I went up the twenty-seven steps to McCabe's room, one knee first, then the other, fifty-four times in total, unable to decide what miracle I would ask for: McCabe ill or sleeping, dead or unconscious, or in perfect and oblivious health, counting her money, signing her sale contracts, looking at the package of Joseph Beuys slides that her German agent had sent her on

Monday, which she was carrying when she brought my breakfast, not knowing that I can read upside down at lightning speed. Anything, anything, anything but gone. Arriving at the landing before her door, I paused like all supplicants must when they reach the top, and their mouths are level with the rotting feet of the saint, being licked by his mangy dog. You lick the saint's feet then, careful not to touch the dog, until he gives you what you want, or before the next sad biped piece of meat in line behind you elbows you away. McCabe's door was locked. I looked through the generous keyhole, an 1820 Cutler Brothers model installed when the house was built, the Judge told me. There was no one inside the bedroom, or in the bathroom, or the closet, whose doors had been helpfully left open. There was nothing on any surface, anywhere: no FedEx packages, books, magazines, candy wrappers, no signs of human occupation. That did not mean the massive oak armoire was empty, or the chest of drawers, two night tables, bureau, medicine cabinet. I had never seen this, or any other McCabe habitat before, so I could not tell if this was the way this room normally looked, or if it had been especially cleansed like the rest of the house, as if State Security was expected any moment. The room exuded a jasmine fragrance. I stuck my nose to the keyhole and inhaled. My stomach rumbled at the memory of last night's delicate rice. I descended the stairs on my ass. The house was empty. McCabe had flown the coop.

20

A Daughter

WHEN SERAFINA WAS TWELVE, her mother, who had lost half of her nose and one ear to syphilis and was waiting to die, told her that her real father was not the man who had been killed in a knife fight when she was seven, nor any of the men who had been in and out of their shack ever since, but the most beautiful man that human eyes had ever seen—white, young, golden-haired, tall, strong, sweet, smart, generous, rich, well-spoken. Jacinto Benavides, the love of her life. She had reached that conclusion after repeatedly reliving their drunken, fornicating week together, which the man that she now thought of as the Beast had put an end to. She told Serafina how Jacinto was killed and dumped in the bay, but not by whom, and how his body had been found a week later by a fisherman, intact, as if he were just sleeping. Jacinto Benavides was then burned and his ashes strewn in the sea, as was done with men like him. Serafina asked what kind of men, but her mother could only tell her that it had to do with some quarrel among Spaniards. "What was this quarrel about?" Serafina asked, with a premature tinge of the sarcasm that would later serve her well. She had been raised in the certainty that Spaniards were quarrelsome, greedy, and stupid. "It was about their dicks," her mother said, in a spasm of laughter so violent and prolonged that she almost died then, and not the next morning. When she recovered, she explained that some Spaniards like Jacinto Benavides cut the skin off the tips of their dicks. Most don't, maybe because they are afraid of pain. They must be jealous of the brave ones, because they have gotten the King of Spain to forbid any dick trimming, and to punish those like Jacinto Benavides who dare to do it. Her mother advised Serafina to keep this information to herself. The less anyone knows about you, the safer you are, as her own mother had told her after revealing why she had been freed. Both of these things were family secrets. Serafina was now their keeper. Her mother made her swear on the Blessed Virgin, and on the holy wounds of Saint Glykeria, Martyr that she would pass on those secrets to one of her children, the smartest one. "Unless you only have one child, like me, in which case you better pray you're as lucky as I've been." This was the first and only time her mother praised Serafina out loud, although she did so to herself every day. She was afraid Serafina would become too vain for her own good. "Children talk too much. Only one of them should know. Don't tell them all, and don't tell too soon," she added, before a gale of coughing carried her away. Serafina went to bed that night with a picture of her father in her mind. He looked just like her, fully grown and in men's clothing. It was not too far off the mark. Serafina was the spitting image of Jacinto Benavides.

Serafina buried her mother near the back wall of the cemetery in the narrow, humid strip reserved for free blacks and mulattoes. Syphilis kills slowly, and her mother was hardworking and thrifty. She finished paying for her burial plot two years before taking up residence there. "I have room for two more," she told Serafina. "Just don't put them on top of me. I want to smell the grass." The burial was swift. The mule-wagon man and his son slid the featherweight coffin into the hole. The gravedigger, who was three times as old as most of those he buried, mumbled a prayer as he began shoveling dirt into the hole. When he finished packing it with the back of his shovel, he looked at Serafina expectantly. So did the other two. She had no intention of giving them a tip after they had extorted from her an exorbitant fee in advance, knowing that she had no brother or husband to fight for her. She dismissed them, politely but firmly. They did not move at first. The old man clutched his shovel until his black knuckles became gray. The mule-wagon man spat and glanced at his son, who always knew what to do in cases like this. The son was distracted by the question of Serafina's age. He could always tell by the shape of the breasts, but the coarse vest that covered Serafina's upset his calculation. She was lucky to be wearing that vest, to be as tall as him, and a head above the two other men, and to look older and stronger than her age. Burying free blacks and mulattoes was unprofitable. You scraped a living only by periodically ransacking a shack while the relatives moaned at the cemetery, or snatching the rare gold chain or ring from the few corpses stupid enough to wear them. The most profitable side-business, however, was snatching the widow, if she was still young, along with the youngest orphans, and selling them to the illegal slave traders, mostly Dutch or French, who were always loitering in the twisted port streets. The mule-wagon man looked at Serafina's long blond curls and light honey skin and knew he could never sell her as a slave. She was worth a great deal, but only to herself, if she was smart enough.

Serafina watched them leave until they were a blur in the distance. She allowed herself, only this once, to spit on the ground with contempt. The mule was the only one of the four departing beasts she could not imagine killing. The other three she stabbed, quartered, and disemboweled with her knife, throwing their livers to the feral pigs that roamed the cemetery at night, and burning the rest until only the teeth and bones remained. Those she left on the ground as a warning to anyone else who dared defy her. With these pleasant images of butchery still lingering in her mind, Jacinto's daughter walked back home.

She kept her mother's washing and ironing clients, but dismissed the men who came late at night. They had deserted her mother when she was unable to hide her disease any longer, but the scent of young flesh brought them back. One refused to go, knocking her against the iron bed railing and trying to mount her. She stabbed him in the left hand in panic, and was surprised at how quickly he let her go and threw himself on the floor, writhing and screaming in pain. Her imaginary bloodletting had been always soundless and in slow motion. She hit him in the mouth and on the head with her laundry paddle while he was helpless on the floor. When he passed out, she dragged him all the way to the sewage ditch, one hundred meters away, dumping him on the edge, so he would not drown. She wanted him alive so he would warn others not to come to her shack. He did this better than she imagined. To save face, he spread the word that she was sick like her mother.

Without the men's money, Serafina could not pay Don Manuel for his lessons. Her mother had taken her to Don Manuel a year earlier, insisting that he teach her reading, writing, and arithmetic. Don Manuel disliked children, girls in particular, and especially pretty mulatto girls like this one, all of them born whores who knew instinctively how to wrap wealthy white men around their little fingers. No need to teach them letters and numbers. Besides, even rich white girls on the island were mostly illiterate. He relented only after Serafina's mother threatened to tell the authorities that he was a sodomite. She had no proof, and no clear notion of what the word meant (it could not be the common buggering all men engaged in, but something else, particularly wicked, that she could not fathom), but knew it was a deadly accusation. Don Manuel did know what the word meant. He also knew the Tribunal of the Inquisition relished accusations without proof, which allowed them to torture you until you provided it yourself. The stench of the seventeen sodomite sailors recently burnt at the stake was still in the air in San Cristóbal de La Habana. It was Serafina's turn now to be difficult. She refused to sit across from the little brown gnarled man with the sour-smelling jacket. She gave in after her mother, physically choking with rage, whacked her hard on the buttocks with the laundry paddle. Serafina was already a foot taller than her mother, who had started small and had shrunk considerably with her illness. She could have easily taken the paddle away from her. She did not, afraid that her mother would die more quickly if she shattered the illusion that she was the stronger of the two.

Don Manuel was about to tell Serafina that he could not continue to teach her for free, when much to his own surprise, he heard himself say the opposite. He did not like Serafina any better now that she had learned in one year what had taken him, the smartest person he knew, at least ten. However, he was bored writing love letters and petitions to the authorities for his illiterate neighbors. Although he didn't realize it yet, he had nearly resigned himself to never seeing his talent and knowledge (one year of law school in Salamanca, Spain!) recognized on this barbaric little island. How far would he be able to stretch the brain of this female mammal that now sat before him, her incongruous yellow locks framing a face that would be handsome if only she were a boy and bathed more often? (Don Manuel, in spite of his musty frock, had a sensitive nose, and Serafina, to keep predator males away, did not wash much.)

Now that Serafina's improved brain became his only reward, Don Manuel redoubled his efforts. He drew up a curriculum, which included geography and history, but excluded Greek and Latin, which were fit only for gentlemen. Serafina would get free lessons only if she accepted his study plan. She agreed after he promised to continue teaching her reading, writing, and arithmetic. "Useful skills for a bodega owner," her mother had said. Her dream had been to turn their shack into a dry-goods store. For that purpose she left Serafina the half of her savings that did not go to pay for her own burial. History and geography made Serafina sleepy. She concentrated on keeping her eyes open in the afternoon heat, while Don Manuel droned on about Julius Caesar, raising his voice above the swarm of flies circling their heads. She was glad that he was so long-winded. You did not have to listen to every word to be able to answer his questions. Serafina learned to nap with her eyes open, a few seconds at a time. Don Manuel was never able to catch her, no matter how quickly he swiveled to face her and throw a tricky question at her. Once, Serafina had no answer; she did not even understand the question. She gained time by furrowing her brow and setting her mouth in a snarl, as Don Manuel did when he was in deep thought. She then rhetorically repeated his question, and reiterated it in the affirmative, embellishing it with the sonorous, well-rounded subordinate clauses opening into more subordinate clauses so dear to Don Manuel. For content she used her common sense. When she stopped to catch her breath, three minutes later, Don Manuel dismissed her for the day, although she had just arrived. That night Don Manuel sat on his narrow bed in the dark looking at the fireflies burning in the tall grass outside his window. Now and then, one would fly into the room and then fly back out after it realized where it was. Whenever he had to bare his soul to himself, as he put it, Don Manuel would sit on his bed in the dark. He couldn't do so in the front room, even with the window shuttered and the door closed. He was dazzled and angry at the way Serafina had bluffed her way out, dazzled at her brilliant sophistry, her daring, her accurate channeling of his voice and intellect, and angry at her for the theft of all he had. Anger soon turned into fear and fear into self-pity, always the last stop in Don Manuel's emotional turmoil. Could Serafina be an incubus, or maybe a succubus? "Why didn't You give me a teacher of Don Manuel's caliber when I was this wretched girl's age, eh?" he demanded, raising his voice, underlining and spitefully capitalizing the "You." The half-bottle of rum he had drunk made him combative. At two-thirds, he turned weepy, engaging in a dialogue with his younger selves and several white women and boys who had spurned him in Salamanca and San Cristóbal de La Habana. The last drop of the bottle had a calming effect. He had dissected his life many times before, but Serafina had handed him a particularly sharp scalpel. He was sixty-five years old. He might not be alive a year from now. There was no time left for his dreams to come true. Serafina was his last opportunity. His genius would be recognized in her. He would be remembered as her intellectual master.

When Don Manuel woke up at noon the next day, unsteady and reeking of rum, his ego had shifted from the aspirations of his younger self to the possibilities of the one he now called, with a touch of hauteur, "my pupil." As often happens when someone gives up what he holds most valuable, he felt an unknown lightness, which he mistook for happiness. Serafina knocked fearfully on his door at their agreed time, convinced that she would be dismissed for good, or roundly scolded. She was embarrassed when he opened the door wearing a dirty nightgown. He noticed, and hid most of his body behind the door. "There will be no lesson today. I am not well. Come back tomorrow," he said, handing her the filthy clothes he wore every day. She was so relieved that she immediately ran home to wash his clothes and hang them in the sun, instead of finding out what had happened to Tirant lo Blanc after he saved Constantinople from the Ottoman Turks. The shirt and undershirt she had to wash and bleach in the sun many times that afternoon and the next morning, until their dull grey turned into a pure white. It was only after the last garment had been ironed and folded that she opened the book and found out that Tirant lo Blanc had died in his bed overlooking the Bosphorus. Serafina was disappointed that his cause of death was a respiratory infection, not a battlefield wound. The violent reaction of Tirant's beloved princess Carmesina, on the other hand, pleased her. Carmesina kissed Tirant's cold corpse with such force that she broke her nose, and her blood flowed so abundantly that her eyes and face were bathed red.

That afternoon, Don Manuel made Serafina wait outside his front door while he put on the clean clothes. Before the lesson started, he announced that he would also teach her the rudiments of Anatomy, Physiology, and Philosophy. She wondered what the three were, and why only rudiments, but dared not ask, still afraid he might be toying with her before kicking her out. (Serafina knew nothing about her mother's "sodomite" leverage.) Don Manuel explained to her the theory of humors, which overlapped all three of these sciences. Serafina paid close attention this time. This theory might be the key to the acrid odor that emanated from the old man, even after he had bathed (his hair was still damp) and was wearing clean clothes. On her way out, he gave her his soiled nightgown and cap to wash and iron. From then on, she washed his clothes once a week.

One afternoon, Don Manuel did not answer the door. Serafina peeked through a crack in his bedroom wall and saw him sprawled on the floor, holding an empty bottle of rum. She forced open the bedroom window and climbed through it. Don Manuel was dead. She did not need his anatomy lessons to know. She had seen her mother die, and she had killed many chickens and one pig. In the three years since she first washed his clothes, he had taught her everything he knew, and she had also learned from his books many things he did not know or had forgotten. The art of writing love letters was the only thing that she was unable to learn. He tried to teach her, hoping to put her to work for him in the port market, where the novelty of a female scribe would have made him some money. Her letters were too short and to the point, and without the indispensable flourishes. When forced, she would try to add some, but they would be either obscure or inappropriate. Instead of flowers, birds, butterflies, dew, sunsets, fair hands, rivers, and so on (he had gone so far as to draw a list for her), she would weave in dogs, pigs, hay, gold doubloons, mud, and buttons. "These are love letters, not a shopkeeper's account book," he told her with his usual distaste (his decision to unselfishly devote his last years to Serafina's education had increased his dislike of her in direct proportion to the admiration of his, and God's, handiwork). "I am going to be a shopkeeper," Serafina thought, flattered by Don Manuel's conclusion, but careful to keep her mouth shut. For the past six months, Don Manuel had nothing left to teach her except for those silly love letters. Everything that was left to learn in his shack she had extracted herself from his books. Now, it was not so much what the books said, but what they left out. Serafina had discovered recently, in awe, the gaps and silences in books. She was now reading between words, beyond words, and without words. It was great fun: Serafina was still a child. She could do it from memory, while washing and ironing, cooking (she had begun selling cod fritters in the market and was now delivering two dozen every Thursday morning to one of her laundry clients), walking, and even sleeping.

By dying when he did, Don Manuel decreed the end of Serafina's formal education and the beginning of her adult life. Serafina was happy that the choice had not been hers. The inevitable felt luckier. She buried Don Manuel under her mother. At first, she had found it distasteful, but a separate grave cost too much, and the pauper's field was out of the question. Besides, she had scrubbed him well before putting him there, and it was only provisional. Once she had the money, she would move her mother into a bigger, nicer, plot. Serafina sorted out Don Manuel's books, moving the good ones to her shack, and burning in a bonfire the stupid and fraudulent ones. The complete works of Thomas Aquinas perished. *Tirant lo Blanc*, *The Praise of Folly*, Aldrovandi's gorgeously illustrated *Ornithologiae*, and the treatises on anatomy, physiology, astronomy, geometry, and mathematics survived. So did Don Manuel's French, English, and Dutch dictionaries and books. When there was little else left to teach, he had plunged her into those three languages, which he could read, but not speak. That did not bother him. He considered all languages to be dead tongues, interesting only in the books that were written in them (Don Manuel did not much care for people). Serafina, on the contrary, had been able to conduct simple conversations in all those languages since she was little. San Cristóbal de La Habana's port area was a Tower of Babel in the early 1600s, and her mother's night clients spoke a cacophony of Malaccan Dutch, French Creole, Wild Geese mercenary English, and all kinds of Portuguese and Spanish pidgin. Learning to read in what Don Manuel reverently called "the major European languages," even if slowly, and aided by a dictionary, was the most useful thing that he taught Serafina. Books in those languages were at once strange and obvious. So was truth, Serafina concluded many years later. After swearing her to secrecy, Don Manuel showed Serafina several foreign books that did not bear on their title page the name of the author or the printer or the place of publication. "They don't want their nails and testicles pulled out by our Holy Mother the Church," he said, crossing himself. "News of the Index of Forbidden Books takes a long time to reach us. So it is prudent to hide all foreign books, including the dictionaries. You don't want a nosy neighbor to see them," he warned her. "How could a neighbor tell, since they were all illiterate?" Serafina was going to ask Don Manuel the day she found him dead, although what she really wanted to know was why Don Manuel was always so frightened. He would have claimed it was just because of his questionable books, concealing his deeper terror that his sodomite past (he had been too sick lately for this to be more than a fond memory) would surface if his books attracted attention, or that some long-forgotten boy uttered his name while being tortured or serviced by a faggot priest, the worst and most common kind. Then he would be accused of heresy in addition to sodomy, ensuring an even slower and more horrible death.

Serafina was fearless, like Tirant. Unlike him, however, she was a realist. When she became one of the richest traders on the island, few knew it because she was careful not to flaunt her wealth, or tie herself to any man. For the rest of her long life, she also kept her voracity for knowledge to herself along with all her foreign books, two thousand at last count, hidden in a priest hole she built with her own hands behind the massive mahogany armoire in her bedroom.

21

Gone

PEOPLE ALWAYS LEAVE SOMETHING behind when they go, a letter, dirty tissue, loose change, a gum wrapper. But not McCabe. It was as if she had never been in the house. As the sun began to set on Thanksgiving Day, I sat on the floor in front of the open refrigerator eating slices of supermarket ham and white cheddar with my fingers. I'll eat here like a pig until McCabe shows up, I thought. "That'll sure bring her back," Reason remarked, blowing cigarette smoke in my face. "You don't know why or where McCabe has gone," she said, ignoring my protestations that McCabe must be back in New York City tending to her gallery. "Furthermore," she added, lighting a fresh cigarette off the butt of the old one, "you don't even know why you care." That was preposterous. One thing I was absolutely certain about: I cared that McCabe had vanished because I was about to kill her. I needed her here for that purpose. This rational certainty was the cornerstone of our domestic happiness since my accident. Reason didn't hear my indignant answer. She had returned to my frontal lobe, where she dwelled, having implanted her poisonous pods.

The more rational a certainty, the harder it is to kill the vulture of irrational doubt circling overhead. The tools of reason fail: the hungry vulture just circles lower, excited by the stench of the logical brain. McCabe's sudden absence, the clean blank page she left, the way she erased herself from the house, amplified the doubt, which was now being played inside my head by a full, bombastic symphonic orchestra, all 230 instruments in thickly imbricated harmony. It was, and it wasn't, the "Finale" of Bruckner's *Seventh Symphony*, in whose tragic reverse recapitulation Goebbels had found the equanimity to admit that two thousand years of Western history were in danger.

I returned to my room on my hands and knees, oozing blood and pus. By the time I was soaking in the tub, my orchestra had stopped playing, and I, too, contemplated doubt with equanimity, even with pleasure. With the familiar (McCabe) gone, leaving a horrific chasm worming with serpents at the end of the map, doubt—musically implanted, repeated doubt—had become familiar. Why and where McCabe had gone, why she hadn't told me, and why I cared now, seemed legitimate subjects of inquiry. Physical pleasure and its concomitant indolence fueled this benign view: the warm water luxuriously covered my body up to my throat. This was my first bath in a month. I left my feet out, propped on the tub ledge, wrapped in clean towels. Tomorrow I might get them wet and see what happened.

I examined McCabe's disappearance dispassionately. An emergency could explain the suddenness of her departure. Could it explain her silence, too? I imagined McCabe getting a dead-of-night phone call from her boy assistant: her gallery, along with Manhattan's southern tip, set on fire by Caliphate terrorists, or flooded, or blown off (all of which had happened more than once before, although her gallery was unscathed each time). McCabe calling Elmira's only cab and rushing to the state capital, where she rented a plane to fly her to Chicago (the lone commuter flight to that destination today, Thanksgiving Day, being at 7:00 p.m. instead of the usual 7:00 a.m., which I knew because I had been keeping tabs on all means of exiting Elmira, for my own sake). McCabe arriving in New York from Chicago to find the tip of the island in flames, or at least her gallery. McCabe caught up in the testosterone hysteria of the heroic rescuers, maybe even escorted away in handcuffs for trying to jump a Firecop barricade to save her precious Beuys, still in its German crate, or hurt by a falling cornice, or huddled with her lawyers and insurance people, unable to place the one call even mass murderers are entitled to, so she could let me know, out of common courtesy, her whereabouts. As I pulled myself out of the tub and onto the cold, tiled bathroom floor, I swore to stop scratching the bloody crust of McCabe's disappearance. Pragmatism and action were all that mattered now. McCabe had to be brought back to the slaughterhouse.

After sanitizing my feet with the washes and ointments in McCabe's nurse's bag and putting on a pair of clean white socks, I crawled on my belly and elbows from bathroom to bed to spare my knees, pushing the bag ahead of me with my forehead. My feet looked less unnatural than when I had taken off the bandages. Whether this was an objective fact or mere habituation, it's hard to tell. My knees, though, looked like raw steak, with strips of dead, bruised skin still attached here and there. I treated them with whatever potions seemed to apply. The storm's howl had turned into a spasmodic whistle. The rain had stopped. A thin sliver of the new moon peeked out from behind the slow-moving clouds, still low and dense like bags of coal, a reminder that the storm could resume if it wished. I fell asleep only after I swallowed a narcotic pill from my pillow cache.

The phones were still dead the day after Thanksgiving. Petrona did not show up for work. The Little Ohio had risen higher than in the celebrated flood of 1863 when two-thirds of Elmira was buried in mud and left there because most able men were fighting with Grant in Vicksburg. Elmira was rebuilt on top of its own grave in brick this time, not wood, when the survivors returned. All day, the local radio played Perry Como and The Beatles in an orgy of self-congratulation disguised as public service. Churches vied with one another to offer sanctimonious, useless emergency services, generally involving prayers and donuts. Idiots who let their dogs and cats roam and shit everywhere pleaded tearfully for their safe return. The pièce de résistance, however, was The Witnessing, as the radio announcers solemnly called it, a fifteen-minute call-in segment every hour, during which the town's remaining whites disgorged family memories of that great flood and heroic war. This is what we have and you will never have: a genetic memory of Elmira's foundation, and second foundation after the great flood. They hammered that in all day long without actually saying it. You just had to listen to their repressive gasps. Forbidden to call a nigger a nigger, a spic a spic, a wop a wop, etcetera, on the radio and in most public forums, Elmira's whites had created a new tongue rich in elisions, and syntactic and semantic black holes, where the now unmentionable were buried and forgotten, as if they had never existed, with no markers left on their linguistic graves. The new flood was a time machine, a tongue-loosener, a fountain from which sprang a fraternity of pale hue. Elmira was jubilant.

The Judge's binoculars confirmed that the river was lapping at the base of the bridge, cutting off Round Hill from the town, just as the radio announced. Elmira's Main Street, however, was nothing like the 1863 photographs I had seen at the local historical society as a child, when I still thought the word "Elmiran" applied to me, too. The windows of shops and parked cars glistened in the morning sun, intact. I could see three high-wheeled trucks slowly making their way from the county building to City Hall. Two rubber boats sat idle on one side next to a building, maybe waiting to ferry white flood victims to a church donut-prayer service. The Firecops were on their way, the radio trumpeted. Elmira could enjoy its day in the water.

Looking at the rich brown river stew of mud and detritus swirling angrily at the Shangri-La bend, the last visible point from my window, I felt the full gravity of McCabe's absence. Gravity in the physical, not just the moral, sense. Skull-crushing, eye-popping, Jupiterian gravity. Would killing her restore the universal laws of physics? My mind said, Yes, Yes, Yes, but my body said. No, Never. You will feel her weight until you die. It was around midday, and the sun seemed to stand still in the cloudless sky. I knelt in front of the window, looking at the river. My shadow was a tiny black circle around my knees. I vowed again to kill McCabe even if it was not to be a cold-blooded, remorseless, liberating crime, but a guarantee of everlasting suffering. Tears poured out of my eyes. They rolled down my face and dropped on my chest and onto the floor, unstoppably.

I couldn't live without her.

I had to get her back. Killing and suffering were better than this unbearable longing. No need to atone or repent: killing McCabe was as righteous now as when the Tongues of Fire first ordered it.

With the phones dead, the bridge to Elmira impassable, and my feet too mangled to drive, writing a letter to McCabe was all I could do on that endless day after Thanksgiving. I sat in bed propped up by many pillows, with one of the Judge's yellow legal pads and a pen found at the bottom of his desk drawer. This was the first time my hands had touched writing tools since the New York meltdown. Hours later, the pad was still pure yellow, and the pen had long been dropped on the floor. If I had been able to write her a letter, one of those brilliantly devious, skillful eighteenth-century frog letters that tease answers without seeming to ask questions, I would have asked McCabe what I had to do to make her want to come back.

I did not want to force her. Other than pretending a serious illness, I had given up on coercion. Besides, if she refused to come back even if I was "gravely ill," my humiliation would be absolute. I could not risk it. More subtle ways had to be found to plant in her the desire to return. Perhaps the way to bring her back could be hidden in the reasons that made her leave. On this second day without McCabe, the business emergency hypothesis seemed ludicrous. Could she be with Bebe? I kept pushing the gaseous suspicion to the back of my mind, not allowing it to acquire shape and volume. Jealousy was the worst advisor at this moment, but the suspicion kept returning. If she was with Bebe, was it for good, or a fleeting relapse? To distract myself from this thought and its complications (who would I be most jealous of, Bebe or McCabe, and why?), I reviewed my last night with McCabe.

Maybe I should not have been so didactic, playing César Franck's entire *Symphony* for her. But hadn't she placed her left hand on her knee, inadvertently pulling up the shirt cuff, so that the naked face of her wrist was visible? This was one of the small gestures of pleasure that I had noticed in her while we listened to music. Another was tilting her face slightly toward her left shoulder, so that her eyes seemed to follow the light coming through the window. Or touching the front of her left wrist with her right index finger, as if she wanted to take her pulse discreetly, without me noticing. Through intuition, which is reason operating on a back channel, I had compiled a catalogue of McCabe's signs of pleasure. Now I was not so sure. They may have been signs of boredom. Had I attributed to her my own pleasure at having such a docile audience? When we listened to music, I felt in my natural state: neutral, equidistant from all feelings and humors. Only with McCabe gone did I realize that my perfect equilibrium could not have been attained without the pleasure directly flowing from her presence. It was I, not her, who had to be put under the microscope. There had never been any carnal desire on my part toward McCabe. Acknowledging pleasure from her verged on indecency, but this was no time for cowardice. She had given me pleasure daily. Incorporeal pleasure. How could that be? Was it just her docility, her willingness to dine with me night after night, listen to my talk about plants, and sit through the lengthy music? I suspected an ulterior reason, but my aching brain refused to dig deeper.

Her docility had a darker side effect, though: it made me miss the signs of her impending departure. Mrs. Crandall's visit was the only red flag, or at the very least, a symptom of McCabe's restlessness. Had Mrs. Crandall helped McCabe escape? I couldn't see her doing much beyond driving McCabe to the airport or calling her a cab or performing some other factotum task. Mrs. Crandall was not the eloping kind. However voluptuous, she was a pillar of society.

At dinner, and when she changed my bandages in the morning, I should have prodded McCabe even more about herself. But it was hard work. Since her answers never expanded into conversation, I was forced to ask one question after another, just to hear her speak. Now that she had disappeared, I craved her voice, and hers alone. Even when they were monosyllabic, her answers were so complete and perfect when measured against my questions that they left me wanting more. The longest I had ever heard her speak was when she told me the story about the Biloxi marshes and the burning corpses.

It was easier to question McCabe in the morning, while she changed my bandages. (When I now thought of McCabe it was the new one I envisioned; the old, voluble, loquacious McCabe had begun receding at that moment on the edge of the Judge's land when I almost pushed the usurper down the ravine.) We were physically close. In the bright light, I could see even the tiniest change of expression in her eyes. My questions the first day were about myself, asking if my feet had been amputated. She said "no" several times until I stopped, still unsure if she was telling the truth. The next morning she changed my bandages for the first time. Each layer she unwrapped from my right foot was more purulent than the preceding. She paused before unwrapping the one closest to the skin. "Your foot is in there. See the shape?" I nodded and glanced away. When she was sure I was not looking, she uncovered the foot. No nurse in the history of nursing had been more devoted than McCabe. Yet she had abandoned her patient.

One day, long after that, she invited me to look at my feet. The intimacy of the offer shook me. She was offering me a part of my body as if she owned it, which she did at that moment. I could see her reflected on the windowpane, waiting for my answer, the careless parting of her lips contradicting the competent hands holding a roll of gauze and a pair of scissors. I was afraid of her. Just for a second. Then I glanced at my foot. It was monstrous. I managed not to heave until McCabe left the room. After that, I was insatiably curious about her.

Questions had to be clear and direct, and seem innocent. They could not be nakedly personal, but nor could they be sneaky. McCabe would clam up in either case. The personal could be reached safely only by starting from the general. A comment wondering whether the Judge's yellow roses risked black spot if it rained too much this fall would slowly lead to a casual question about fall weather in her hometown, which turned out to be Bangor, Maine. That was a logic-defying upset. I was sure Bebe had told me that McCabe was from Concord, where she had been raised in an orphanage. Someone was lying. As I learned more about McCabe's childhood in Bangor, a tiny fact a day, I added this fib to Bebe's catalogue, which was almost as long as mine.

McCabe did not like to fish. In Bangor, this was the only leisure activity available to her other than church. So she worked, from the age of eight, to make money and kill time. She liked to have her own money. Her aunt was neither rich, nor poor, nor too stingy or young. She had died in a retirement home a few years earlier. McCabe was her only survivor (from which I inferred no parents, siblings, etc.). Fibulous Bebe had told me that McCabe did not remember her parents and (maybe—at the time I hated McCabe's guts so much that her life story made me want to puke) that her mother may have been unmarried, or that her father had walked out on her and the baby. I now wished I had paid more attention to Bebe's gushing reports. On the other hand, she may have been feeding me misinformation just for the hell of it. Bebe could have had a career as a double or triple agent.

It is also possible that McCabe had deceived her. After all, what did anyone know about McCabe before she took SoHo by storm in the winter of 2002? What did anyone know about anyone in New York, the Mecca of self-reinvention, the born-again capital of the universe? Haven't you noticed, dear listener, how the eyes of New Yorkers glaze over when one of them imprudently mentions their original place of birth? How the room tone acquires a frigid buzz if the remembrances go beyond the geographical fact? How, if they persist, standers-by will drift away, afraid that they, too, may have to expose their loathed original selves?

As the second night without McCabe fell, I reviewed those facts, one by one. They ranged from her childhood diseases (whooping cough) and pets (a frog, a snail) to why she became an art merchant ("Just looking to scrub my money," then finding out that "I dug selling trash"). I had memorized them. I counted them now (arithmetic had not deserted me). There were 676. In her voice, each of them had seemed uniquely hers, filled with meaning and possibilities. Now they were brittle shards of generic trivia that could be used to assemble anyone's portrait. Her voice is what I missed most on that second night. A voice so ordinary that I can describe it only as what it was not: not loud, raspy, shrill, breathy, nasal, guttural, sweet, booming, soft, deep-throated, or high-pitched. Nothing special distinguished it. That is what was moving and, in retrospect, magnificent about her voice: it was an apotheosis of the generic. The transubstantiation of everything and everybody. The Holy Wafer of Sound. I craved a fix. A craving so brutal that my stomach cramped, my skin crawled and itched the more frantically I scratched, leaving bloody ruts. When my chest began to hurt, I settled for some aural methadone. I managed to crawl out of bed, gasping, and turn on the music player. I sobbed, dry-eyed, while the Antiochian soprano sang Reynaldo Hahn's remorseful *"Dis! qu'as tu fait, toi que voilà, de ta jeunesse."* Openly, shamelessly sobbed. Softly, though, so I could listen to her. It was not McCabe's voice, but a palliative. My chest was about to explode when she began to sing. Before she finished, I was asleep on the rug in a pool of tears.

22

Searching

PETRONA RETURNED THE NEXT DAY. She left the lunch basket by my door and then began to vacuum. Chicken bones flew out of my hands as I quickly devoured the food. They landed where my tears had pooled on the rug the night before, grease dissolving in salty residue. I am a careful, civilized eater. Near starvation could explain my lapse that day. More ominously, it may have been the beginning of the degenerative slide that propelled me under this bed, encased in a crumbling, inhuman shell.

After brushing my teeth, I wheeled myself out to the landing and called Petrona. She came trailing the vacuum cleaner. I asked her to turn it off. She did so in slow motion, a one-second delay for every century of Aztec enslavement. Things were back to normal. For an instant, I imagined McCabe strolling in the garden.

Petrona did not know anything, or claimed not to. Miss Maké had not mentioned any trip. Petrona had no idea where the food they cooked with the church señora had gone. It was still in the kitchen when Petrona had left that evening. She had not come to work because of the flood. Even getting here today had taken her twice as long because the Elmira bridge was still closed, and she had to cross using the only bridge that was still open, in a neighboring county about twenty miles to the East. As I suspected, the food the three of them had cooked together on the eve of Thanksgiving was not the quail banquet McCabe and I had eaten during our last dinner together, of which Petrona was the sole, proud creator. I praised her inspired cooking, item by item, the way a restaurant reviewer would, observing the ingenuity of the sauces in one sentence, the perfect braising of the meat in another, and the presentation in yet another. There is nothing I liked more than praising a subordinate like Petrona for an exceptionally well-executed job, the accomplishment of the quail banquet redoubled by the pleasure of congratulating myself on my shrewd judgment in hiring her.

The mysterious Thanksgiving Eve meal, the one that had disappeared from the house without a trace, had been cooked under Miss Maké's direction, with Petrona as executioner, and Mrs. Crandall as witness. This, according to Petrona. Mrs. Crandall just sat on a stool by the refrigerator and chatted with Miss Maké. About what, Petrona could not tell, given her limited English. They laughed a lot (I knew that: I could hear them from my room). Petrona did not know the names of the food she had helped prepare: one was some sort of vegetable stew, another a rice dish, a third some sort of dumplings. The dessert had been some kind of tiny balls covered with confectionery sugar. As to what Mrs. Crandall had brought wrapped in a blanket, Petrona was on firmer ground. That was the main dish, which took all day to cook, and turned out fine even if it was not prepared the way Petrona would have done it, with bitter oranges and cumin, garlic and oregano: "It was a suckling pig," Petrona said.

In every nineteenth-century novel there comes a moment when the main character is left speechless. This was mine. Did I notice a malicious glint in Petrona's eyes after she dropped the depth charge, or was it a glimmer of pity, or a reflection of the sun streaming in through my bedroom window? She stood frozen, holding the gray vacuum coil, a Mumbai python charmer about to feed a mouse to her star performer. I don't know how long we were in this face-to-face frieze, me in the wheelchair of defeat, placed in a slightly elevated position to signal my rank, she displaying to me the snakelike machine. I may have lost consciousness for a while, because the next thing I remember is dialing McCabe's gallery on the Judge's black Bakelite phone. A voice assured clients in several languages that their calls would be quickly answered. I hung up without a word. The voice was not McCabe's, as it had always been—a personal touch for the immensely rich—but that of a male computer surrogate. Was that a good or a bad sign? I couldn't tell. Had it been her voice, I would have left a message for her, which she may or may not have answered. Either way, it would have advanced my investigation. On the other hand, I might have gotten hooked on her voice, and spent the rest of my days calling back at briefer and briefer intervals just to hear her for thirty seconds. Craving not just her voice, but increasingly her flesh.

Mrs. Crandall had slapped me in the face. She had stolen a four-legged creature that belonged to me, to people like me, not to her, never to her kind, never. She had brought Shangri-La to Round Hill, bypassing me, the gatekeeper. From a place she knew nothing about and had never set foot in, to a place she knew nothing about but in which she resided, thanks to her native husband. She had had the chutzpah to give the emblematic creature—my creature— to McCabe; it was a gift that should have come from me. She had done all of this under my nose. Brazenly. Don't tell me she would not have done any of this if she had known where I was from! You know perfectly well she would have. The only difference is that she would have tried to curry my approval, to show off how down she was on all things spic. Mrs. Crandall had challenged me with the suckling pig. To what end? She was also telling me something about McCabe and something about herself—perhaps something about them both, together. I didn't know what. Her message was opaque. I would have to extract it directly from her.

I am proud of myself for the way I handled Mrs. Crandall. I kept my anger in the icebox until I was ready to confront her face to face. After I let it out, I did not allow it to deter me from my goal of bringing McCabe back. It helped that Mrs. Crandall had tapped an old and boring reservoir of hatred, one that I had wallowed in even before I learned to read and write. This is what the tattered scrolls mired at the bottom of that fecal pit proclaimed: White people despise us. No exceptions: homo and hetero, Rapturous Evangelicals and Malthusian fanatics, resettlement camp bait and fortified city dwellers, sympathetic elites and xenophobic white trash, and every white piece of shit within and between them, whether true whites or honorary whites, including but not limited to Beulah-ish spics, gooks, niggers, and chinks; white-nosing heebs, yids, and kikes; gyros, polacks, russkies, guineas, and Kosovars and their Serbian torturers fresh off the boat after their third genocidal war in a century, thankful to America for this gift of a common ground, at last. There are epithelial and stylistic differences among them, but their contempt for us is one and indivisible. We, the other people, reciprocate with bitterness, wrath, disdain, delusion (pretending the *cabrones del coño de su puta madre* don't exist), melancholia, murder, suicide (drugs, alcohol, holding up a 7-Eleven in plain daylight), circling the *raza* wagons so tightly that we asphyxiate, wearing ridiculous and spurious folkloric rags, and so on. We are not nice, we, the other people. We know it, and that makes us even more choleric. We would like to be nice like Mrs. Crandall. Hatred eats you. Repressing hatred, however, eats you twice as fast. I am only skimming the reservoir that Mrs. Crandall stirred, just to give an idea of how deep and old it is. At a moment like this, I think of sly, hypocritical Petrona and her five-hundred-year-old bilious cesspool. Am I her Mrs. Crandall?

I went looking for Mrs. Crandall, not to avenge a slight, but to find McCabe. (The slight I was willing to stuff in the bottomless reservoir for future use. It is important to clarify this in view of how things turned out.) I spent the rest of that week teaching myself how to walk again, aided by two of the Judge's walking sticks. It was sweaty and painful. Relearning to stand on my own two feet took several hours. I wore the Judge's wonderfully padded slippers over two pairs of soft socks. In between rehab sessions, which lasted seconds at first, then minutes, I slapped on my feet everything I could find in McCabe's nurse's bag, trying not to remember the way she narrowed her eyes in ferocious concentration while she changed my bandages. My knees also had begun to heal. They were still swollen and oozing, but I did not have to walk on them. I congratulated myself for my stoicism. I had been a stoic child. Then I had lost that quality under the indulgent gaze of scores of girlfriends. Perhaps it was coming back. At the end of the week, my feet were more or less functional, though they remained paler and flatter, their shape hesitating between foot and stump. I was never again able to walk without pain. Later, as my body began to change, stump became the predominant shape. But that was still in the future.

I was exultant when I actually managed to get myself into the cab that would take me to the Elmira library. McCabe had been gone for seven days. I was dressed as myself, my real self, the one McCabe saw at dinner every evening. Señora Mirtila was dead and buried, wig, scarf, and rosary, in the same grave as the Fujianese mathematician. It was madness to have thought that with all their ingenious machines, State Security could be fooled by amateur disguises. As the cab spiraled down Round Point at top speed, I glanced back at myself with the eyes of the newly sane. I had been mad. For months, maybe even two or three years, perhaps longer. The search for McCabe had sharpened and cured my mind.

Mrs. Crandall was behind the library counter when I arrived. She was wearing a severe ensemble, which clung salaciously to her body: a navy blue, knitted skirt, just long enough to cover the knees, a white, long-sleeved silk blouse with a discreet bow on the round collar, and a short jacket matching the skirt. In her black pumps, she was almost a foot taller than me. She did not recognize me at first. When she did, she jumped a little. I pretended not to notice, to give her a chance to rebound. She flashed her kindest smile. I returned *Fathers and Sons* and asked to be taken to the Turgenev cache in the basement. Not in all those words: "I want more," is what I said, poking the returned book. I spoke uncertainly, not as badly as Mirtila, yet not as well as myself. I wanted Mrs. Crandall to transition from Mirtila to me without a shriek of horror. Not that she would have shrieked. She was tougher than I thought. Mrs. Crandall hesitated. "I am alone here today," she enunciated with a sweeping gesture of her open arms that lifted her breasts and caused her blouse to open, revealing sumptuous cleavage. She caught my eye, but did not immediately re-button her blouse. I took a few steps toward the basement stairs, then looked back at her and said, in my own voice, "Please . . . It won't take long." Mrs. Crandall thought about this for a moment, then sighed loudly and locked the library's front door, after hanging a Back Soon sign. When she rejoined me to lead the way downstairs, I noticed her blouse was again tightly buttoned.

The library basement was lit like an old church, with large pools of darkness and half-shadows. Mrs. Crandall switched on a tiny lamp clamped to the nineteenth-century fiction shelf, and a soft golden light bathed the leather-bound spines of the books. We held our breath together, transfixed. Mrs. Crandall was the first to return to the valley of the dead. She crouched in front of the bottom shelf, where the Turgenevs lived. Running a finger slowly over the embossed titles, she read each of them in a whisper. I stood next to her, unable to tear myself away from the seductive golden glow, the murmur of the millions of perfumed and brittle pages, the trillions of words—oh, sweet Arcadia, why would anyone want to leave you? Mrs. Crandall extracted a book. "You haven't taken this out yet," she said, handing it to me. It was *Home of the Gentry*, the theme book for my unrequited love of Bebe. In a vicious one-two punch, Mrs. Crandall had yanked me out of my beloved Arcadia and punctured poor Mirtila. Did she know about Bebe? Was this the knockout jab? I crouched next to her, to better gauge her answer. "Have you read it?" I asked. "No," she said, "I haven't read any of these books." We were inches apart. I could see beads of sweat forming above her upper lip, her blouse sticking to a tiny wet patch above her left breast. It was hot in the basement, but not that hot. "You should," I said. Mrs. Crandall studied the book's spine for a long time, sliding her gaze up and down the golden curlicues. Then she grabbed my right hand by the wrist, gently but firmly, and pulled it under her skirt. Her cunt was as delicious as expected. You can fill in the details on your own, or aided by any jerk-off book on the market. I have no time, or inclination, to offer you Mrs. Crandall's cunt on a silver platter, rhetorically speaking. We did it until my hand, wrist, arm and shoulder hurt, until I drew blood, until we heard footsteps above on the main library floor. I picked up *Home of the*

Gentry with my dry left hand. Mrs. Crandall disappeared into the basement toilet. When she reappeared, she was again her voluptuously starched public self. She showed me the basement emergency exit, a metal plate with a safety lock that could be opened only from the inside. It led to a narrow, little-used alley sandwiched between the back wall of the library and a high evergreen hedge. "Will I see you again?" she said. She was at the bottom of the stairs that would take her back to the main floor. "Where's McCabe?" I snapped. She looked at me as if I was naming an exotic shellfish. "Miss McCabe. My employer. Where did she go?" There was a crash upstairs, more footsteps, and laughter. Mrs. Crandall crossed her index finger over her lips. "Tomorrow morning at eight, I'll leave the back entrance unlocked," she whispered and ran upstairs. I scrubbed my hands in the sink and left through the alley. Waiting for the cab by the corner pay phone, I found what I was looking for in Turgenev's book: "Her image rose most vividly before him; he seemed to feel the traces of her presence round him; but his grief for her was crushing, not easy to bear: it had none of that serenity which comes from death."

The next morning, shortly before eight o'clock, I had the cab drop me off at a nearby corner. Better not to be seen near the library. The basement emergency stairs were harder to navigate than the main ones. The Judge's walking sticks were useless on the high and narrow steps. I let them slide down to the ground as gently as possible, gripped the handrail on either side and began lowering myself like a gymnast on parallel bars. Mrs. Crandall descended the stairs at eight fifteen. We had an hour and fifteen minutes before the library opened. I wanted some answers up-front, but she pulled me toward her before I could open my mouth. She was hungry. I liked that. In her, that is. Hers was a generous hunger. I did not feel exploited and overworked, as with certain insatiable, selfish fucks

I'd rather forget. She did not know how to touch me, but was eager to learn. I don't let strangers paw me, and I'm no one's guinea pig or teaching aid. Glorita and unattainable Bebe came to me fully formed. If anything, I was their pupil. The long string of one-night stands and opportunistic flings in between them, and during and after Bebe, were either ambidextrously skilled, or incompetently passive, which can have an ephemeral charm. All, however, had been much girl-handled before me: being first is as unappetizing to me as cod-liver oil. I ignored Mrs. Crandall's suggestions that I take off my clothes. To humor her, I let her poke me through my pants. She did it clumsily at first, disruptively, busily, annoyingly, until in time, she found out on her own that less was best, and timing was everything. She discovered that her cunt was driving us both. Proud and grateful, Mrs. Crandall began to worship her cunt, and offer it to me in every way she could think of. She must have known, however, that this by itself was not enough to bring me back, that finding McCabe was my Holy Grail.

Mrs. Crandall sold me her information bit by bit. Slowly. Expensively. With fornication as the currency. She wouldn't talk unless she'd had her (provisional) fill. The ratio was four-fifths fucking, one-fifth talking. I was quartered between exasperation and pleasure, longing and carnality, McCabe and Mrs. Crandall. I wanted McCabe. She was the one I took home with me after the increasingly violent pleasures in the library basement. But I got hooked on Mrs. Crandall. She was nearly the best fuck I'd ever had, almost as good as Glorita, and, unlike her, without the help of anything other than pure flesh. No emotions or history. Mrs. Crandall ceased to be high-gentry librarian, Saint Glykeria, Martyr, proto-deaconess (and closet white-trash social climber) the instant she grabbed my wrist and directed my hand to her cunt. She became pure cunt and buttocks, all wetness, exactly as I had envisioned her. I had not had a fantasy about Mrs. Crandall, but a premonition. "You knew me better than I knew myself," she said. She was now openly whorish.

It took me a week of sweat and cunt to piece together the bits. Seven journeys of Gomorrah in the library basement, each containing many others, like each day of the Creation—in this case, exactly seventeen and two-sevenths of the legendary one hundred and twenty-one sodomitic journeys. We began on a drizzly Monday morning. On Wednesday, after an increasingly violent and abject session yielded little information, I ordered her back to work as she was, wet and naked under her pleated skirt. On the top step, an inch away from the assistant librarian whose footsteps could be heard in the main room, she lowered herself onto my fist, slowly and deeply, and listened to my instructions. From that moment on, she was to sit from now on at work with her thighs slightly spread so that her naked cunt and buttocks were kept firmly in contact with the slick seat. She was allowed to rub her cunt against the seat, but not to touch it until she got home. The seat should be left unwiped, for anyone who might enter her office to see and smell. She was not to wear panties, pants, or any skirt that could not be easily lifted above the chair. On Thursday, she begged me to discipline her. She had touched her cunt once, late in the afternoon when rubbing it against the seat had ceased to alleviate her. I made her wait until Sunday afternoon, after her Holy Communion at Saint Glykeria, Martyr. I fitted her with a double plug held firmly in place by a leather strap. She was to wear it at all times. I ordered her to go upstairs to the main floor, naked except for her strap and shoes, so that she would begin to get accustomed. She was not to come down until I called her. I let her wait a good half-hour before going up. I found her standing by a window, the blinds slightly opened. Any observant passerby could have seen her. It was very risky. She was ready to answer my questions. This was the day: I could not let her leave until she talked. The plugs slid out of her, wetly, the moment I loosened the strap. She was lying on a table on her stomach, spread-eagled, her ass slightly raised so I could better see her cunt and her newly opened butthole. I fucked her for the rest of the afternoon, with my fingers and both of my fists, reinserting and removing the plugs. The table was drenched with cunt wetness and blood. I fucked her against walls and floors, on chairs, in a sweating frenzy, pinching her nipples, twisting the plugs inside her orifices to open them more. We stumbled down to the basement and lay there on the floor as the sun began to come down. She brought me a glass of water from the bathroom sink. When I was done drinking, she gave me the last and meatiest piece of the puzzle she had been feeding me bit by bit all week. That night, in the Judge's study, I finally assembled the puzzle, only to discover that there was another puzzle hidden within it. This is what Mrs. Crandall told me during our seven journeys. I have put it in chronological order and added a few comments.

Shortly before I regained consciousness, McCabe had called Mrs. Crandall at the library to make an appointment, in private, at Mrs. Crandall's office after the library closed for the day. Mrs. Crandall did not know how McCabe had gotten there, or returned home. She had offered to drive her back, but McCabe declined. Mrs. Crandall knew by then everything there was to know about the public McCabe, heroic SoHo art merchant. She was shocked by the physical change, but accepted McCabe's explanation that she had been on a strict diet. Besides, her voice was the same as Mrs. Crandall remembered from their brief encounter at our kitchen door—the first time, she swore, that they had met. (I was puzzled by Mrs. Crandall's assessment, but did not want to interrupt her first substantial flow of information: I thought McCabe's voice had changed as much as her body, perhaps even more.) McCabe had been extremely gracious. She thanked Mrs. Crandall for receiving her on such short notice. It was a confidential matter. Her employee was gravely ill; the prognosis was not good. McCabe wanted Mrs. Crandall's help to locate a relative who had lived in Elmira a long time ago and might still be here: *Her name is Glorita*, she said. "She thought that as a librarian I would know who's who in town. I explained to her that Shangri-La was not really part of the town, although technically it was. I had never been there. None of them had ever come to the library in my fifteen years here," Mrs. Crandall told me. (I had, almost every day, but that was long before Mrs. Crandall's arrival.) McCabe had left, graciously, but visibly troubled. (How had Mrs. Crandall, at first glance, learned to gauge what was going on behind that bony, impassible face?) Mrs. Crandall was curious, though, so she made some discreet enquiries. A few of her friends had Mexican maids who lived in Shangri-La. All were recent arrivals. None knew of any Glorita. A few days later, a $20,000 donation was made anonymously to the library fund, of which Mrs. Crandall was a trustee. It came from a private account at J.P. Morgan in Manhattan. The bank would not say more when Mrs. Crandall called to express her gratitude. She was sure McCabe had sent it. Mrs. Crandall almost drove to the Judge's house to thank McCabe personally, but changed her mind at the last minute. "She was so shy and polite that I did not want to embarrass her," she told me. Instead, she redoubled her efforts to find information about Glorita. "The least I could do," she added. She searched the library records and confirmed that no one from Shangri-La was registered. She checked the phone book for any spic named Gloria or G. anywhere in the county. There were about a dozen Gs, but they turned out to be Gregorios (which Mrs. Crandall charmingly pronounced Gorgorius, like the current Basileus), Germanes (which she did with a hard G and a sibilant s), or Gladyses. She canvassed in vain the tax rolls and the High School yearbooks from the 1970s (but did not recognize me in my shag, I cackled inwardly, keeping that and my local origins to myself; as for Glorita, she did not graduate). Mrs. Crandall then sent McCabe a brief letter reporting on her investigation, which was delivered by the butcher boy. She had decided against even a tactful mention of the anonymous donation. "I did not want her to think that I was trying to help just for her money," she told me. I could barely control my urge to slide my hand back into her prodigious cunt. Mrs. Crandall was most whorish when smarmy. She sensed my skepticism, but not my lust, fortunately, because her story would have been truncated. "I also did it because I was bored at the time," she said, giving me a hungry look that could have degenerated into another wall-splattering blood-and-secretion orgy if my mind had not been all tangled in Glorita's sudden appearance in the story. Much to Mrs. Crandall's surprise, McCabe called her as soon as she received the letter, and asked if she would drive her to Shangri-La to look for Glorita. They went on four consecutive Sunday afternoons. McCabe insisted on remaining inside the car while Mrs. Crandall, Greek New Testament and Spanish phrasebook in hand, knocked on doors, pretending to be on a church mission. There was no street map of Shangri-La. The only available map of Elmira, a wispy black-and-white ink drawing printed by the county fifty years earlier, did not even show its site. It also stubbornly refused to show most of Elmira's side streets, featuring the less grandiose houses. Mrs. Crandall, who had dabbled in Chinese ink and watercolor painting to alleviate her boredom, drew a street map of Shangri-La on the first Sunday, as she and McCabe drove around trying to understand the shape of the neighborhood. This was Mrs. Crandall's idea. She drew the perimeter and the one access road, looking in vain for the main streets before concluding that there were none. Small concrete-block houses sat next to rusty trailers and wooden shacks on the same block. All streets seemed equally important or unimportant, or maybe their importance depended on signs that they could not yet decipher. Mrs. Crandall divided her map into four large grids. McCabe picked the upper left quadrant to begin their canvassing. They would cover the other three in a counterclockwise sweep on the following three Sundays. Mrs. Crandall's canvassing system was based on cleanliness and prudence. She only knocked on the cleaner-looking houses that showed signs of female habitation. Her quota was two per block. She also approached the few women she saw lurking in the freezing porches and backyards. Some directed her to the home of an older resident; one even took her there herself. Mrs. Crandall kept a log of her interviews. None of the Shangri-La streets had traffic signs or nameplates that she could see. How did people know where they lived? How had mail been delivered? (We know the way ants and bees know, Mrs. Crandall. The late-lamented USPS never set foot in Shangri-La. They dumped their whole load inside that concrete bunker with the locked, rusty side door located on the left side of the access road, where it joins County Route 37. Some old guy paid under the table by the residents—so he wouldn't lose his equally late-lamented food stamps—then delivered the mail door to door. He was the one who would have known about Glorita, if anyone did. These were my parenthetical thoughts, which remained unsaid.) Mrs. Crandall numbered the streets running west–east in a north–south progression, and named with letters the ones running north–south, in an alphabetical west–east order. So 1st and A streets both began at their intersection on the northwestern corner of the upper left quadrant they canvassed on that first Sunday. Her logbook registered date, time, street, and both cross-streets; location of house within the block; description of interviewee (only three gave their surnames); and KN for knows nothing, NR for new resident, R10, R20, R1987, or RL for those who had lived there ten or twenty years, or since 1987, or "for a long time." On their fourth and final Sunday, as they finished canvassing the last quadrant of Shangri-La, they had yet to find a trace of Glorita.

Mrs. Crandall reached for her dress. She had to go home. It was almost dinnertime. Now was my turn to beg, cajole, and abase myself, even cry. I could not let her go. That night I had to squeeze from her the last drop of information about McCabe. My pain must have been real, even if my theatrics weren't; I couldn't tell anymore. She was moved. She held me like Mary held the Baby Jesus, giving me her breast to suckle, putting my tiny hand inside her warm cunt. I cross-questioned her gently, careful that her cunt did not come to a boil too soon, enjoying the slow release of her wetness, the swaying of her hips, delicate at first because we were sacred mother and child. "Mercy can be very funny," she said. I did not immediately realize to whom she was referring. McCabe hated her given name and never used it. She was plain McCabe to all. Was Mrs. Crandall that distant from McCabe, or that close? No, she could not remember if she ever called McCabe that name to her face. Unlike her jolly predecessor, New McCabe had no sense of humor. The few jokes I tried on her fell flat. Music, birds, food, wine, bandages were our only shared language. "She can be quiet, but she can talk up a storm." About what? I asked. "Oh, everything, and nothing. Art and life. She's been everywhere and met everyone. But she's not stuck-up. Deep down she's still a healthy Iowa farm girl," said Mrs. Crandall. I exhaled, surprised. "She says so herself," Mrs. Crandall added soothingly, with a maternal tremor of her hips. I asked her what they and Petrona had cooked together on Thanksgiving eve. "Your Thanksgiving dinner. What else?" she said, kissing my ear while her cunt wrapped itself tighter around my hand. She had bought the suckling pig in Shangri-La at McCabe's request. Tears rolled down my cheeks. Mrs. Crandall kissed my eyelids and held me tighter. "That's all I know," she said, declaring the interrogation closed as her hips warmed. I believed her. She was innocent. "Poor baby," she said, tenderly, her cunt arching and flooding my fist. I kissed her on the lips, for the first and only time. Mrs. Crandall then abandoned herself entirely to me. Passion made her body more voluptuous than ever. Her cunt was fleshier and warmer, her breasts more bountiful. She had kept most of herself out of my reach until this moment, while I had thought she had nothing more to give or show me. I put my ear on her belly to listen to the palpitations of her cunt, the sound of my fingers touching her deep inside. I was so stunned by how passion had transformed her flesh that, when her cunt began to quiet down, satiated, I lowered my guard and, in turn, abandoned myself to her. She fucked me like the Mother would fuck the Child. Licking, whispering, sucking, touching. She had learned. I came a dozen times, on her lips, hands, and breasts. I was inside her milky womb when she was inside me. When she stopped, breathless, my face still buried in her breasts, I almost retched in disgust. I had let a stranger touch me. Worse: a stranger with an opaque connection to McCabe, someone who could have been lying to me all along. "I don't want to fuck her any more than you do," Mrs. Crandall said sweetly, as if reading my mind. She held my gaze long enough for me to check her sincerity, then said: "Mercy and I just had the beginning of a beautiful friendship that might have flowered if she had stayed in Elmira." That was Mrs. Crandall putting me in my place. How foolish of me to think that McCabe would stay here with me until death did us part.

I let Mrs. Crandall get dressed, pretending not to notice when she hid the double plug strap at the bottom of her bag. I followed her up the stairs until she reached the main door of the library. When she turned around to say goodbye, I shoved her on the ground and mounted her. She was bigger and heavier than I was, but I caught her off-balance. Weeks on the wheelchair had built up my upper body. She giggled first, then struggled, not daring to make a noise so close to the street. She put up a fight, twisting, kicking, biting, spitting, punching. She broke my lip, which bled all over her face. I strangled her with my left hand. When she was about to pass out, I released my grip so she could breathe, and shoved my right fist into her cunt. I slapped her until her lips and her nose bled. She tried to slide away but ended half-sitting against the door, which allowed me to push her legs wide open over my shoulders and push my fist into her ass. She screamed, but no sound came out of her mouth. When I shoved my fist back into her cunt, she came in a flood of cum, piss, and blood, over and over and over. Exhaustion stopped us a long time later. We lay side by side, listening to the sound of snow falling outside. She was the first one to move. When she returned from the bathroom, she was wearing her blue knitted ensemble. Her face was almost normal, except for a slight swelling on the upper lip. It would look much worse tomorrow. She shoved her soiled, torn dress into her bag. I did not know what to say or do. I was ashamed of myself. I still am. This is the most shameful thing I have ever done in my life. I have confessed it to you in vivid detail at the risk of appealing to your basest instincts, as a way to mortify myself and perhaps, in time, gain absolution, not from you or some improbable god, but from my best self, which watched me in horror and repulsion. I did not know what to say to Mrs. Crandall that night. I stood before her majestic blue-clad figure silhouetted against the library's storm door, a ragged, stinky pygmy before a towering Athena. "Make sure you lock up behind me," she said, not unkindly. Then she was gone.

23

Ashes to Ashes

THE NEXT MORNING, there was a small brown parcel in my break-fast basket addressed to "Miss Mirtila" and bearing no stamps or sender. Inside was Mrs. Crandall's Shangri-La logbook, wrapped in a silk scarf so old that its crisscrossing threads hung in the air like a cobweb. The scarf smelled like overripe blackberries and wet soil, Mrs. Crandall's smell at the beginning of our daily sessions, before the more potent animal odors set in. Was I forgiven, or was this a set up? Had she lied to me some, a lot, or not at all? I sniffed her scent on the scarf with the indecent voracity of a dog. Then I folded it care-fully and put it inside a vacuum-sealed plastic bag, the kind used for frozen leftovers and forensic exhibits. Mrs. Crandall's scent would be preserved for future use. I was her dog. She was my mistress. Mrs. Crandall whistles; I stand on my hind legs and shove my hairy dog dick up her ass. The Archangel Raphael sweeps down from above, burning sword in hand, and slashes the whore and her dog down the middle. I took a freezing shower, grinding my teeth, until my gnarled toes began to turn blue. I had to flush Mrs. Crandall away, purge her from my body in order to regain my human form. I could not allow her back until I had found and killed McCabe. For that I needed to be human. McCabe was my true quest, my only enigma. Everything else, even Mrs. Crandall's cunt, would have to wait.

Hardened by the icy shower, I examined Mrs. Crandall's logbook with the necessary sang-froid. It was, like her, an imbrication of order and debauchery. The entries were surgically precise and systematic. The handwriting was in black ink, with an architect's small, perfectly even capitals. The map was impressively accurate and detailed. Mrs. Crandall had been modest when she had called it a sketchy line drawing. The book itself told a different, more hedonistic story. It was made of heavy Canson paper with a Belgian watermark, hand-stitched and bound in luxurious black leather. A red silk string page marker was attached to it. An entry on the final Sunday showed that Mrs. Crandall knocked on the third house on the south side of my old street, but that no one answered. Did Mrs. Crandall know that the National Security Advisor, Rafael Cohen, had been born in that cinderblock shack? If so, had she told McCabe? Had McCabe asked?

Rafael's official bio listed Elmira as his birthplace, and then jumped to Harvard, Oxford, and Rhodes Scholarship glory, with only a discreet wink to the spic vote ("the son of hard-working Hispanic immigrants"). Not a word about Shangri-La. Rafael despised that name, but was infatuated with his own, believing himself named after the archangel—a felicitous name, he once remarked, embraced by all three great monotheistic religions. "I can pass as anything anywhere," he boasted to Glorita, who promptly informed me with tomboyish glee. I knew better, but did not want to torment him. Didn't I cling to my own conceits to survive in the belly of the beast Glorita had named Aracnida, the Beautiful? Rafael Cohen had not been baptized after the Prince of Light, but after El Chino Rafael, the fat, ageless Chinese who for half a century pushed his bountiful fruit and vegetable cart through La Esperanza's pig-stained streets, my grandmother confided, after swearing me to silence. El Chino doted on little girls, particularly Rafael's mother, who was pretty as a picture and adored him, my grandmother added, willfully blind to the unsavory implications, as the custom had been in La Esperanza. There, Chinese men were highly prized and thought to come in only two flavors: the industrious eunuchs, like the ostensibly celibate El Chino Rafael, and the good fathers and providers, those openly shacked up with the black or mulatto women who always swarmed around them in the hope of catching themselves a Chinaman.

One place they hadn't looked was Shangri-La's cemetery, not to be found on Mrs. Crandall's map. It was hard to find. An impassable field of hawthorns and thistles hid it from the barrio. The only access was through a narrow, muddy path that began near the river. The sun was high and bright, melting the snow on the Judge's rosebushes. I decided to go visit the dead.

The cab left me at the end of the paved street. I went up the slippery path on foot, keeping my balance with the Judge's walking sticks. I found my grandmother's grave first, overrun by thorny weeds. I'd paid seventy-five dollars to lease the plot in perpetuity, and three times that for a fancy pink granite marker with her name and vital dates. My father went in next, then my mother. There was space for one more. "I want my ashes to live with a woman who loves me." The phrase popped into my mind accompanied by the humiliating blare of mariachi horns. If only I could express with dignity and simplicity the horror of being abandoned underground, or encased in a marble wall, or describe the longing to be remembered, loved, and kept forever at home. Turgenev would have pulled it off even if he had been born a spic. Torn between ridicule and fear of death, I stood before my grandmother's tomb and did all my limited talent afforded me: I sang for her the maudlin, pitiful phrase in my uncertain Spanish, so she could understand. "*Yo quiero que mis cenizas vivan con la mujer que me quiera.*" I cut my right index finger trying to remove a big weed. A drop of blood fell on the snow, perfectly round for a few seconds. This was my red flower for my mulish grandmother, my belligerent mother, and my puzzled father. "Talk to me," I asked my grandmother. "What should I do now?" She tickled the soles of my feet but did not say a word. The sun began dropping behind the cemetery hill.

Rafael's parents were buried across from mine. Weeds also lurked there under the icy surface. A small Christian cross was etched on the gray stone marker, as tradition and superstition, rather than piety, dictated in La Esperanza. Genoveva had demanded it and Ezequiel had acquiesced, "with some repugnance," he confessed to me at my grandmother's wake. A day after I purchased our plot, they had gotten their own on an installment plan, and ordered a marker. I had to battle with the stonemason to keep the wretched cross off our own pink marker. My mother was too shrewd not to have noticed its absence, and too beholden to La Esperanza not to lament it. After a lifetime in Elmira, her arbiter in all matters of custom, morality, and aesthetics remained La Esperanza, somewhat softened by distance and changing times, but still clad in its imperious certainty.

I searched the cemetery looking for Glorita's grave. I wanted to find her there. Dead at nineteen, the last age I saw her, or not long thereafter. Forever young and wicked, my enchanting Glorita, font of all yumminess, begetter of Bebe and all other scrumptious, crazymaking girls. Glorita, whose subterranean genealogical links with Mrs. Crandall and McCabe I sensed but did not yet understand. I wanted to find Glorita's grave to immortalize her divine girlishness, protect her honeyed pussy, coddle her tiny velvet ears, keep her alive forever, even give her new life: bring her back from that valley of death where vultures pick at the bones of the young grown old. A skinny black dog with red, mangy patches on its back watched me from behind a tree, then followed me at a distance, as I moved from one row to the next.

Dusk washed out the inscriptions on the tombstones. I had to get close to read them, often aided by my fingers. Each smelled different from the other, even when they were the same type of stone and from the same year. Polished granite, impermeable, had the faintest smell, but its deeply etched inscriptions released unique scents produced by the particular mix of animal, vegetable and mineral debris caught in them. In gray stone I detected the earthy, smoky, or mineral aromas of mushroom, iron, and, unexpectedly, red wine aged in oak barrels, none of which were physically present. I also caught a whiff of late menstrual blood, dark red and richly clotted.

On my last station of the Glorita cross, when I had almost given up hope, I found the grave of her godmother, Altagracia. Hers was the only name on the tombstone and on the gaily-colored plastic wreath. Oh, how I wished my Glorita had been there. I would have kissed the soil, I would have talked to her, I would have sung to her. Disappearance without physical death is the worst torment. In time, like Glorita's. Or in space, like McCabe's. Sitting by Altagracia's grave, I understood that killing McCabe would be the reverse of death. Had I known back then what I knew now, I would have killed Glorita thirty years ago. But we thought we were eternal and eternally young. I did not any longer wish for Glorita to be in Altagracia's grave. As much as her loss without death anguished me, I did not want her here. "Forgive me, sweet Glori, for I failed to kill you," I said.

I had never given a thought to what would happen to McCabe's body after I killed her. My mission began and ended with the act itself, followed by my ecstatic liberation. I had envisioned Firecop harassment—and was prepared for it—but not McCabe's funeral, burial, or memorial. I stood up holding on to Altagracia's monument, embarrassed by my egotistical blindness, shaken like someone who had taken one step into the abyss and then retreated. I thanked Glorita for setting me straight. I thanked Altagracia, my parents, my grandmother, Ezequiel Cohen and Genoveva, and all the lonely and forgotten dead in this cemetery. The thicket of brambles and thistles that hid them from Shangri-La showed how much they were wanted. They were not tricked by any Day of the Dead tomfoolery. I swore with the dead as my witnesses, and my shining Glorita as my patroness, that I would not allow McCabe to be treated like a piece of dead meat. I would place McCabe on an altar, honorably preserved in full blood, gore, piss, shit, and saliva, before rigor mortis set in and secretions were congealed. I would burn her with my own hands, and spread her ashes over the Little Ohio.

McCabe came back to me at that moment. Vividly. Helped by the dead, I had finally emptied my body of Mrs. Crandall. I heard McCabe's voice describing the Biloxi marshes and the migrating birds. I saw her listening to the third movement of Franck's *Symphony* with her eyes closed; crouching by the rosebush holding the Judge's secateurs in her right hand, and in her left, a diseased stem which she was about to prune; silhouetted against the noon sky, standing at the edge of the ravine.

Once while she was removing the bandages from my feet, I asked her why she stood there. My head was turned toward the window as she had instructed, so that I would not see the soiled underside of the bandages and the oozing lumps of raw meat that my feet had become. She was surprised that I even asked. Wasn't that view the reason the Judge's house had been built here? I agreed that it was a fine view, though far from spectacular. I myself used to stand there before the accident (to cover my tracks, I had begun using her tactful word for what had happened to my feet), but never as long, or as often, as she did. It was as natural for her to look at the ravine as it had been for me, she said, even if, unlike me, she had no memories attached to it. Perhaps that is why she lingered there, she said. A stone was a stone for her, and a tree was a tree. Nature was the same everywhere.

"You can look now," she said. The fresh, white bandages gleamed in the sunlight streaming through the window. McCabe drew the gauze curtains and was gone before I realized it. Moments later I saw her splitting logs by the garden shed. Next to her was a woodpile on a pallet, half covered with the usual blue tarp. She split wood for the rest of the week, until the woodpile was gone, along with the pallet and the offensive blue tarp. I grew up with those blue tarps. They were my playpen, poncho, camping tent, and picnic blanket. Our emergency roof weighted with bricks over leaky spots by my poor, inept, beleaguered father, who bared his teeth in an obsequious grin before pushing open the service door of the "whites only" hardware store.

At the cemetery, McCabe first came back to me in snapshots seen through a gauzy curtain. Then with sound, volume, depth, motion, and emotion. She moved me, McCabe—she tore my guts out and I still did not know why. She came back as a perfect hologram, more real than real. Smell, touch, and taste were missing, but not missed. That was Mrs. Crandall's fiefdom. I had never touched or tasted McCabe. Her smell must have been too subtle to penetrate the ample space that always separated us. The closest we had been was when she had cleaned my feet, her face about sixty inches away from mine.

McCabe also came back to me through my mouth. I inhaled her until my chest hurt. She had to return because I was holding her soul. I had not stolen it: she had given it to me. She could not live long without it. She would be like a zombie. Wherever she was, she must now be feeling the pull of my lungs. I had her essence in my possession. I did not want to keep it, or deprive her of it. I wanted to exhale it and return it to her, thankfully, lovingly, for her to have and cherish one last time before her apotheosis. I swore to protect her after the killing, to never betray her. The word "desecration" fluttered in my mind. I quashed it.

Half an hour later I caught a ride to Elmira in a pickup wreck driven by a handsome young Mexican dyke in a black heavy metal *en español* tee shirt. Her voice soon betrayed her as a girly, long-black-haired, smooth-faced Mexindian boy whom I thought hermaphroditical and not older than sixteen, until he told me in broken English that his wife was expecting their first. I was shocked. A baby girl-boy with a wife and kid! I thought I had misunderstood, so I made him repeat it, which he did, verbatim. He had been most alluring in his second permutation, as a hermaphroditical boy. I regretted to hear that this was not who he was, at least at present. The boy was a demon driver, careening around curves on two wheels, passing colossal live-poultry trucks within seconds of incoming traffic, and flashing his road lights at the ancient and lethargic Chevys and Buicks most white Elmirans had been reduced to driving. My head was in a whiplash with so many adjustments of real and libidinal perspective. "Where you of?" he asked me sweetly. When I answered that I was from there, he didn't believe me. I insisted. He giggled nervously and shook his head, unsure if the joke was on him. When I persisted, with a gentle but heartfelt *"Yo soy de aquí,"* he got so pissed that he swerved and almost landed us in a ditch. He dumped me right there on the road, a quarter of a mile from Elmira, giving me the finger as he sped away.

24

Mercy

A FEW DAYS LATER, I was in the kitchen when an unknown car pulled into the driveway. Its chassis was as putrid as Saint Lazarus' skin. I grabbed a kitchen knife. Then I saw Petrona get out, and circle the car several times like a mad hen, opening her mouth wide and gesticulating. The kitchen windows were shut. No sounds came through. The sun was beginning to rise.

Petrona came running into the kitchen. She let out a whimper and clutched her heart with her right hand when she saw me standing by the sink. I had put away the knife and pasted a Mary Mother of Christians smile on my face, suspecting what was coming. (Why is it that we spics clutch our hearts at the least provocation: joy, terror, surprise, disappointment, sadness, hope, etcetera?) When Petrona stopped wheezing, she regurgitated a convoluted stream of Spanish words on the subjects of loyalty, duty, gratitude, sorrow, regret. She spoke in the neutral third person: *"uno,"* one. It was not Petrona, but one, who regretted being forced by circumstances beyond one's control to suddenly quit. It was not I who "one" was leaving in the lurch, but "the fellow human being." One was doing so not out of disloyalty or lack of consideration. Not without pain, since one was pained (*"A uno le da pena, señora, mucha pena,"* she bleated) because the fellow human being needed one to eat properly, wear clean clothes, sleep in an orderly house. Not without anguish (*"Uno siente angustia al dejar al prójimo aquí en estas condiciones tan tristes,"* she wailed). Petrona, whose known vocabulary had hovered around twenty Spanish words, who never spoke unless spoken to, who, when forced to answer by the unspoken threat of dismissal ever present between housemistress and maid did so stingily, sourly, drawing a clear moral line between obedience under duress and willing cooperation, Petrona was now a flood of words, unstoppable. She was scared. Bug-eyed, piss-in-pants, shitless scared. I was afraid she'd have a heart attack and drop dead in the kitchen. "Petrona! Shut up," I said in English, in the firm tone of a dog trainer's "heel." She stopped and sat down. "Is *la migra* after you?" She shook her head, "No, señora, no. No es la migra." Then who? I cooed. Petrona began to cry. She threw herself on her knees, begging me to let her go. When I tried to help her up, she clung to my legs, leaving a trail of tears and mucus on my freshly pressed pants. I told her she could go, but that was not enough. I had to tell her that I wanted her to go for her own good, and mine, that no offense was taken or given, that I would have told her to go today even if she had not told me first that she had to go. I gave her a month's wages for the road, and walked her to her car, consoling her for her treachery.

The tailpipe barely cleared the road under the weight of children, mattresses, chairs, and impractical black iron pots—undoubtedly precious heirlooms—lovingly strapped to the passenger seat. A shriveled tobacco-colored man shared the back seat with four or five children (they were hard to count through the steamed windows). He appeared to doze while the little ones jumped and fought around him in atrocious Elmira-twanged Spanglish. I did not know that Petrona had a family. Were these her children? Could they be siblings, and the old man their grandfather? I fought against the repulsive suspicion that he might be her husband. I wished Petrona a good trip. *"Cuídese, señora,"* were her last words. Take care, or beware—depending on intonation, facial expression, body language, and context. Beware, or take care. I could not tell which.

Petrona left on Wednesday, December 12, at about 6:15 a.m. Exactly thirteen days before Christmas. That period now feels more remote than any of the preceding ones. I know what I did, but not when: each day is not a free entity in my memory, but part of an unbreakable block of ice in which "thirteen days" has been carved. This was the ice age, inside and out. I worked hard to keep myself serene, so I could reach that state of icy resolve that distinguishes the successful criminal. Subzero temperatures set in after a heavy snowfall. Sleet turned into ice-sheets on the ground, topping the snow. Chunks of ice began to form on the river bend that led to Shangri-La. In the ravine, the gnarled tops of bushes stuck out of the snow like zombie fingers. The gutter outside my windows cracked in two places under the weight of the ice. Two icicles the size of mammoth fangs soon hung from the cracks, partially obstructing my view. One morning I went up on a ladder and managed to free the gutter drain of ice. First I chipped at the ice with a hammer and a broken chisel from the Judge's prehistoric toolbox. Then I melted the bottom ice crust with a crème brûlée torch. McCabe's funeral pyre would be like that: fire on ice.

The melted snow finally trickling down the drain reminded me of the icehouse. It was a classic circular vaulted structure hidden in the midst of an old cherry-tree grove on the side of the property opposite the ravine. Round Hill descended there gradually, through two meadows and, at the very bottom, a one-hundred-and-fifty-acre woodland for hunting. All were part of the Judge's property. The nearest farm was a red dot on the horizon. The red dot was the top of the silo, locally known as "Dick's tip," after the owner's grandfather, whose artistic idea it had been. A row of cypresses planted by Mrs. Wilkerson's own grandfather—"after Van Gogh," she always reminded you—fortuitously shielded the icehouse from "that abomination." I used to play in the icehouse while my father raked the leaves on the Judge's lawn, muttering about Mrs. Wilkerson's latest demand. "Don't let the Missus see you there," he always said, not without glee. I would tiptoe down the three steps, peek at the scary dark vault, and run back to Papá and his leaves with my heart beating hard against my chest. "Your heart is in your mouth," he said one day. After that, I kept my lips tightly pursed every time I ran from the icehouse, afraid I'd spit out my heart and die.

The icehouse door was blocked by snow. When I shoveled it away, I saw that the door was chained and padlocked. None of the keys I found in the house over the next few days fit. In the end, I managed to pry open a chain link, without breaking it, and slide out the padlock. Inside, the icehouse was bigger than I remembered, and filled with dry leaves. I bagged them and burned them in an oil drum with a chicken-wire cover that my father had kept nearby for that purpose. I burned the leaves a little at a time, every other day, along with small chunks of frozen meat. If anyone were watching, or smelling, in the distance, they would not think it odd to see smoke and smell burnt flesh on the day after Christmas.

Once again, I began my days cleaning and polishing the contents of the Judge's studio, reclaiming the carefree routine of my first weeks here, before McCabe's transformation. I found serenity in the struggle against brass and silver stains, the dust that clogged the ears of Dresden shepherdesses. That serenity was the anesthetic that allowed me to confront the second task of the day: calling everyone and everywhere, in this shrunken and beleaguered land

and abroad, who could possibly lead me to McCabe. I even tried to track down Bebe.

I did not care any longer why McCabe came back, as long as she did. I did not care what I had to say. Mrs. Crandall had taught me the virtues of carnal humiliation. I had to apply her lesson to my heart. I ached for Mrs. Crandall during those thirteen days, through freezing showers, naked runs in the snowy meadow behind the Judge's house, and sleepless nights. More exactly, my flesh ached for hers, while my heart longed for McCabe, and my mediocre mind stood between the two, puzzled.

Every night since I had given up Mrs. Crandall's carnal protection, I had dreamt of a sea monster in an ink-black Sargasso Sea. It had McCabe's long limbs and Bebe's silky shoulders, with their hands, eyes, and backbones intertwined. It was majestic and dangerous. I had to find Bebe. To get to McCabe, or for Bebe's sake, or both. It only took a dozen calls to Bebe's bewildering array of phone numbers. She had left a frothy trail of outgoing messages from L.A. to New York to Budapest to Constantinople, the increasingly tenuous queen of cities, where she was headlining the Army of the Levant's Grand Millennium Concert. Bebe was still Bebe. A will of steel under deliciously frivolous icing. Her messages were champagne drops, truffle crumbs left for the lucky dog to lick. I had not spoken to Bebe in years. We had not fought. I had run out of steam, and she never pursued anyone. It was not in her nature. Bebe was The Pursued. She had rewritten the Belle Époque hetaera's manual for New York's new dyke century. I was afraid she would chew me up and spit me out the moment she heard my voice. Bebe did not forgive lapsed admirers. Even after years of apparent domestic bliss with the first McCabe, she expected boundless devotion and fealty from me—and a dozen others.

I got lucky in L.A. Bebe picked up on the first ring. "Hello, sweetie," she said. I was tongue-tied. A long time ago, she used to call me sweetie, swee'pie, shrimpie, munchkinik, and spicchik, when I had sufficiently pined at her feet. I would have slapped anyone of any color who would call me spic anything, but not indulged, adored, authorized Bebe, mistress of cold and hot. Bebe of the rancorous elephant memory. I thought she was sweet-talking to me now on the phone as if a bitter decade had not gone by. I head-over-heeled again. Not that I had ever stomped her out. Bebe, and Glorita, burned in my heart like an unknown soldier's flame. Ignored, yet eternal. "Hello, sweetie" melted space and time. Bebe was smoking reefer at night under the Brighton Beach boardwalk while I lusted for her. "Spicchik," she said, caressing the word; "spicchik," she said, giving me the gift of Glorita painting her toenails red on the porch, Glorita wading the creek in her Smokey Bear panties, her flat brown chest glistening in the sun, Glorita in a cloud of dust receding from the back window of the refugee bus, not waving, just standing on the road, arms folded, yellow dress fluttering. "Spicchik," Bebe had said, giving me Mrs. Crandall and McCabe, who now watched these scenes through my eyes. For a microsecond, I loved them all equally and simultaneously. Then Bebe broke the news that her marriage to McCabe had ended. "I got tired of being a kept woman," she said on the phone. I untied my tongue. "Hello, Bebe," I said. "Hello, sweetie," Bebe said. "I got tired of being a kept woman." And I understood that it was not she in the flesh, but her incorporeal voice. "I'll be back home before Christmas," she said before hanging up, leaving no space for a message.

Was Bebe talking to McCabe? I listened to her message at least twenty times. Sometimes I heard "sweetie," who could be McCabe, but not necessarily; other times I heard "sweeties" followed by muffled giggling, which was more like Bebe. One minute I'd think Bebe would never leave an intimate message for all to hear; the next minute I'd remember Bebe dancing on tables at the Odeon hours before it burnt down during the Second Great Fire, flinging a martini on a simpering heiress at the Four Seasons, stepping out of the elevator naked at Cardinal Gonzaga's office with "Suck My Dick" painted on her chest and her back (I was left on the ground floor guarding the mink coat from which she had emerged "as God brought her into the world," my grandmother had said upon hearing the story in one of my infrequent phone calls. My granny despised priests ("a bunch of perverts") as much as she lapped up my bad-girl stories from the big city. They all had a double in La Esperanza, where everything that ever happened in New York had already happened long ago.)

On my twenty-first listening of Bebe's message I finally understood its true meaning. It was McCabe's final dismissal ("I got tired of being a kept woman") in all three of its possible versions. If "sweetie" was McCabe herself, it was an added slap, sarcastic rather than endearing; if it was a new paramour—or if it was in the plural, "sweeties"—it was as meaningless as an air kiss, and "I got tired of being a kept woman" was still an indictment of McCabe for the whole world to hear.

I had stuck my finger in a live outlet: Bebe had settled the score. The jolt almost made me give up McCabe. I packed my bag and threw out my pitiful McCabe mementos: the wine corks and cheese wrappers, the rosebush twine, a button fallen off her hunter's shirt, the nurse's bag. Bebe would be thrilled to see me in L.A. now that she was back in play. She might even get me a job there. We would let bygones be bygones. I would rein myself in, keep to best-friend behavior. We would go clubbing again. Everybody would think once more that we were lovers. I wanted to be envied. I wanted to be seen in public with the most handsome, inaccessible, expensive of them all. This fantasy lasted only one evening, complete with images of the long-extinct palm trees, blue frothy drinks, Technicolor smog sunsets, red convertibles, Pacific beaches, and balmy weather, and a newly incestuous Bebe, as alluring as ever, but now protected by the strongest taboo. What burst the bubble was not just the illogic of severing "Bebe" from "lust," which could not be done, but realizing that she had ceased to be the emblem of all my failures. Bebe was not why I had to kill McCabe. Her revenge on McCabe was not mine. The McCabe connected to my Bebe-related humiliations had long ceased to exist. She had purged herself from this world, without my intervention. I retrieved from the wastebasket the corks, wrappers, and twines that were the only proof that my McCabe had ever existed. The suitcase I left packed. From then until the end, I dressed out of it, keeping it always ready to go.

The search for McCabe now filled every minute of my days and nights. I called every major art gallery and museum in New York City, Barcelona, London, and all other strategic points east and west, pretending to be a foreign collector. McCabe's SoHo gallery was open. It had never closed. In fact, it was expanding upward and sideways, to the floors above and the adjacent buildings. They had just sold a Beuys for a record figure. It had been the biggest ever private sale of a living artist. McCabe, on the other hand, had not been seen lately on the Manhattan social circuit. Some thought that they had glimpsed her at her gallery recently, or that someone they knew had, but when pressed could not remember when or whom. Others said that she was on a roll after the Beuys killing, flush with cash and anointed with the mystique of winners, that being picked by McCabe was now every living artist's obsession, that she was lying low these days to keep them off her back, planning her next coup.

Others put her variously in Germany, India, or even China, where she was opening a branch across from the Guangzhou Opera, or signing the new hot young thing, someone whose name no one could remember given how one Chinese name sounds like the next, but who, everyone said, was the Chinese Basquiat, not at all Basquiat-like in his art, but Basquiat-like in sexy boy-genius raw power.

McCabe was a high-risk gambler. She had seized her chance, taking her business to the stratosphere from her Elmiran woods. She had fired and hired, bought and expanded, slashed and burned the competition from a distance. She had done in weeks what would take others years. All while playing nurse with you, Reason's wormy voice hissed. No: while nursing me back to life, selflessly, devotedly, graciously, I said out loud, quashing the worm. Where did she find the time and energy to do so much? I began to admire her. Admiration had not been on my list of McCabe-related feelings until then. Now I was overflowing with it. I admired her intrepidness and intelligence. Making money wasn't only a craft for the cunning, yet stupid. In McCabe's brilliant hands it became art and science, war by other means, purview of the new Caesars, Napoleons, and Clausewitzes. McCabe calmly pacing the garden while planning her next campaign, her long legs the only part of her skinny body that moved, McCabe interrupting her inspired cogitations to take care of me, to be with me: I felt humbled by these images from our daily life whose meaning had been opaque and was now clear. McCabe was great and she was merciful. Oh, yes, she was merciful. That is why she shied away from her name. She did not need to trumpet her nature. Her deeds spoke for her. She was merciful as only a ruthless general can be. Did she know that I was planning to kill her? Had she shown mercy to her killer to prevent or to forgive the killing, or did her brilliant strategic mind conceive other outcomes? On the other hand, she may not have known or suspected anything, a lamb when not on the battlefield, her mercifulness flowing innocently from her to me and back to her, without beginning or end, goal or motive. It was in that returning ebb that her mercy carried back to her whatever little I could give: a piece of music, an ear for her bird tales, rotting feet, and moral misery.

I fell asleep to the image of McCabe, the merciful lamb, and the river of mercy flowing between us. I did not dream, but held on to a reality sweeter than dreams.

It was still dark when I woke up. I left a last message with the gallery's voicemail android: "Hey, McCabe. There'll be someone here on Christmas Day who you want to meet, and who's dying to meet you. Come over." Christmas was forty-eight hours away.

25

In Labor

TWO DAYS BEFORE CHRISTMAS, McCabe's work-booted feet followed me everywhere as I got the house ready. I vacuumed, waxed, polished, dusted, and washed floors, rugs, walls, furniture, doors, silver, windows, and china. I cleared snow off the driveway. Drove for eight hours to the state capital to bring back all that Elmira lacked: the deep-yellow Danish butter that McCabe liked to lick off her index finger; the Rocamadour cheeses that she had inspected with suspicion until I cut a piece and put it in my mouth (she hated destroying the little cheese's perfect roundness, so I always had to cut them for her when she wasn't looking); the honeyed Anatolian peaches and pears, near-extinct from war, which she stared at, but did not taste; the mangoes, guavas, sugar-apples, nísperos, and guanábanas she smelled and touched with great curiosity so often without eating them that I asked Petrona to hide some in the back of a cupboard as a reserve for Sundays, Petrona's day off; and the side of venison I knew would delight McCabe, the insatiable carnivore. In Elmira, I arranged for the delivery, at the last minute of Christmas Eve, of four dozen yellow, red, white, and pink roses after bribing the flower-shop owner into forgetting an order previously placed by the wife of a prominent orthodontist. I also bought cornmeal, molasses, and the county's sublime ham, its only world-class product, lamentably still unknown to the world at large. I did not mind showing my naked face in town. Secrecy was no longer needed. It was a relief that the Elmira public library was shut for the holidays, though I'm embarrassed to confess that I peeked twice through the darkened windows, half hoping and half dreading, against all logic, to find Mrs. Crandall there. The table where she had lain naked was still empty. She had removed the heavy dictionary that I placed under her buttocks, so I could reach deeper into her cunt. The memory and the example of Mrs. Crandall kept my body going those forty-eight long hours before Christmas as I slaved to prepare the house for the return of McCabe. I had no doubt that McCabe would come back. She would take the bait. She was too much of a gambler not to. I had lied to McCabe, the great and the merciful: I expected no one else on Christmas. It was a necessary lie for the greater good, hers and mine, a lie that, retroactively, when it had accomplished its beneficial end, would cease to be a lie.

On Christmas Eve, I was in the kitchen at daybreak, needing four hours to do what Petrona would have done in one. Now her terror again filled the kitchen. Something far more malevolent than la migra had chased her. Had the English-only vigilantes who roamed the backwoods at night threatened her? Had she or her shriveled man stolen from one of the Negro drug dealers who lately controlled the outer edges of Shangri-La? Had I seen the contours of the Aztlán eagle on her car's putrid chassis? The side of venison wrapped in transparent plastic drove Petrona out of my mind.

The venison had spent the night in the Judge's king-size Sub-Zero fridge. It now stretched on the heavy oak kitchen table as luxuriantly as Mrs. Crandall's body on the library table. The color pattern was different, though: here pale red meat, pure and fatless, over light brown wood; there, sumptuous, creamy flesh overflowing a polished cherry slab. I had never butchered venison before. I followed an illustrated primer self-published by a Pennsylvania resettlement camp butcher that I found tucked inside a cookbook. It was much more difficult and time-consuming than he claimed. Separating the meat from the bones and the muscle tissue required considerable strength and precision. At one point I moved the venison to the floor, to get better leverage. Six hours later, the pieces of venison were neatly stacked in the refrigerator, ready for cooking. Cleaning the butchery required another three hours: the table and the surrounding floor were splattered with blood, bones, and scraps of discarded meat. Blood had dripped between the planks, where it coagulated. I discovered it while looking for the source of the stench that persisted even after I had washed all floors and surfaces, and dumped the securely bagged venison waste in the garbage can outside the kitchen. It took me another hour to scrape the blood out of the floor cracks with a rusty scalpel I found in the Judge's toolbox, and to apply bleach onto each crack with an eye dropper, precisely, so as not to damage the polish on the wooden planks.

McCabe had loved meat. I thought about it in the past tense while butchering the venison. I could not bring myself to put it in the present, even when I imagined her at that very moment eating a bloody sirloin for lunch in Manhattan, or dining on *Eisbein mit Erbspüree* in Berlin, or breakfasting on kaorou in Beijing. Wherever she was, she would be either eating, digesting, or preparing to eat meat. Meat and birds, dead or alive, were her only bodily interests, but her expanding empire was her true passion. I had imagined McCabe bored with her art dealing, content with the money and power she already had, and eager to move on to something that fed her spirit. Wasn't that why she had become a nurse, an ornithologist, my patient pupil? Wasn't that why she so quickly dispatched the fresh load FedEx brought her every morning from Manhattan? I had mistaken her tactical brilliance for lassitude, my material poverty for wisdom. Butchering the venison, I searched for a quality in my person. I found none. McCabe's immolation would become my only quality.

The bone structure of the deer is not unlike ours, though the backbone is thicker and wider because it must support a full belly. The muscles that prevent backbone and belly from collapsing from the pull of gravity are also twice as fibrous and numerous than those of the average Caucasian human male. The legs, however, are similar, except that there are four instead of two. The animal kingdom consists of pieces of walking, breathing, jumping, fornicating, dim-thinking meat, on two or four legs. I am referring to us, mammals. I once dreamt that I was a pig rooting for truffles on the banks of the Little Ohio. Another time I dreamt I was a prairie dog running in the snow in the last remnant of the Great Prairie, which almost touches Elmira County in the west. In the summer, you can see it swaying in the distance if you climb a tree in Shangri-La's cemetery. The Great Prairie was my Sargasso Sea, my Caribbean, boiling or frigid, my Red Sea parting, my home within home. I sat in the tree with my father's binoculars trained on the golden waves. There I saw Moses, Billy the Kid, and Captain Morgan, who had set fire to San Cristóbal de La Habana centuries ago according to my father. The binoculars warped the tips of the prairie grasses and the line of the horizon. I took this to be proof that the earth was flat, even when I knew it was round. The Judge, who hated opera, had slipped his binoculars to my father before his annual fall trip to New York with Mrs. Wilkerson, hoping to avoid yet another *Forza del Destino* at the wretched Met. It did not work. She forced him to go anyway, my father later told me.

ANA SIMO

By the time I finished cleaning up, the sun was a pale yellow smudge dropping behind the icy rosebushes. The saddest winter sight in Elmira is that pale yellow twilight that replaces the afternoon. It made my mother walk around the house with pursed lips and a glare in her eyes. My grandmother advised me to keep clear of her daughter on those days. "She has a malignant streak," she told me, hesitating between regret and pride. "But," she added (and I knew what would follow: an indictment of my father), "He provokes it in her; he's no saint." As usual, she clammed up when I asked her what exactly he did wrong. I couldn't see it and was afraid that I, too, might be provocative and un-saintly. "You haven't done anything," my grandmother said, pulling me into her fat lap. This was the beginning and end of many of our conversations. To her mind, I could do no wrong. I nevertheless mimicked my father, scurrying around the house, eyes glued to the floor to avoid my mother's incinerating gaze until the whistling in the kitchen signaled that all was back to normal. My mother couldn't whistle a tune any more than she could sing, but it was the happiest sound in the world for the three inmates in her fearsome prison.

My mother's choleric winters continued until the day she died. And one year, winter drove Ezequiel Cohen mad. The sixth-grade English teacher had explained the meaning of "the dead of winter," which in Elmira fell in February. Despite our protestations, Rafael and I were paired to do a five-hundred-word essay on the subject. We fought whenever we tried to write together, so this time I wrote the text and he did the illustrations. One showed a boat trapped in the ice in the Little Ohio River. Another showed a woman and a boy at table while snowflakes swirled outside their window. On a couch, nearby, a man slept under a green tartan blanket. All three had curly black hair. The teacher asked who the man was. Rafael said it

172

was the grandfather. I knew it was Ezequiel, who had been lying in exactly the same position under a green Army surplus blanket for almost a week. When Ezequiel first failed to get up from the couch to go to work, Genoveva ran in tears to my mother, as she always did. My mother and my father, separately and together, went to talk to Ezequiel, who didn't answer them either. It was then decided to leave Ezequiel in peace until he ran out of sick days. We were to pretend he was not there. Water and food were left on the windowsill by his couch. They remained untouched during the day. In the morning, they were gone. I was sitting alone at his dining table, revising my "In the Dead of Winter" essay, when Ezequiel spoke from his couch, slowly and laboriously, in English, a language he officially could not speak. "He was uncircumcised in flesh, but not in heart," he said. He looked like someone who had chewed on something bitter. Then he shut his eyes, exhausted by his first and only bout of eloquence in the alien tongue. I never told anyone. This happened on a Saturday. By Monday Ezequiel was back to mopping the school hallways, all smiles as usual.

At four o'clock, the roses had not yet arrived. I needed them to lift the winter shroud that was enveloping the house. The flower shop insisted, for the third time, that they were on the way. The Yellow Pages listed no other flower shops outside the state capital. Thirty years after I had left, a decrepit Elmira was still the only semi-civilized outpost in the heart of the heartland. I found a flower wholesaler about sixty miles west of Elmira, in an adjacent and otherwise unpopulated county, surrounded on all sides by the shreds of the Great Prairie. The owner agreed to sell me $200 worth of assorted Colombian roses that were sitting in his refrigerator. He was not sure how many there were, but it should be more than the four dozen I wanted. He said he was giving me the Colombian price without me having to go to Colombia and risk being kidnapped and having a finger chopped off, or an eye gouged out and mailed to my family. This went on for a long time while I commiserated with him about Colombian florists, winter blizzards, the unfairness of military subsidies for unused grasslands but not for flower importation, the disrepair of county roads, the venality of soldiers and politicians at the local, state, and federal levels, and other matters.

The world has the wrong idea about the white rural inhabitants of this corner of the heartland. They are supposed to be wise, hardworking, honest, dignified, and silent, only a tad less taciturn than, say, Minnesotans of old. That is a big load of baloney. This contradiction is lost on them, but not on smart little spics like Rafael Cohen, who pointed it out to me during a sixth-grade visit to a nearby milk farm. The farmer was a chiseler, his wife a whore, their four children violent and moronic giants, the assorted adults hanging on (in-laws, farmhands, the inevitable junkie younger brother in a black Metallica tee shirt) were bloodsuckers, and the entire group a collection of degenerates of the Bible-thumping, sister-fucking, speed-and-sanctimony-addicted persuasion. Rafael did not say it like that. These were, and are, my own words. "Witness the decline of America!" was all Rafael whispered in my ear as we entered the milking barn. We both tittered.

I arrived at the flower wholesaler when the family was finishing dinner. The man and his two sons loaded the flower boxes into the Land Rover. He was pissed, but held his tongue when I insisted on checking the contents of each box before it was taken out of his warehouse. As I began to drive away, he told me to watch out for prairie dogs crossing the road. "We don't want some dog guts splattered over your nice car now, do we, Miss?" he said, baring his yellowish canines.

I saw no living creature on my way back. The snowy flatlands on both sides of the road were perfectly white and empty under a sliver of moon. I wished I had taken McCabe to see the remnants of the Great Prairie before the snow covered them. She would never see them now. Regret twisted my stomach the rest of the drive. I may even have shed some tears. When I pulled into the Judge's garage, the Elmira roses were there waiting for me. It was around eight o'clock. I spent the rest of the evening matching all one hundred and twenty roses to vases, bottles, tall glasses, and any suitable container I could find, and putting the finishing touches on the Christmas meal. I arranged the flowers in large bunches, which I spread around strategically so that the house did not look, or smell, like a funeral parlor. I put the prettiest vase with yellow roses in McCabe's empty bedroom. For the dining table I created a muscular arrangement with red roses at the center, surrounded by concentric circles of white, pink, and, on the outer ring, yellow roses. McCabe's proximity must have inspired me. I am not the artistic type. Putting flowers in vases is alien to my nature. When I went to bed, drunk on a 2002 Pouilly-Fuissé that I had been keeping for a special occasion, the venison was the only thing left to do. I had even set the table with the best the Judge and his wife had to offer (I had found the delicate white tablecloth in Mrs. Wilkerson's armoire, still wrapped in tissue paper.) The table was set for three. I was going to lie through my teeth until the end.

From my bed, I could see the thin moon rising behind the rose-bush. McCabe could not keep her hands off that bush. Every morning, hands in pockets, she scrutinized it, bending over to look at some microscopic detail or kneeling to peer at an inaccessible branch. After the inspection, which would sometimes take a good fifteen minutes, she would bring the shears out of the garden shed and nip here and there. I suggested that she save herself the extra trip by bringing the shears with her the first time around. "You can keep them at the entrance with the Judge's walking sticks," I said. She refused, saying that she did not always need the shears. "But you always use them," I insisted. There may be a day when she wouldn't use them, so she preferred not to prejudge, she replied (not in those words—she would not have said "prejudge" or even known the word, but that is what she meant). She reflected for a long time, then added: "I don't want to prune the rosebush just because I have the shears in my hands." With this, I fell asleep, content.

26

Navidad Blanca

BINCRÓSBI WAS WAFTING UP from the kitchen clock radio.

"We're all white on Christmas. That's what my man says," Ezequiel Cohen spat in La Esperanza Spanish, each word ending in an acid air clap. How sweet it was to wake up to Bincrósbi on Christmas morning. You floated upward on his foamy white spiral until you reached the surface of the sea of tranquility. That was how white people woke up all year long, except Trailer Trash down the road, who woke up to his dogs.

The howling of dogs was Shangri-La's relentless soundtrack. Dawn of the Dogs, with mutts playing the walking cadavers; or a topographically incorrect *I am a Fugitive from a Chain Gang*. Night and day they howled, so we would not forget our delicate geopolitical situation, a brown island on Bincrósbi's foamy white prairie. Hundreds of bloodthirsty, big-fanged canines fighting for a length of tripe in the trailer park, ready to rip out your guts if you looked them in the eye. It wasn't tripe they wanted, but to be let loose, so they could tear through Shangri-La, ripping off limbs, flattening our houses, which suddenly seemed so small and weak, and running off with bloody baby torsos in their jaws. Trailer Trash had the power to unleash his dogs. Every day he didn't was a day we owed him. Yet I did not hate him.

"I'm as white as they are!" my grandmother bellowed, so they could hear her all the way in Elmira. She was dyspeptic at the lack of racial logic of the *americanos* (i.e., white Americans, black ones being *negros americanos*). With her fair skin, blue eyes, fourth-grade diploma, beautiful penmanship, and La Esperanza birth certificate, she knew that she was better than the americanos, and, through sheer luck, better than the *inditos*, the little Mexican Indians, across the road. My grandmother's conviction of her superiority was so absolute and so rooted in chance that she could be generous and unassuming in her daily life. Thus, she became godmother to several generations of inditos. Noblesse oblige, Rafael once admiringly remarked. The lack of this quality in white Americans, so rich and lucky, is what she resented them for most. Even Bincrósbi she distrusted. Had this been her house, she would not have let him preside over our Christmases.

Bincrósbi was the only americano who ever entered our house. Rafael and I did not count. We were not americanos, just "born here." That was how Shangri-La saw its American children. To compensate for withholding our souls, the neighborhood binged on blind loyalty and flag-waving patriotism any time there was a disturbance against our adopted country anywhere on the globe (except south of the border, lest we betray our own, offend a neighbor, or give satisfaction to the americanos, ever ready to tar all of us with the same brush). To further appease the giant, Shangri-La boys were offered to the army in sacrifice. Half came back with tattoos and some of the same bad habits picked up at the state penitentiaries by their more numerous jailbait peers (drug and steroid use and dealing, bitter depression, terminal ethno-racial confusion, and a fat chip on their testosterone-swollen shoulders). The other half came back in the proverbial body bag, allowing their mothers the coveted status of *mujer sufrida*, a martyr.

Had I set the kitchen clock radio last night? I was still too drunk to tell. I drifted into that zone of clarity between wakefulness and sleep where McCabe dwelled. A scene from two months ago uncoiled with serpentine dread. I was still confined to bed, with my feet raised and thickly bandaged. McCabe was sitting on a chair by the foot of the bed. "I didn't know that you followed Washington politics," I said, trying to sound casual. "I don't," she answered. When I remained silent, she added, "They don't matter." She looked at me with curiosity. My hands got clammy and shaky under the covers, but I pushed on: "Yet you ran out to tell me about the National Security Advisor and the bomb . . . ." It was now McCabe's turn to be silent. "I thought that you'd want to know," she finally said. "Why?" I asked. "Because you like to know everything," she answered evenly. I tried to decipher the meaning of that terse statement but hit the glass wall that was McCabe's open and candid face. Did I see a slight tremor of fondness at the corner of her mouth?

She had a strong mouth, generous but not fleshy, perfectly in proportion with her nose and chin, both equally well defined. The new McCabe could not be called pretty. Her ears were a little too large and separated from the head, her neck perhaps too long. I decided this was only noticeable because the rest of her features were so harmonious. Hers was what used to be called a handsome and noble face. There was something Byzantine about McCabe. Not Byzantine as in classical paintings, but as you can still see in the faces of Anatolian refugee women who have just arrived on the streets of Astoria, before Aracnidan cuteness infects them. McCabe's body and head were slightly mismatched. Her body was too bony and elongated, more suitable for the narrower elfin faces so common in Prague. What allowed her face and head to sit gracefully on her body, in spite of the mismatch, were her shoulders, slightly wider than what her body required, but perfectly adapted to receive the neck and head. Breaking down McCabe into her architectural components was not something I did in our everyday life. It was only in that zone of light, cushioned by a hangover and Bincrósbi's fecally sweet voice, that I began to pull her apart.

In real life, as distinct from uncoiled memory, McCabe was as alive and human as Mrs. Crandall, even if I perceived no carnality in her. Was flesh necessary for life? Thunder, lightning, wind, music, and, come to think of it, birds did not bring flesh to mind, and yet they were alive. McCabe was the most splendid specimen of the breed. I knew that life and passion existed outside the flesh. I had seen it in McCabe and experienced it with her, but I did not understand it. My brain was too small to grasp this in any but the most general way. Whenever I tried to understand McCabe and her effect on me, I would feel the vertigo of the starry sky. Just as on the Night of the Dead at Shangri-La's cemetery, when praying to heaven with my grandmother for her indito godchildren's forebears. *Abandon yourself. Do not think.* Who said that? I could not identify the voice. The zone of clarity has lousy acoustics. Bincrósbi, for all we knew, could have been a sadistic pedophile, the kind who shoots videos of six-year-old girls sticking pencils into their tight little assholes. Saint Bincrósbi, Protector of the Spics. He had the narrow, sharp features that McCabe's body was made for, but mercifully did not get. Things would not be what they are if McCabe had Bincrósbi's mug. This curious thought finally woke me up.

The house was mute. A robin sat on the rosebush. Don't they migrate? McCabe would have known. I missed her. Unbearably. Odiously. Just one more day of suffering. I may have held her soul in my mouth, whatever that meant, but it did not stop my longing. It made it worse. My appetite for her was as insatiable as Mrs. Crandall's had been for me until the day she imposed her will on herself and dismissed me. Exemplary Mrs. Crandall. I was tempted to go to her, drown in her overflowing and uncomplicated breasts, but I pulled back on my leash as she had on hers. Mrs. Crandall and I understood each other perfectly well. We were dogs in heat—prairie dogs, not the horrific kennel-dwellers. Two cowardly, but free, prairie dogs.

With the logs split by McCabe, I had built a pyramidal pyre inside the icehouse. After stuffing the pyramid with fire starters, and placing a large gas can in a corner, I had removed two stones from the upper part of the icehouse wall so that the smoke could escape. Oxygen to keep the fire alive would come in through the heavy iron door, which I would keep open as much as necessary. The stone could resist a temperature of about twelve hundred degrees Fahrenheit without cracking. I would lay McCabe's naked body on top of the pyramid face up, arms open, eyes closed.

I had seen her naked body twice before. The first time was from my window on a balmy October morning, after the snow that had frozen my feet had melted. She had been splitting logs for about an hour by the gardening shed when she took off her clothes and work boots and doused herself with the hose. The water must have been cold, but she did not seem to mind. She coiled the hose on a low sycamore branch and stood underneath, face upturned, drinking the water and letting it run down her chest and belly. I could not see her face. From my window, she looked about six inches high by the distant shed. I hesitated before I picked up the Judge's binoculars. I was afraid to disturb the flow of events. That was one of my phobias. Curiosity was stronger. Like a doomed time traveler in a

Saturday morning show, I trained the binoculars on her face. Her lips were parted to receive the water, the tip of her tongue visible inside her mouth, waiting, her eyes closed in the heavy-lidded way of someone sleeping. Her face was transfigured. She was so human that she was inhuman. I dropped the binoculars as if I had stepped barefoot on burning coals. The second time was at night. My own moaning woke me from the fever long enough to catch a glimpse of her standing naked at the foot of my bed, then walking to the window to close the shades. Oh, merciful one, who rushes in the dead of night to the sickbed of the worm without thinking of covering yourself! I had seen her naked twice, yet I still had not seen her flesh. The fire would.

McCabe's pubic hair was a deep red. I had not trained the binoculars on her body. That would have been indecent. I had seen the red splotch with my own eyes on the distant six-inch figure, right before water began to pour out of the hose, darkening and flattening the hair on her head and body. The hair on her head was almost black, like her eyelashes and the hair of her armpits. Her tee shirt sleeve receded to reveal the dark armpit hair when she lifted her right arm above her head to get me a book from the Judge's uppermost shelf. I was next to her and happened to look up from my wheelchair at that very instant, catching the dark underarm shadow. Behind the book I had asked for, whose title I don't remember, she found a 1904 edition of Audubon's *Birds of America*. During our last meal together, she told me that finding that book, on that precise day, had been a good omen. Of what, she wouldn't say. Perhaps as a consolation, she volunteered that she had grown up watching birds in Maine, which in the summer was the bird capital of the world. More than two thousand different species had been sighted. The cliffs near Portland were a favorite nesting spot for albatross. McCabe almost convinced me she was from Maine. What does it matter now?

McCabe took the Audubon book to her room the night she found it. She must have taken it with her when she left, along with what I always assumed was her birding notebook. Now everything is subject to reinterpretation. The Audubon book, as all other items in the Judge's house, was in an inventory attached to the lease that McCabe had signed. Early on, before her transformation, old McCabe had given me the lease to keep along with ten thousand dollars in twenties and tens for household expenses. I had insisted on a cash economy. "Ain't no more where dat come from, so make it last," she jabbered in her phony Afro-Brooklynese. The time when I was devoted to covering my tracks, with alibis, with taking my revenge on that bombastic but ultimately harmless creature also named McCabe, seems so remote now that I wonder if my brain is finally going dark under this mattress, or if the remoteness is of a moral nature, an acknowledgement of my insignificance. I am not today who I was at the end, and I was not then who I was at the beginning, or even in the middle. This is not a riddle, dear listener, but a statement of fact.

In the silence after Bincrósbi's posthumous white dream, I wondered what the Judge's heirs would think happened to the Audubon book. I could ask McCabe when I saw her. I sat in bed, sobered by this unappetizing possibility. My curiosity was beginning to flicker already. I was, until then, the most curious person I had ever known. It was my pride, my sole accomplishment, the only respectable entry in my private Guinness Book of World Records, chock full of petty excesses. That Christmas morning, however, I did not want to learn anything more about McCabe. I knew little, or nothing, but it was enough. I would not ask her about the Audubon book and her notebook, or where she had been, why she had left, why she had come back (although this was not a mystery: she would come back because, unlike me, she was still curious—she who had no flesh, she of the eternal mercy, she of the impassible face which was the face of kindness because hatred is never impassible—she, unlike me, was still in the world). It was a sublime contradiction, that of mercy and power, whose deciphering would have delighted me not long ago, but now left me indifferent. A lifetime of curiosity was over. The time of acceptance and action had begun, a twenty-four-hour cycle that would end the next morning at this hour with a pyramid of smoldering ashes. Did anyone know the precise hour of Mary's accouchement? We should drink a toast to her, McCabe and I.

I scrubbed my body with a stiff brush until my skin was a reddish brown. How I wished I could keep that vibrant color, instead of my dull beige. The bathroom mirror showed a naked female of the human species emerging from a sulfurous cloud. She was short and solidly built, with some roundness of ass and belly to balance the muscular arms and back. Her breasts were small and not yet sagging. Her face was older than her body. It told her real age: old, but not irreparably old. Her short hair was dyed brown to match her eyelashes, eyebrows, and eyes. Her hands, feet, and ears were surprisingly small. Her nose strong, her lips fleshy, her teeth regular but slightly yellowish, her chin weak, her face square. This was the person known as I.

I put on my best clothes for my Christmas dinner with McCabe: black corduroy pants and jacket, beige button-up shirt and socks, black leather boots I had shined the day before, all much worn, but of good quality. For the pyre I would change into work clothes and old sneakers. I took my time brushing my teeth, clipping my toenails, combing my hair, rubbing lotion on my body, getting dressed. It was nine o'clock. I did not expect McCabe to arrive before noon. There were only two flights she could take: the daily flight from Chicago to the state capital, one hundred and eighty miles southeast of Elmira, arriving at 1:00 p.m., or the weekly Penal Colony transport arriving there at 10:30 a.m., in time to catch the 11:00 a.m. air taxi to Elmira. Traveling all the way by land, or on a privately chartered plane, seemed far-fetched options. If McCabe arrived on the earlier flight, I would offer her a light, cold lunch; if on the second, an apéritif. Dinner would be served at eight o'clock. The venison would go into the oven around six o'clock. Her bed was freshly made in case she wanted to take a nap before dinner. I opened her bedroom windows to let in the clean winter air.

Ice floes lumbered down the river toward the Shangri-La bend, where they got stuck. Soon the bend would be frozen solid. Once, Glorita had dared me to walk on the ice. When I refused, she stepped on it alone. I watched her walk toward the middle of the frozen bend until I could not stand my fear. I grabbed a sturdy tree branch and followed her. "What's that for?" Glorita said when she turned around and saw the branch. "Nothing," I said, embarrassed. "I can take care of myself," she said. I thought she had read my mind and knew the branch was to save her if she fell through a crack. "I know," I said. "Then why do you keep butting in?" she yelled. Glorita was scary when she got pissed. I was afraid she'd melt the ice and we'd both drown. She was angry that I had gotten into a fight for her. A big moron called Ñico pawed her at the bus stop in front of the school, so I jumped on his back and tried to strangle him. He whirled around like a mad elephant with me hanging on to his back, my hands too small to circle his thick neck. Two of his pals ended up pulling me off and kicking me on the ground until Glorita threw herself on top of me screaming at them *assholes, mothafuckas, pendejos, cabrones, hijoeputas, chingones,* etc. They hesitated for a second because she was a pretty girl, even if she let the fucking dyke suck her pussy, come suck my big fat Mexican dick instead, you *puta.* Glorita seized the moment to pull me away. The three orangutans jumped up and down in a frenzy of crotch-grabbing rage. Ñico screamed he was gonna stick it up my filthy tortillera dyke ass. I yelled at him to go home so his daddy could shove it up his fat ass: "He's waiting for you, *maricón!*" The three gave chase, but the school bus pulled over in the nick of time. I was spitting blood. My left eye was closed and my lips swelled. Breathing was painful (a broken rib, as it turned out). I told my parents I had fallen down the stairs trying to catch the bus. They didn't believe me, and I was grounded for a week. The truth I told only my grandmother. Glorita and I were thirteen. There had been other fights before, and much taunting, but this was my first big match. In the next five years, until I graduated from high school and Glorita dropped out, I got another rib and an arm broken, lost two teeth, and saw my clothes periodically ripped and my lips, nose, eyes, elbows, and knees bloodied. I was not a victim. I gave almost as good as I got. I never ratted on anyone—not out of a sense of honor, but because it would have made matters worse: everybody hates queers, even those who say they're our friends, and a lot of queers hate themselves. To compensate for my size and inferior muscle power, I began to wear, and use, brass knuckles decorated to look like rings. I always aimed at their snouts. I also carried a box cutter in my pocket, which I used more than once, and a hunting knife in my knapsack that I often flashed, but never used.

High school taught me that my enemies were everywhere, and my people nowhere. I was still one with Shangri-La in what concerned white people, but not in what concerned me. The benevolent

Shangri-La of my childhood, all for one and one for all, turned into the envious, narrow-minded, bigoted, gossipy, hateful, brutal Shangri-La of my youth. It loathed me and I loathed it back. Just like Elmira, although Elmira is unforgivable. Even Rafael avoided me in public, afraid to call attention to himself. I did not hold that against him. Rafael did not know how to fight. No one was unhappy to see me board that refugee bus, except Glorita and my grandmother. I lost them both that day. Do not try to find any larger meaning in any of this. Mine was an unexceptional adolescence. Glorita and I did not fall through the ice. She told me to turn around and start walking back to the shore. She would follow, keeping a distance between us, so as not to stress the ice. I did as she said. Not once did I look back to see if she was following me, despite my doubts. On the shore, I kept looking ahead and just waited, and waited, and waited. I was about to turn around when I felt Glorita's arm over my shoulder. She was already taller than I was and liked to feel proprietorial.

I reluctantly shut the windows in McCabe's bedroom. Glorita was vividly over there, on the icy shore. I could not tear myself from her. In the end, I did. I betrayed her. But it was only provisional, until I took care of McCabe. In the kitchen, the clock radio was still on, now spewing static. I ate breakfast, then went up to my room and brushed my teeth again. Trying to read Turgenev's *Home of the Gentry*, I got stuck on "the little girl stretched her hand out of the window the little girl stretched her hand out of the window the little girl stretched her hand out of the window." I read and reread it without understanding it, unable to move on. This has happened to me in airplanes during takeoff. A newspaper intended to calm me down trapped me in a groove in which terror replaced meaning. I put the book back on the shelf. I knew it by heart. I could close my eyes and walk through it. That is what I did until the Judge's grandfather clock announced that it was noon. As if on cue, I heard the crunch of the gravel on the driveway.

A dark-blue sedan was approaching. Was it the same one that McCabe had taken that night in September? It disappeared from my view as it pulled into the front entrance. I heard the car door slam and steps on the pebbles. I controlled my urge to run to the front door and fling it open. I began to descend the stairs, measuring my breathing as if the plane was about to take off. The doorbell rang. Had I left the door locked? Had she lost her house keys? McCabe was being formal. I did not know how I should greet her. I decided to take her bag. It would be my sword of purity. Until I had it, my hands would remain deep in my pockets. They should not touch McCabe. It was not myself I was restraining, since I had no desire to touch her, but social convention, with its enforced physical contact, its collisions and accidents. The doorbell rang again.

I opened the door with my right hand, keeping the left in my pocket. The door traced a fluid, dignified arc. It had taken me much practice and oiling of the hinges to remove all hints of anxiety or reluctance from my door opening. A banality, you will say, but a loose screw sinks the big ship. Nothing, not even the color of the roses in a particular vase, had been left to chance. The path from McCabe's arrival to her apotheosis on the pyre had been minutely mapped. The door opened with an elegant sweep. I heard a breathless "Hi, there." Then I heard myself say, "Hello." Then, "Could you please open the garage door?" I did as I was asked. When the blue sedan was parked in the garage, hidden behind the Land Rover, I offered to take one of the two small bags. "Thanks, but I think I can manage," was the polite answer. We stood in the dim light of the garage, unsure of what to do or say next. "I owe you an explanation," I heard. The acrid body odor was distracting, as were the soiled shirt, muddy shoes, and greasy dark-blue suit. "Motor oil. Had to pour it in the dark. Got it all over me." Where had that telegraphic form of speech been learned? "So . . ." I said, searching for the right balance between distress and panic. "Sorry to barge in on you like this . . ." came the insincere answer. I slammed the car top with unintended violence. "Whatcha done?" said a mean, deep voice coming out of my chest that I had not heard in years.

He looked at me reproachfully. That is what saved him. I had grown up cosseted by his reproachful gaze. It made me feel daring and modern where he was meek and old-fashioned. I took him to the maid's room in back of the garage. Unused since the Judge died, it smelled musty. "Take a bath. You stink," I said, handing him a large garbage bag for his filthy clothes, a towel, and a bar of soap. He was anxious to tell me his story. "Later," I said. I had to throw the kitchen window open, so McCabe would not smell his presence. I warned him not to leave the room, or make any noise. "You can't stay long. This is not my house," I said. "I know that," answered Rafael Cohen.

27

The Grand Vizier

WHEN I RETURNED WITH FOOD, booze, and an air freshener, Rafael was dressed for summer cocktail hour in the Vineyard in a pale blue shirt, white and blue seersucker suit a size too large, and sockless penny loafers. He was scrubbed clean and imperfectly shaved (his perennially blue jowls always lent him a Nixonian truculence on TV, which his soft, high-pitched voice belied). His big, swarthy head, though, was pure La Esperanza. All he was missing was the moustache. Those were the only clothes he had in his car when he left, he said, devouring the ham and cheddar sandwiches.

I found him a forest-green parka that had belonged to Mrs. Wilkerson. It was a little tight on his waist, but not too girly. The Judge, who had been six foot four, could only provide socks, scarf, and woolen cap. I personally contributed a large grey cable-knit sweater that fat McCabe had given me before she melted away. Nothing could be done about the penny loafers and the seersucker pants. He would have to freeze in them. The jacket, on the other hand, was returned to the bag it came from, which I noticed was otherwise empty. What I had taken for a second bag was in fact a large, hard-cased briefcase. Rafael had shoved it under the bed, but insufficiently, so the top and handle stuck out. It was 1:30 p.m. He had been here only an hour and a half and it felt like a century. The elasticity of time is one of the themes I wish I had had time to study. McCabe would not arrive now until four o'clock at best, if traffic out of the state capital were miraculously light. I had two and a half hours to get Rafael back on the road.

He sat on the maid's bed, licking the mayonnaise off his fingers and finishing his second beer. I sat across from him on the only chair with a bottle of Evian at my feet. The food tray on the night table was a repellent mess of chewed ham fat, gnawed bread, and ketchup-soaked napkins. Rafael belched before his hand could reach his mouth, and thanked me for the first time since his arrival. I removed the tray from my line of vision and hoped he would go wash his hands and greasy mouth, from which still hung a few distracting crumbs. Rafael had always been a slob, but I could not believe he ate like this in front of his masters. His down-home minstrelsy was for my benefit, I suspected. He took a wallet out of his back pocket and showed me a picture of a blond girl and boy standing on the exact kind of fastidiously clipped lawn that calls for a seersucker suit. They were twins, he said, just turned twelve. A good-looking blond woman could be seen in the background. The kids were almost as tall as the mother, who was not precisely short—"Five foot eleven," said Rafael, flattered when I asked. (He was five four and a half in his socks, although he always lied about his height. Had he dared lie about it to his current employer?)

So far, my day with Rafael had been a succession of rancid clichés, from his unannounced arrival, haunted and hunted, to the picture of the predictable blond, white giants. We were trapped in a B-movie medley. I was not I anymore, but a ventriloquist's dummy channeling my own discarded voices from the past. Who was he? "This situation is spiraling out of control," I heard myself say, teeth martially clenched. Some malicious prompter was feeding Rafael and me these trashy lines. I sank deep into the chair. When I opened my eyes, Rafael was leaning over me with a wet towel. "You passed out," he said. I was still clutching the proof of his successful safari in Upper Blancoland. He pried his trophy family out of my fingers and sat on the bed to look at them. It was considerate of him to let me be, to spare me from further embarrassment. I had never fainted before in front of him, although I had been on the verge twice: when they drew blood from my wrist at age eleven, the Elmira school district having gotten it into their heads that all spic children were either asthmatic or tubercular, and when I cracked the back of my head on the curb during an after-high-school brawl.

"I haven't done anything illegal," Rafael finally said, cleaning his black-framed glasses with a corner of the bedspread and putting them on. He now looked like the Kissinger of the Paris Agreements, down to the kinky hair creeping up under the thick pomade. "Nothing at all that could get you or," and here he hesitated, searching for the prudent term, "the main tenant of this house in trouble." Lawyerly mendacity had replaced the telegraphic style. He stole a glance at his family picture. Did he wink at them? "You gotta leave right now," I said. The corners of his mouth went up slightly. "I swear you're gonna be sorry if you don't. You're gonna lose your job and bring grief to your family, and shit's gonna rain on your boss if you stay here." He blinked twice behind his thick lenses, but his mouth remained almost gleefully upturned. "You'll lose everything, Rafael," I said. He studied his family picture under the bedside lamp. Did he get his instructions from them? Was he trying to find his genetic imprint in the two Brobdingnagian children? Where I saw none, a father's eye might see a dozen tiny hereditary signs such as curved toenails or unusually thick earwax. He put the picture back in his wallet. Then he retrieved the wet towel from my lap and hung it from the shower curtain rod. "I already have," he said from the bathroom.

Rafael told me his story in the one hour of grace I consented to give him. He promised to leave when he was done if I still wanted him to. I assured him it was unlikely I would change my mind. He finished at 3:15 p.m. McCabe must have landed two hours and fifteen minutes earlier at the state capital. She might already be in the car that would bring her here. Rafael put on the borrowed winter clothes and took his belongings to the blue sedan. I did not follow him. I was already traveling with McCabe inside a black limo moving through the snowy flatlands. The snow was bone-yellow at this hour. When Rafael came back to say goodbye, I asked him to stay.

I will not repeat here the many twists and turns of his story, its tortuous illogic, logistics, and soap-opera betrayals. I did not follow half of them. Many of the characters, and there were dozens of them, I had never heard of; I cared for none. Nor did I know the meaning of most of the government agency acronyms involved, although at the end of his account each had become a living character, with its own morality, face, smell, and body mass. My physical and political topography of the nation's capital and ruling elite is willfully inadequate. Growing up in Shangri-La, I never paid them much attention. None of us did. Then, I erased them entirely from my mind when the grotesque venality and hypocrisy that have been both the strong and the weak points of my parents' adoptive country thoroughly tipped in the direction of the latter. That was in 1984, the year the Great Hunger erupted, killing or displacing half of the country's population, and emptying the heartland; the year the Caliphate opportunistically gobbled up Anatolia, cutting off Constantinople from Asia. Two utterly avoidable cataclysms provoked by our rulers. In 2008, the year Rafael entered government, I was happy to see his picture in the paper behind the President-elect. I would have been equally happy if he had been made capo. There is only one measure of success. Six years later he was in a maid's room telling me how the other side suffers.

"Allow me to recall Rafael's swift ascent to power," Rafael said. Even if the official media had rehashed it ad nauseam, "our memories are short." He relished telling his story, in spite of the melancholic third person. Eight years ago, when the Caliphate first started digging anti-nuclear bunkers on either side of the Bosphorus near besieged Constantinople, Rafael, then an obscure adjunct at MIT, published an essay in *Foreign Affairs* provocatively entitled "The New American Racialism." In it he proposed a simple and elegantly final solution to the Caliphate menace: mix and ultimately replace the genetic stock of the border populations threatened by the Caliphate—and in time, that of the Caliphs themselves—with the DNA of America's black, yellow, and Hispanic peoples, with its unmatched genius for sociocultural malleability. NAR's race-based Wilsonian idealism would succeed where centuries of mutual mass slaughter had failed.

The essay caught the eye of the presidential front-runner, who asked to meet the author. They hit it off. Rafael took a leave of absence from his university to devote himself to the task of sharpening the candidate's capacious, if mediocre mind. When she was inaugurated, in 2008, he was rewarded with the number-one position at the National Security Council. When she was re-elected by a landslide three years ago, the President asked Rafael to remain in his post. He hated the limelight as much as the President loved it, was unconditionally loyal to her, and carried out the NAR revolution with the ruthlessness often found in shy, selfless people.

At first, most of the action had been internecine. As DNA harvesting centers went up in suburban ghettos and refugee and resettlement camps, drawing enthusiastic and patriotic crowds, the White House, hiding behind the National Security Advisor, purged enemies and doubters from government and military-industrial bureaucracies, among them the remaining, ossified neocons, liberal multiculturalists, White Canon lovers, Bible literalists, and assorted fellow travelers. The battle had been won last summer. NAR was then projected worldwide. It had been glowingly received abroad, not only in the proud ancestral homes of America's spics, niggers, and chinks—all of whom dreamt of their own genetic Trojan Horse empire spreading after America fell, as it inevitably would one day soon—but also in Europe intramuros (except France). All praised its enlightened realism, its preference for humane intervention instead of force, and the entente of races and civilizations it promised.

Rafael's nails were still bitten to the flesh. The Patek Philippe watch and the J. M. Weston shoes were new developments. A lighter line on his finger betrayed an absent wedding ring. "They're going to drown them," he said, hiding his watch inside the cable-knit sweater's sleeves. "They're going to drag them out of their beds after midnight tonight, once it's not Christmas anymore. Then they're going to shove them in a container and dump it off the coast of Delaware. Near international waters, but on our side, so they can keep away nosy people. Not that anyone will know what's in there." His eyes got watery. "They," he explained, were the President's loyalists; "them," soon to be at the bottom of the Atlantic, were the leaders and intellectual instigators of a failed coup, "a rabble of white evangelical Air Force majors, Negro notables, white supremacists, embittered neocons, and Aztlán fundamentalists," Rafael spat. The coup had been attempted yesterday, on Christmas Eve, and had lasted seven and a half hours. The White House had been the sole target. Officially, it had never happened. Few inhabitants of Washington, D.C. had

ANA SIMO

heard or seen anything, given the one-mile restricted zone around the White House. And those who had would never talk. Neither the media nor history books would record it. The President had managed to escape unharmed and was now safe in a bunker somewhere along the Mexican border. Rafael had survived by locking himself in an East Wing broom closet until the loyalists regained control. He had seen hundreds of dead, both assailants and defenders.

"So your side won," I said brightly, standing up, ready to show him the door. He looked past me, his head mournfully bobbing up and down. "She wouldn't listen to me," he said. "I tried to reason. Then I pleaded. I begged her." He stood up and flapped his arms as if about to take flight. "A container! In the Atlantic!" He sat again on the edge of the bed and began to pull the sweater sleeves over his big hands. "And you know what?" he said. I shook my head. "She's right." The star pupil had outgrown the teacher.

I was relieved by his tone of resignation and was about to say something cowardly, like "You did what you could," or "Maybe you could take some time off from your job," when he rasped, "I think she's gonna pull a Vince Foster on me." That is why he had fled his office in a panic after hanging up on the President's secure line, first on a stolen motorbike to a refugee camp far beyond the restricted zone, then several miles on foot to a derelict garage in a suburban Salvadoran slum where out of sentimentality he had kept his old used car, still registered to the original owner and bearing its original Maine plates. He had driven directly here "because I know you won't rat on me." He refused to say how he had found me: "The less you know, the safer you'll be," was his noble answer. I almost socked him in the nose, but his glasses steamed up. "They'll get me in the end, you know." He wanted me to drive back to New York immediately, so he could wait for them, alone. He wanted me to tell his wife

196

and kids that he had not killed himself. "Suicide is contagious. I don't want to put that curse on them, and their children, and their children's children."

It was three thirty when I told Rafael he could stay. He gave me a bear hug. It made me unexpectedly sad. Without knowing it, I had been thirsting for brotherly affection. Now that I had it briefly, I felt its painful lack. Since my father, Ezequiel, and Rafael had disappeared from my life, no other men had taken their places. Rafael felt beefier than the last time we had hugged, while my mother's ashes were lowered into her grave. I did not want to cry in front of him, so I ran to the kitchen with the excuse of getting him more food. I'm not sure whether the ticklishness in my eyes and throat was impeding tears. It's been so long since I last cried that I'm not sure I can recognize the warning signs, even retroactively. A few trips to the kitchen were needed before I was satisfied with Rafael's stock of food and drink. He had enough for a week. To humor him, I promised I would leave before sunrise, as soon as my guest was gone. She was due to arrive any time and just stay for dinner, I explained. It was imperative, for her safety, that she did not see him, or vice versa. He fought me tooth and nail on this, wanting me to cancel the appointment, or at least leave with my guest as soon as she arrived. He did not want our deaths on his conscience. "You should have thought about that before coming here," I said. That shut him up.

It was hard not to feel vindictive toward Rafael for having fallen from the sky at such an inopportune time. Once the warmth of the hug faded, the best I could do was to soften my vindictiveness with selected childhood memories, deliberately played over and over. This behavior modification exercise produced a semblance of kindness that Rafael mistook for the real thing. Luckily. He had learned about wines at his masters' table, so I brought up half a dozen good bottles from the cellar. It was almost four thirty. Before going back to my bedroom lookout, I gave Rafael several blank notebooks and the Judge's Mont Blanc pen. "Write your story," I said. He looked at the writing materials with suspicion. Was he paranoiac? Did he think I was trying to extract a confession from him? I could be part of the presidential cabal. I could have phoned the authorities from the kitchen. I would not trust me if I were him. For the first time ever, I was afraid of Rafael. He had never lifted a finger against me or anyone else, as far as I knew. He was more the doormat type. But he would not have risen as high if he was not, in some way, a fighter. Besides, insanity makes people superhumanly strong, and he was not entirely sane. That coup story was a madman's fantasy. Dumping a container full of political enemies in the Atlantic was a cheesy remake of Pinochet's discharging them from a plane into the Pacific (a less costly option). True, the inconceivable had become ordinary. I could not tell which articles of our yo-yo Constitution were suspended at the moment. Years ago, the first time it happened, the country roared, or so the already tattered media said. Even I, still a child, sneered. Now no one cared. No one was keeping the score. A coup? In Aracnida, the Beautiful, nothing was too grotesque anymore to be true.

"You could write a letter to your children," I said ingratiatingly, promising to deliver it. How many promises had I made already, none of which I seriously considered keeping? Rafael asked me to swear by my mother's ashes to do it. He became agitated when I tried to weasel out of that. So I was forced to look him in the eyes and reluctantly swear on my mother's memory to hand the letter to his daughter and son. Do broken promises have any consequences for the dead on whom you swear in vain? I didn't think so, although I would not have been surprised if St. Augustine had a different opinion. He was a vindictive fellow himself. I decided to check the *Confessions*, and do whatever had to be done to lift the burden off their souls. I was, and still am, a cautious unbeliever.

Back in my room, I took a lightning-fast shower and changed my underwear and shirt. My travails since Rafael's arrival had left me smelling sour. Through the binoculars, I saw a rabbit hopping across the driveway as it looped down the hill. The rabbit stood in the middle of the road, my advance lookout, the first that would hear and see McCabe's car coming up the hill. I had cleaned and oiled a Mauser Gewehr 98. It was the only rifle in the Judge's collection that was specifically made for war. The other seven were all antique hunting shotguns, even if humans were often killed with them, the earliest being an 1866 Winchester Henry Iron Frame Rifle. The Gewehr 98 had a glorious history. It was the German army's standard rifle between 1898 and 1935. It killed or wounded Rupert Brooks, Apollinaire, and hundreds of thousands of others in World War I. I would have never used a hunting rifle: McCabe was not an animal, but all too human, a sublime woman, fit only for the company of poets and heroes. Honor, purity, and cleanliness were owed her. If I had had the guts, I would have chosen a sword; but I am a coward. I do not mind acknowledging it. On the contrary, my cowardice enhances my accomplishments. Never did someone do more with so little, morally speaking.

The rabbit was now a grey smudge on the road. The Mauser was back in the Judge's gun cabinet, first from the left. It was loaded with the only two bullets I had found, one in each of its twin chambers. The second bullet was there in the unlikely event the first one missed, or did not finish the job. I did not want McCabe to suffer. The key to the cabinet was in the right pocket of my jacket. Target practice with the Judge's rifle had been out of the question: too noisy, too risky to try buying bullets online, let alone in person. I was not concerned anymore about my future; I just did not want to be stopped from doing what I had to do. So, I had practiced my movements with the unloaded gun until I could do them with my eyes closed. Every day I slashed a few seconds from the sequence of unlocking the cabinet door, grabbing the Mauser, loading it, pointing at her forehead, and shooting. I would drive a bullet into her forehead, right above the nose, while she was sitting at the dinner table, between dessert and coffee. I would approach her from behind and to the right, call her name, and when she turned her head to look at me, I would pull the trigger. At such close range, about ten feet, I could not miss. I was a pretty good shot; I grew up shooting rabbits with Ezequiel, which my mother stewed and we all ate, except for Rafael. Even now, when I had not shot at a living creature in twenty years, my hands did not shake. I had been an avid carnival shooter in New York City, a provider of ugly stuffed animals to embarrassed dates. That had kept me sharp.

The flight from Chicago had arrived on time at one o'clock. Airport information would not tell me if McCabe was on board. It was six o'clock now. Five hours to drive the 180 miles from the state capital airport to the Judge's house on a secured military expressway? Not impossible, but like Rafael's operetta coup, unlikely. Even then, I did not doubt McCabe would come. That was my only certainty. Everything else, even the roundness of the earth, could be questioned. The dilemma was whether I should start roasting the venison at once, even if McCabe had not arrived. My faith in McCabe's arrival, however absolute, lacked a precise time frame. I peered into the dark with the binoculars, not expecting to see anything, but to help myself think. My brain worked better when my eyes were focused on the light grey landscape turning into charcoal grey and then black velvet. I would start cooking the venison at 6:30 p.m. sharp. The outside lights went on, circling the house in gold. I again aired McCabe's room and turned on the lights throughout the house, which now glowed with Christmas warmth. After removing a few tired flowers from the vases, I put the venison in the oven, at a slightly lower temperature, anticipating a longer cooking time than the recipe called for. To give McCabe time to get home.

At seven o'clock I went to see how Rafael was doing. The kitchen had a door that opened to the outside, and another opening onto a covered hallway leading to the cellar and the garage. The maid's room could only be reached through the garage. It was unlikely that any noise in that room would be heard in the house. McCabe would never know we were not alone. On the other hand, Rafael could be screaming his head off in there without me hearing anything from the house. The boy I had grown up with would never go mad or kill himself. But the man with the Patek Philippe watch who talked about coups and containers was more opaque. I rapped softly on his door. When he did not answer, I went in. I did not see him at first. The room was in shadows. He had moved the chest of drawers away from the door and the only window, and was writing on it by the light of the table lamp, his back against the wall. That might prolong his life by ten seconds if his presumed killers came through the door, twenty if through the window, provided they did not first throw in a grenade, as they always do in the movies. He did not lift his head from the notebook or stop his hand, which was flying over the paper. I envied him. I wished it were my hand on that paper. But I had been marooned on a white sheet of paper for a long time, long before the loss of nouns and verbs made denial impossible, marooned from the moment "Benbassa" had won me that Blue Ribbon almost forty years ago. Perhaps it was Benbassa's curse that had shaped my life, the punishment for pretending to be a writer. Benbassa's curse, and not McCabe, even if I sensed an undercurrent between the two.

Sitting on the maid's bed, I watched the shadows cast by Rafael's hand flit over the paper, left right, left right, a squadron of black moths taking off one after the other and disappearing into the night sky. Turgenev would have heard the scratching of pen on paper. I had to content myself with what my eyes saw, unconfirmed by my ears. Pens glided silently these days. Technology worked hard to silence our little helpers, while cacophony swamped the world. I envied Rafael his writing, as I envied McCabe sauntering up and down the stairs when my bandaged feet kept me tied to bed. And I envied him his tale, particularly if it was a paranoid mirage: then it would be tragedy instead of political drama. Above all, I envied him his readers, the daughter and the son, and their descendants, who would turn his tale into an immortal myth. I wished I were Rafael, even if a death squad was on its way. I had my own coming, anyway. I wished I were him, but without leaving my body. I could not conceive of myself inside a male body. And look what I inhabit now: a carcass, a shell. At least I don't have a dick. Watching Rafael's hand I soon began to feel his words flow in my mind. His hand and my mind were synchronized as if he was taking my dictation. My rhythm, intonations, hesitations, commas, and periods were all there in his hand. I never read Rafael's letter to his children, that is, the one he recorded on paper, but I remember every word I dictated to him. It went like this:

"Dear beloved children:

"I'll be dead in a few hours. You're going to hear many bad things about me. Don't believe any. The worst that can be said about me is that I was mad with love of country. Falling in love is a kind of madness. When the love object is a person, sanity eventually returns. When it is your country, or an ideal, you become increasingly delirious and infect all those who surround you. I was mad until a particularly horrible event suddenly cured me a few days ago. My eyes are now wide open. Many terrible crimes have been committed before this even more terrible crime. I'm responsible for them. Not because I committed them myself, or even knew about them, or approved them, but because they may not have happened if I had not thrown the dice. Mad love of country was my motivation, but I do not absolve myself with it.

"I wanted you to begin life freer than I did. That is why I never told you much about my parents—your grandparents whose names you bear, Genoveva and Ezequiel—or the place where I grew up. The past can nail you down. I've been trying to remove the nails since I was born. I kept of the past only what I could bear. I thought I would tell you the whole story later, when it could do you no harm, when you were my age and had your own children. Don't think I was covering up some big family secret. Ours was an ordinary story about ordinary people. It is just that, until recently, these two places were my black holes: La Esperanza, the sugar mill town where my parents came from, and Shangri-La, the fetid subdivision where I was born and grew up. You have never heard those two names; neither has your mother. The 'Elmira, a small town in the heartland' listed as my birthplace in my official bio means nothing to me. My parents, your grandparents, are buried in Shangri-La, an orphan settlement straddling the border between Elmira town and county, and forgotten by both. Go visit your grandparents' grave when you are older and can travel alone. Do not bring anyone else with you, not even your mother. Go to La Esperanza, too. Maybe I have a double there! I wish I could go myself.

"My dear, beloved children: I was not gifted for fatherhood. Every time you asked me to play with you I was scared. Even before you learned to speak, you seemed to have things in mind that I could not begin to imagine. I felt shy in front of you, so discipline was my only language. At least I never hit you, but I know I bored you with my lectures. I want you to know that your father is dying an honorable man. I am not hiding behind anyone. I am not saying that I just obeyed orders. I was mad, blind, wrong. I'm sorry.

"Your loving father,

"Rafael Jacinto Cohen Martínez"

That was the end of my dictation. I do not know the names of Rafael's wife or children, but I distinctly felt his hand writing "Genoveva and Ezequiel." The florid, Esperanza-style signature, with full surname and both of his parents' names was, in my opinion, a childish affectation. It was bound to confuse the twins and become fodder for the Aztlán fundamentalists, whom Rafael reviled. Maybe he was just trying to be intimate, maybe his public name, Rafael J. Cohen, was too intertwined with "National Security Advisor" to be a father's name. Rafael's hand stopped. He had filled the entire notebook with his large handwriting. The last half was the letter that I "dictated" to him. The first half he had done before I came into the room. Was it a letter to his wife? A last-minute will? I say quote-unquote "dictated" to stress that I knew, and know, in spite of my present diminished circumstances, the difference between the literal and the truthful. My dictation was truthful, but not literal, as in facts happening in the physical world. Hence the quotation marks. The difference between one and the other should be evident to you, dear listener, without me pointing it out at every turn of my account. Rafael put the notebook inside a manila envelope. I noticed an incipient bald spot on top of his head. "Give this to my kids, but don't read it, please. It's kind of embarrassing," he said, acknowledging my presence. I later wrapped the envelope in plastic and hid it in the safest place I could think of: in the cellar behind the old boiler, which was no longer in use. It must be there still.

Rafael was suddenly cheerful. He jumped and clicked his heels in the air, sideways, like he used to when he finished his homework. That was his only physical trick and he did it amazingly well even now, when he was at least thirty pounds heavier. Rafael had always been chatty. I didn't like to talk. So we got along fine. He wasn't just chatty anymore. Words poured out of him now in every direction, frivolous and hectoring, indignant and lyrical. One moment he launched a vitriolic diatribe against Aztlán fundamentalists: "They've repackaged the old Aztlán tripe. They're selling it as ersatz identity for the identity-deprived white masses. I mean, how cynical can you get?" he said, gasping angrily in between words, and giving himself a burst from an asthma inhaler that he pulled out of his pants pocket. The next moment he exulted in remembering a heavenly Sachertorte he had tasted last month at the Café Demel in Vienna, neither of which would have existed had the Caliphate not been savagely repelled there a generation ago. The possibility of loss increased his gustatory pleasure, he said, words desperately pouring out until he checked his watch. "It's halfway there, already. Even in rough seas." He fell silent and slumped in bed, his eyes half closed. His face was more revealing then than when he was talking. I would have learned to read it if he had stayed for a while. "They must be burning my library by now," he mumbled, his eyes now fully closed.

Rafael seemed to be dozing. It was time for me to check on the venison. When I was at the door he suddenly said, "Do you ever hear from Glorita?" I shook my head. "Me neither," he said. Why would

ANA SIMO

he, anyway? He hardly knew her. Was this just gossipy intrusion,
or vampirism? Some people live to suck the memories of others.

The fragrance of rosemary, thyme, and wild meat basted in red
wine filled the kitchen. The venison was almost done. I stuck a fork
in a tiny roasted potato. Still a little hard; they needed a few more
minutes. The Pennsylvania butcher said you could keep them warm
in the oven for a couple of hours after cooking without the venison
drying out, or the potatoes getting mushy. Just make sure to baste
the venison from time to time. Do not touch the potatoes! Set your
oven at the lowest possible temperature. Some newer state-of-
the-art ovens had a warming function, specially designed for that
situation. I inspected Mrs. Wilkerson's oven closely, oven manual
in hand, but did not find that function. When the time came, I just
set the oven slightly above zero, keeping my ear on its door until I
heard the gas swoosh on.

Snowflakes swirled under the garden lamp. Soon they thickened
into a light snowfall, enough to add a picturesque touch without
disturbing traffic. The Celestial Designer was still on my side.
McCabe was not being driven from the airport: she was driving
herself. Why didn't I think about this before? It's always slower
when you drive yourself instead of having a local driver who knows
the roads. She had certainly rented a car at the airport. Add fifteen
minutes for pickup, at least. Add another, say, half hour, to look at
a map, hesitate while approaching an exit, even take the wrong one.
What kind of a driver was McCabe? I had never seen her drive. One
summer she drove a rust bucket from Bangor to British Columbia
to work in a fish-canning factory, she told me. She was fifteen. That
was about twenty-five years ago, at the tail end of the Great Hunger,
but driving is an indestructible skill. McCabe's wealth dated from
a little over a decade ago, as far as I or anyone else knew. What had

206

she done in the fifteen years between the fish-canning factory and SoHo? Where had she been? "It was brutal," was all she would say. Driving cars likely figured in her years of wandering through the desert before arriving in Manhattan, where you did not need a car, and a great many people never learned to drive.

McCabe's life had been harder than mine. I never worked in a factory. I managed to survive on my wits and America's ebbing guilt toward my kind. McCabe had not gotten a break. She deserved every penny she had.

Rafael feared a marriage of convenience between the Aztlán fanatics and the Caliphate. "They've been secretly courting each other for a while," he had said. Both abhorred the mixing of races and civilizations. The Caliphate would gain credibility and a new, multicultural fifth column, the Aztlanites, access to the Caliphate's Swiss bank accounts, recruiting wizardry, and fat VIP rolodexes. When Rafael talked shop, his face would begin to blur before my eyes. The familiar traits would become unfamiliar: the nose too small or large to be his, the ears too high up or low, the Adam's apple less visible than I remembered. I would no longer recognize this compact man with the large gestures. Then he would fall silent, and it was again him.

McCabe had no gurus. She would never fall for Aztlán and their ilk. She was serene in her non-identity. I worshipped her supreme blankness. Rafael must not see McCabe. He was not as perceptive as I was with the particular and the unique—a weakness of theoreticians—but McCabe's glow was hard to miss. He might kidnap her, intellectually speaking, and use her in a new ideological stew. McCabe could be a powerful weapon in the hands of a philosopher-turned-advisor to the prince. I even had a name for it: supra-essentialism. An old idea stolen from Leibniz by each succeeding generation. Rafael could re-brand it. In an accidental world, McCabe was pure essence. It's not an identity that you need, but an essence, he could tell the identity-deprived white masses that were imperiling the stability of the Republic. McCabe will give it to you. She will restore purity and glow to America. That's how Rafael could snatch the white masses from the lusting Aztlán viper. A delirious scenario? Maybe, but no less so than Rafael's NAR, or such archaisms as neoconservatism, Islamic fundamentalism, neo-nativism, Communism, and the homebred thicket of Christian heresies from the Reconstructionists to the rapturous, all of which became the truth du jour at some point, with the revolting consequences we all know.

I did not give a rat's ass about America. There was no such place. It had been a postprandial dream of the Enlightenment, kept artificially alive by the feeding tubes of self-interest through the end of the twentieth century, until its fat throat was slit in the Jacobean gore of 2008. Mrs. Crandall was all that was left of America, the Accidental. She was the healthy limb, heavy with fruits. The tree was rotten. The limb would one day wither. In the meantime, it was the most sumptuous of meals. Poor Rafael, had he tasted Mrs. Crandall as I had (an impossibility), he would not be fretting now about the clueless white masses. They could always sing "Aracnida, the Beautiful."

At the fish-canning factory, McCabe had started on the assembly line, and ended as a class "A" forklift operator. Those were the biggest forklifts, used to carry heavy loads to the waiting container ships. The factory had its own docks in the back. McCabe said it was hard not to run over the seagulls when you put the forklift in reverse to disengage from the load. Seagulls swarmed over the dock day and, she discovered, night. She had chosen the night shift thinking that there would be fewer of them. But there were just as many. "The floodlights were very bright. They thought it was sunlight," she said. An ornithologist from a nearby college stopped by one night to take Polaroids of the seagulls on the dock. He told her that lack of sleep might render them infertile after a couple of generations. He was chased away by security before he could answer her question: Were seagulls throwing themselves in front of the forklifts on purpose? This was the only time when I felt a bodily impulse toward McCabe. I could have lifted her in the air, held her tight against my chest, and put her safely in my pocket, if any of that had been physically, or morally, possible. The sea was never far from McCabe in her early years. Saltwater, fish, and birds were in every story she told me about herself. They weren't actually stories, but snippets, flashing images. The only full story she ever told me was the one of the Spanish sailors burning corpses in the Biloxi Marsh in the seventeenth century.

McCabe would come. Mrs. Crandall was in town. I considered going to see her after everything was over; she would not say no to me. Bebe existed somewhere, eternally, promising the rapture like a careless, provocative god. Only Glorita was truly absent. I fought the impulse to fall on my knees and beg for her to be alive. No matter how old, sick, or unlike Glorita she was. Please let her be alive. Lucky Petrona, who had my legs to grab, and my pants to smear with snot. I had only the venison, visible through the oven's glass window. I am an egoist, I told the venison. I declared Glorita dead because time had gone by, yet I did not sign my own death certificate. If I am the same now as I was then, more or less, why wouldn't Glorita still be my Glorita? The venison sneered. I lowered the oven temperature a bit more. Then I put on a pair of McCabe's surgical gloves and went to inspect Rafael's car.

It did not take long. The inside was impeccably clean. It smelled of rug shampoo and leather-nourishing cream. The glove compartment held only the car manual. The flashlight revealed no signs of the mud that covered Rafael's shoes and clothes when he arrived. The trunk was empty and equally antiseptic. I lifted the trunk rug, but there was nothing underneath apart from the new spare and a gleaming jack. The undercarriage was mud-free. The tailpipe shone. The chassis had been recently washed and waxed. It was a high-quality detailing done by hand—I could tell because there was no wax residue on the windshield. How could a car this clean have been warehoused for years in a crummy Salva garage, and then driven 1,033 miles from D.C. to Elmira? Unless Rafael stopped nearby and got it cleaned. If he did, his coup yarn was undoubtedly a lie. I closed the car doors carefully, so he would not hear me. I found no traces of old McCabe in the car. Yet, the more I shone the flashlight on the blue sedan, the more it looked like the same car that had picked her up that night.

Back in the kitchen, I turned on the clock radio. A golden retriever was lost along Elmira County Route 24. The President had spent Christmas with her parents in her hometown of Laredo. She was expected to tour a war orphanage tomorrow. Servicewomen and men abroad had made a record 11,375,086 Christmas calls home. I gagged. Print, TV, radio, and Internet so-called news had a vomitive effect on me. They were a wad of lies, half-lies, and quarter-lies (the latter now anointed as truths by professional skeptics). I had avoided them for years, for health reasons. I did not realize it then, but it was a sign of incipient panic on my part to think I might be able to deduce truth by comparing the radio version of the world to Rafael's. They were so far apart that only faith, in one version or the other, was possible. That was, after all, why I had stopped consuming "news" in the first place.

The snow had begun falling thickly. How long could a dog survive in this cold? McCabe had to take Route 24 to reach Elmira. She might see the dog. Rescue it. Or run over, maim, or kill it. A golden retriever would be visible against the snow, but it was hard to stop a car suddenly in this weather. You might crash into the icy ramparts that formed on either side of the road. McCabe would get out of the car anyway, whether or not she had hit the dog. She would rescue the dog if it was unhurt, or if it could be healed; if it was beyond help, she would finish it off, I didn't know how, perhaps by snapping its cervical vertebra with her big hands; then she would drag the dead dog to one side of the road so that other vehicles would not disfigure it. Wasting time with a stray dog on a night like this was risky, especially if you were driving alone and were not accustomed to the fierceness of winter storms in this part of the country. It snowed in Maine, but nothing like this. What I was seeing through the kitchen windows could not be called a heavy snowfall anymore. It was a winter gale, the kind that buried Shangri-La for days, until we dug ourselves out with hand shovels and a snowplow that Ezequiel would chain to the corner Negroes' decrepit pickup truck. He had found the snowplow in an illegal car dump down that same Route 24 the golden retriever was now wandering down. After one of his performances in front of their porch, he had asked the Negroes to help him fetch it. They did. Chained to their pickup, it became Shangri-La's official blizzard buster. The Negroes were known to accept tips from grateful neighbors. Most went to keep their truck running. It was perennially being repaired in their yard. Ezequiel claimed he never saw a penny, nor did he want to. But I saw him exchanging bills and coins with the head Negro several times. I don't know what he spent the money on. He did not smoke or drink, and Genoveva must have kept him fully occupied. My mother's cousin was too "young and appetizing" for her own good, according to my grandmother. She preferred Ezequiel to her own niece. She sided with him in all their marital squabbles while pretending to be neutral. "It's a pity that Rafael takes so much after his mother," she used to say. Her pronouncements were absolute. Once uttered, they stuck to the person forever, at least in my mind.

I imagined McCabe and the dog in the snowstorm against all reason. The chances of her encountering that dog on that road at that time must have been staggeringly slim. Besides, McCabe was not a dog person. There had been no dogs in her stories. No mammals, in fact. But she had rescued me on a night not unlike this. And, genetically speaking, 85 percent of me, or any human, was doglike. On the other hand, she may have rescued me in spite of my genetic links to dogs and other inferior mammals. Perhaps it puzzled or amused her that, while genetically so close, nothing else in me was doglike, except my physical addiction to Mrs. Crandall. I was not loyal. I also thought that I was smarter than a hound. I'm not so sure anymore. It was one of those persistent images that cannot be dislodged by reason or sophistry: McCabe and the dog in the snowstorm. I stopped fighting it. I felt her large, warm hands touch my muzzle, then my furry belly, to see if my heart was still beating. I could not open my eyes. They were frozen shut. I felt her take me in her arms and walk with me for a long time. My head flopped to one side. I was dead or sleeping.

The grandfather clock brought me back to what we doubtfully call reality. It was 9:00 p.m. I was still sitting in the fragrant, darkened kitchen. The storm had eased for a moment. I went to the window. Something white and large was moving at the far end of the driveway. A large snow-covered branch swaying, I first thought. Then it seemed to move forward as well. A large, furry animal.

A gigantic white bear. As it lumbered toward the house it became clear to me that this was no four-legged creature, but a biped sunk almost to the waist in the snow, and fighting its way forward. This was not McCabe. It was taller and wider. A tall man covered in a long, white fur coat and hat. Rafael may have been telling the truth after all. I considered grabbing a hunting rifle and blasting off his face the moment he came through the front door. But that would only alert the rest of the death squad. He wouldn't be alone. Better lure him sweetly into my bathroom so that he could relieve himself, and hang up his wet coat. Get rid of him there, quietly and cleanly. Rafael might try escaping into the meadow behind the icehouse, and onto the road past the farm. I'd take him all the way to the icehouse. We'd both be wearing the Judge's snowshoes. I would make him walk behind me, stepping in my tracks, so it would seem that only I had been out. On my way back to the house, I would create as many confusing and interlocking tracks as possible. I would explain them to the interrogators as healthy exercise. But the corpse of this first killer, what could we do with it? He was almost here. As he came up the last stretch of driveway, I moved away from the window so he wouldn't see me. He had a large satchel across his chest. His chin was tucked into his coat, and his hat covered the rest of his face. I waited behind the front door holding my breath. I heard him stomp the snow off his boots on the front steps. I opened the door with a big smile.

McCabe smiled back at me. When I did not move, she picked me up in her white bear arms and delicately put me down to one side. Then she stepped in and closed the door behind her.

28

The Future Generations

WHEN RAFAEL COHEN realized that he had little time left in this world, he was terrified first by death, then by oblivion. He could do nothing about the first, so he waged war against the second with the only weapons that he had left: pen, paper, and the certainty that he was right.

"I am leaving life," he wrote. "I am helpless before an infernal machine that uses medieval methods, possesses a titanic power, and fabricates lies according to a carefully mapped plan, a machine whose audacity is matched only by its arrogance.

"The great traditions of our nation—the democratic ideal that inspired all our actions and justified our cruelty against our internal and external enemies in order to defend ourselves—have little by little sunk into oblivion. Once our government and security agencies deserved our trust and respect. Today, our government is disfigured and our security agencies have become degenerate conglomerates of well-paid, morally bankrupt bureaucrats. Avid for medals and glory, they wrap themselves up in their past credibility to feed the sick mistrust of our rulers. They invent sordid stories, not realizing that they are digging their own graves. History will not forgive them.

"These omnipotent agencies can annihilate in a second any member of the government, Congress, the military, or our servile media, to make him or her look like a traitor, a saboteur, or a spy.

"I knew nothing of a coup attempt. I am not guilty of anything, yet I will drag down thousands of innocents with me. A fictitious organization has already been conjured: the 'Cohen Gang.'

"I have been at the service of my country since the age of eighteen. My entire life has been dedicated to a single goal: the survival of our nation and the victory of democracy. I can already foresee the front page of the newspaper that usurps the hallowed name of the *Times* trumpeting that I, Rafael Cohen, wanted to destroy our nation's prosperity and security, and weaken it so that it would fall like an overripe fruit into the Caliphate's gluttonous mouth. What despicable slander!

"I have made more than one mistake in my efforts to serve my country. I only ask posterity not to judge me more severely than I already judge myself. The President and I took a road never before taken, to save our country. At cabinet meetings, everybody expressed their opinions, freely. We butted heads, vigorously, for the sake of our country, whose very survival was threatened. It was a golden era.

"I am speaking to you, future generations of leaders of our nation, who have the historic mission of untangling the monstrous maze of crimes that, in these terrible times, is catching fire like a dry prairie, asphyxiating our nation.

"In these days, perhaps the last of my existence, I am convinced that historical truth will cleanse my name from all the mud that is already soiling it.

"I am not a traitor. I would have given my life without hesitation to save the President. I loved the President. I never conspired against her.

"I ask the future generations of leaders of my country, young and honest men and women, to read my letter before Congress, and to rehabilitate my memory.

"Know that the banner that you carry in your triumphant march toward a more perfect union also has a drop of my blood!"

When Rafael Cohen finished writing, he went back to the beginning and spent a long time considering a title. He knew that the wrong one could land him in the dreaded dustbin of history, mocked by the reading elites and unknown to the functionally illiterate masses who, by definition, could not get past the title. His heart wanted to cry out loud, "Save Our Dying Land!" But his immoderate sense of dignity made him settle for "Letter to the Future Generations." His last minutes of life were consumed by regret at his own lack of audacity.

29

White Fur

MCCABE SWEPT INTO MY BATHROOM, leaving a trail of snow, mud, and ice. I crouched by the front entrance, my swirling head between my knees. Had she worn this white fur coat when she picked me up from the tree hollow and brought me back, unconscious? White fur was preferable to the cadaverous latex gloves through which she had always touched me. It was softer, more animal. I am stating this as an objective fact. I neither wanted nor did not want to be touched by McCabe, skin to skin, or to touch her.

Steam filled the bathroom and was invading the Judge's studio. McCabe's coat, boots, and clothes were in a heap on the bathroom floor. She had not even bothered to close the door. I did, on my hands and knees, still fighting off vertigo. Then I cleaned her filthy trail all the way to the front door. Her behavior was disquieting. McCabe had always been laboriously polite with me, almost courtly. That is, after her transformation. Was old, boorish McCabe resurfacing? Even that fat pig had never crashed my bedroom and used my private bathroom. I'm not your maid, I muttered, using the mop handle to stand up. I cleaned after her because filth had no place in my house, particularly not on this day of days. I did it for me, the mistress of the house, not for her. When I was done cleaning, I locked away

McCabe's odd return in the same box as her unexplained absence. My eyes had to stay fixed on the quarry.

McCabe came out of the bathroom sooner than I had expected. I heard her slam the bathroom door and walk around my room. When she appeared in the kitchen, I was uncorking a bottle of Veuve Clicquot Ponsardin, more precisely a La Grande Dame Brut 2005, kept by the Judge, and me, for the grandest of occasions. She hung her fur coat from the back of a chair, and balanced her hat on top of it. Her boots were now clean. "Happy New Year," she said incongruously when we clinked glasses. I tried to steer her to the dining-room table, with its appetizer display. She preferred to stay in the kitchen. It was warmer there. She was not hungry, yet. She drank most of the bottle, as if it were water. "I'm thirsty," she said, when she realized I was staring at her. I uncorked a second one. This she drank at almost human speed. She surveyed the kitchen, as if taking an inventory of each item. "Why do you crawl?" she suddenly asked. My throat narrowed, choking me. Could she see through doors and walls? "Your feet must hurt still," she said. "No," I lied. While I was mobile, my feet were permanently deformed and pain kept me awake at night. "That happened a long time ago . . ." I blurted out, trying to cover up my terror. "Not that long ago," she said. I had walked into my own trap. We were dangerously close to a subject I wanted to avoid: McCabe's absence. Time, dates, calendars would unavoidably lead us there.

A month and two days ago, McCabe and I had had our last supper together. That was the last time I had seen her. Thirty-one days ago, I had last heard her voice in this kitchen, along with Petrona's and Mrs. Crandall's. But I had not seen her. She had been totally absent for thirty-two days, and absent in all but voice for thirty-one. McCabe, not I, should have been the one eager to avoid the subject of time. "Thirty-two days is not long to learn to walk again," she persisted. Was she being guileless or cruel? I often asked myself that question about McCabe. It was misdirected. She did not know the difference. Her purity of intention depended on that. I was the only one who could answer the question, (self-) helpfully rephrased: did I feel like the target of McCabe's cruelty, or of her innocence? A nonsensical question for a rationalist like me.

McCabe went to the window. The snowfall had stopped. Low dark clouds were moving northwest, toward the footprints of the Great Prairie. The moon was struggling to come out. "Let's go," said McCabe, grabbing her coat and hat. When I didn't follow her immediately, she added, "please." Her car was stuck in the mud at the bottom of Round Hill. She needed my help to bring it up. We got into the Land Rover. McCabe sat on the passenger seat as always. She slammed her door shut. I tried to close mine noiselessly. Her eyes were fixed on my hands while I fumbled with the lock. She leaned over me, opened the door and slammed it shut so hard that the Land Rover shook. Rafael must have heard it. With McCabe watching my every movement, I had been unable to warn him about our little spin. Before he could stick out his head, I careened out of the garage. I was afraid he would run away or kill himself, thinking we were his executioners gone to get reinforcements. McCabe did not seem to notice the blue sedan opposite her in the garage. There was no way she could miss it when we got back.

The black Lincoln had its left front wheel stuck deep in the mud. McCabe insisted on doing everything herself. I was there only to drive the Land Rover. "Keep them warm," she said, throwing her coat over my feet. She quickly chained one vehicle to the other, back to back, and wedged a piece of wood under the Lincoln's sunken front tire. Both the chain and the wedge came from the Lincoln's trunk.

McCabe sat on its driver's seat and signaled me to start the Land Rover. After a few pulls failed to dislodge the car, McCabe asked me to trade places with her. "I'm too heavy," she said. She did seem taller and wider than before, but that could have been the effect of heavy winter clothes. The Lincoln had D.C. restricted-zone plates. Inside, it smelled like apples. The registration in the glove compartment listed McCabe as the owner, at a Dupont Circle address. She rapped on the glass. I lowered the car window. "You can look at that later," she said, evenly. McCabe never got angry. That was her advantage. Before I could say I was sorry, she was striding back to the Land Rover. McCabe always fled ahead of my apologies. The Lincoln was freed on the second try.

The Washington, D.C. restricted zone was the last place on earth I would have associated with McCabe. With his tall tale, Rafael had uncovered fear behind my cynical loathing of the place. I was shamefully afraid of our rulers. That is why I pretended all my life that they did not exist. McCabe was powerful, but she was not one of them. She had taken care of me, who was planning to kill her. Her goodness was beyond doubt. It was also inexplicable. Would McCabe have helped Rafael? A logical question I should have asked myself. I didn't. It was as if he inhabited a different plane. Someone of McCabe's caliber could have a car registered in the D.C. restricted zone for any number of business reasons. Nevertheless, I wished I had brought the Mauser with me.

McCabe agreed to drive to the last vestiges of the Great Prairie. The moon was now out. We might see swift foxes hunting for rabbits. First we drove back to the house. While she waited outside in the Lincoln, which she insisted on taking, I parked the Land Rover in the garage. Inside the maid's room, Rafael had fallen asleep fully clothed. He was snoring. Saliva trickled from one corner of his open mouth. I wrapped him in a blanket just as I wrapped the Mauser. The extra bullet went into my pants pocket. McCabe followed me with her eyes as I placed the bundle on the back seat. Unasked, she moved to the passenger seat. "I'll drive so you can see the landscape," I said, redundantly. She nodded. McCabe was always kind to me. The roads had been freshly plowed, and traffic was light, so we got to the prairie's ancient edge in less than an hour. The moon shone brightly on the snowy flatlands. McCabe leaned forward in her seat, glancing left and right the way people do at tennis matches. There was nothing to see other than endless snow and sky. Yet she radiated excitement. I told her the names of the different prairie grasses and flowers, and the seasons in which they appeared. "You should see this in the spring, when cardinal flowers lap at the clumps of bluestem grass; it's like a sea on fire," I rhapsodized, forgetting time was running out for her. "I can see it," she said. My words were that vivid. Flattered, I described for her the martyred prairie dogs, poisoned, torched, gassed, drowned, or quartered by the government and military farmers, and the near-extinct black-footed ferret, whose main meal had been prairie-dog meat. We were silent for several miles. Then she said, "When are you going to write again?" I stopped the car, ran out into a field, and threw up in the snow. My mouth stank. I cleaned it with fresh snow. When I got back, McCabe was not in the car. The motor was running but the headlights were off. The Mauser was still in the back seat. McCabe was standing on the opposite side of the road, about fifty feet away, her back toward me. I grabbed the rifle and walked toward her. When I was about twenty feet away, I stopped, aimed the rifle at her, and called her name. She did not turn around. I called her again. She remained still. I cocked the rifle and called her a third time. She turned around and faced me. It started snowing again, softly. We were there for a long time, facing each other, until my shoulders hurt and I lowered the gun. She let me reach the car and wrap the gun in the blanket, before she started walking back and got inside. "I'm hungry," she said, as she shut her door.

On our drive back, McCabe mentioned that Constantinople had fallen to the Caliphate shortly before dawn, which was around midnight in Elmira. The city was in ruins. Its inhabitants slaughtered. The Emperor and the Patriarch, executed. All foreign military and civilians safely airlifted. Total war had begun worldwide. I did not believe her. I never could tell with McCabe's deadpan. Its flatness could hide many meanings, or none. Before she left, I had decided that she always meant what she said, literally. That's how much I had ended up trusting her. Driving now through the ghostly Great Prairie toward the glow on the horizon that was Elmira, I was both sure that she was lying and ashamed to doubt her. "What are you going to do now?" I said, just to break my shamed silence. I must have looked like a clown out on that field with my shoulders shaking under the weight of a World War I gun. At least the frisson of fear at McCabe's D.C. car registration was gone. That's what's good about shame. It wipes out everything else. "Nothing," McCabe answered. I stepped on the gas so I wouldn't have to talk. We flew through a red light at the entrance of Elmira. A Firecop car was soon on our tail. They pulled us over on a side street. Two Firecops got out. The younger one shone a flashlight on my face, then on my hands, which I kept visibly resting on the steering wheel. Even in lowly Elmira, hiding your hands from a Firecop could cost you your life. He swept the back with his flashlight, missing the Mauser on the floor under the blanket. The bullet in the chamber would have been hard to explain. The older Firecop shone his flashlight on the car plates, punching them into his tablet. He asked McCabe for her registration. He swiped it on his device, and the yellow light of the screen bathed his face while he read. Like Ezequiel, he moved his lips while reading. I was about to turn over my driver's license to the younger Firecop when the older one said sharply that it would not be necessary. He shut down his tablet, returned the license to McCabe, thanked her, touching the brim of his helmet with two fingers, and walked back to the patrol car, followed reluctantly by his younger partner. "It's Christmas," McCabe explained to me. She sat back, stretched her long legs, and crossed them at the ankles, as if getting ready for a long trip. Ten minutes later we were back inside the Judge's garage. McCabe went into the house without a glance at Rafael's blue sedan.

Rafael was now sleeping on his left side, his back toward the door. How easy it would be for a killer to walk into the room, stand where I was, and blow out his brains with, say, a Finnish Glock 17-Pro fitted with a silencer. They must have ways to bypass the alarm on the garage door. I returned the Mauser to the gun cabinet.

McCabe was sitting at the kitchen table. She asked that we eat in the kitchen, because it smelled so good. It was hard to say no to McCabe. She asked so humbly and was so happy when you said yes. After many trips back and forth, I managed to transfer the beautiful dining-table setting to the kitchen table. The venison was slightly overcooked on the edges, but otherwise excellent. The roasted potatoes were still firm. Lowering the thermostat in the dining room on our way out had kept the appetizers fresh. McCabe ate with relish the stuffed trout, the mushrooms vinaigrette, and the avocado slices; then she attacked the meat with both hands. She soon had that blissful look on her face which I had missed so much. It was almost like old times, except that there was no music. "Tell me a story instead," she said when I offered to put something on for her. "What about?" I said. "From your book." Fighting off nausea, I said, "I don't have a book in me." She had heard that expression before. It was an odd expression. As if a book was a bodily organ, or a virus, or a fetus. Was that true? "That's what they say, those who know about these things, those who have had books inside them, or knew someone who did," I said. I believed them. "But maybe some books were not inside people, but outside," she replied. Maybe others were not inside your body all the time, but came and went, slowly or suddenly. "People say lots of things that are not true," she said. "You too?" I jumped in, recklessly. "Yes," she said. "Me too." McCabe then dropped her head on her chest. I was afraid that she might begin to cry. I didn't want her to. She must not. Her grief would be unbearable, I tell her. She says it is unbearable for her, too. Stop it, then, I say. Use your willpower. I kneel in front of her, take her hands and kiss them. She lets me. They're big, raspy, dry, and repulsive to touch, like the skin of a stuffed reptile. Yet, the overall effect is one of rough beauty, in spite of the large knuckles. Grief makes McCabe quiet and still. It makes her close her eyes and surrender her naked hands. Now that her grief is overflowing, I realize that it has always been there. When she watched the birds, chopped wood, cleaned my feet, obsessively pruned the yellow rosebush, carried armloads of packages to the waiting FedEx truck, even when she or the former inhabitant of her skin boarded a blue sedan in the middle of the night: didn't that McCabe walk toward the car with hunched shoulders, her chin also buried in her chest? Open your eyes, I say, please, look at me. Her hands are cold. Are you ill? I say. Is she going to faint? Is she dying? Her hands are resting on her knees. I bury my face in her hands. They smell of venison, mushrooms, and, faintly, apples. I'm fine, she says. It's nothing. I've been driving for two days. Don't worry about me. When I look up, her eyes are open. She's looking at me, and through me, at the same time. Thanks, she says. I stand up. Sorry, I say. She puts her hands in her pockets. What about some music, she says, too brightly. Good idea, I say. In the Judge's studio I hesitate between the obvious, the trite, the strident, the maudlin. No music is good or bad enough for this moment. I would have chosen silence. But she wants music, for my sake, not hers. I choose pure joy, the saddest thing in the world. I return to the kitchen and the French horns announce the return of the briefly homesick American to Paris by night. McCabe is smoking a cigarette. Her head rests in her right hand. Her right elbow is propped on the kitchen table. She holds the cigarette with her left hand. She seems to be far away. I did not know that McCabe smoked. I stand on the threshold. "Do you like this music?" I say. "It sounds familiar," she says from that faraway place. "What is it?" I tell her. She turns around and sees the rifle in my hands, then she looks away. "What else can I do?" I say. "I don't know," she says, putting out her cigarette. I load the rifle and pull the trigger. I hear a scream, then a thud, then a gurgle. The rifle butt kicked me hard in the shoulder. A donkey-kick. Good shot. Right between the eyes. McCabe is on the floor, covered in blood, eyes and mouth wide open. Soundless. Frozen. Time stops. Then she howls like she's being skinned alive. Shows her teeth, bloody, too. Spits blood. Howls and howls and howls like a wolf. She is holding him in her arms. He looks small and dark. I saw him jump in front of her as I was pulling the trigger. I couldn't stop.

She howled and rocked him in her arms all night. I did not dare get near her. He was dead. What could I do? I cleaned the Mauser, inside and out, and put it back in the cabinet. The other bullet was still in my pocket. From the dining room, I kept watch on them. Waiting for her to fall asleep or quiet down, so I could pry him away.

Her, I could not comfort. She was suffering for the three of us. Me, I felt nothing. That's how great my grief was. Stuck in my inner freezer. I sat on the floor, too, wrapped in a blanket when it got too cold. It seemed indecent to sit on chairs. Her howling became almost a screech at one point, a growl at another, a murmur, wail, whimper, scream, cry. This was her native language. She was eloquent in it. I began to understand it. Animal sounds are coarser than words, but more moving. "Exalted and sanctified," she wailed. With her intestines, "May his salvation blossom." With her lungs, "Exalted and honored, elevated and lauded." With her stomach, growling, "In the world which will be renewed." Rafael could recite the Hail Mary backward, "thee with is Lord the, grace of full, Mary Hail." Rafael and I took our first communion together. His grandfather, Moisés, still alive in La Esperanza, did not get a picture. He was not supposed to know. He hates priesters, Rafael said. Ezequiel had been baptized in secret by his mother, "just in case," but had refused the First Communion. He did not know how to pray.

I must have dozed. How long, I don't know. It was less black outside, but not yet dawn. The house was silent. The kitchen lights were off. She was still sitting there, with him. Their shapes were visible in the dark-grey half-light. She was moving in place, jerking her elbows. Small movements. There were sounds, too, soft sounds. Could he be alive? I crawled to the threshold of the kitchen, for a better view. She was putting something in her mouth and tearing it with her teeth. It was his arm. I fled to the icehouse, wrapped in my blanket. In a corner, away from the pyre, I lit a small fire. My stomach wanted to vomit. I didn't. I won. In the morning, I returned to the house. All I could manage was a quick glance through the kitchen window. She was still sitting in the same spot. Chewing. His limbs and head had been ripped from the trunk. She was now pulling out his intestines.

I ate snow. It was my sedative. Several times that day I returned to the kitchen window. Each time I was able to watch a little longer. By nightfall, not much of his body was left. The last time I peeked she wasn't there. Neither was he. The stove and the table seemed to float in the grey twilight. A charcoal shadow was visible on the floor. She crossed in front of the window, barely missing me. From behind a tree, I saw her haul two heavy black garbage bags to the icehouse. Soon smoke was coming out through the icehouse roof. She tended the fire for a while before returning to the house. The lights went on in her bedroom. She drew the curtains across the windows. My feet were numb. I couldn't stay outdoors any longer. I was still afraid of her, but physical pain often trumps common sense, as any torture subject will confirm.

The kitchen stank like a slaughterhouse. A faint smell of bleach could not mask the stench of blood and feces. I barricaded myself in Rafael's room. I drank some of his orange juice. When that did not make me heave, I ate his saltine crackers. I have been on a saltine cracker diet ever since. It's all I can eat. He had left his wallet, keys, and wedding ring on the night table. Inside the wallet I found a picture of the three of us at a school picnic. I am lounging on the grass, with my head on Glorita's lap and my gaze sourly fixed on something to the side. She is leaning with her back against a tree trunk and looking straight at the camera. He is standing slightly behind her, looking at me. She is tanned and radiant in her yellow halter top, cutoffs and big hoop earrings. He and I are not as ugly as I remembered. We are just scrawny and tense. He is cross-eyed behind his cheap plastic eyeglasses. That is not visible in the picture, but I know. Four deep white creases show that the picture has been folded in his wallet for a long time. The date is 1976. We were not yet twelve.

I picked up his car keys with a tissue and stuck them in the blue sedan's ignition. The photo, the ring, and the other keys I hid behind the old furnace, along with his notebook, and Mrs. Crandall's scarf and Shangri-La logbook. They still must be there. His empty suitcase and his briefcase were gone. Had she also thrown them in the pyre? Wrapped in Mrs. Wilkerson's parka, I ventured to the icehouse shortly before sunrise. The pyre was still burning. It was now shorter, blacker, and wider. Only a charred bit of femur was visibly human. The rest of his remains must have been sandwiched in the middle of the pyre to ensure incineration. I added more wood to the pyre. The sun came out. Light vibrated in the dark-blue winter sky. A few fat robins sauntered on the holly branches. It was one of those perfect winter mornings that made my mother weep, so rare and splendid were they in this new land. For the past thirty-one hours, my mind had been empty of all thought or feeling. Fear, repulsion, cold, nausea, painful feet were all bodily reactions, like when you cut off a lizard's tail and it keeps jerking. All I knew was what I saw, heard, touched and smelled. Looking at the luminous sky I felt sorry for McCabe. Why had she done any of this? She had not killed him. I had. A warm and dense fluid filled me, clogging my nose. I couldn't breathe. Pity is entirely physical when you experience it for the first time so late in life. As I made my way back to the house and slowly up the stairs to McCabe's bedroom, fear and pity racked me, neither strong enough to dislodge the other. I stopped several times to catch my breath. Her door was slightly ajar. She was sitting by the window. Her hair was still wet from the shower. She was wearing jeans, grey socks, and her red plaid shirt. All clean. Her boots, shiny, were by the radiator. The flowers still looked fresh in their vases. The room smelled good. She must have burned her bloody clothes, I thought. McCabe turned her head toward me. "I'm sorry," I said and she nodded.

I saw the car as it crossed the Elmira Bridge. Long before it started coming up Round Hill. I knew immediately it was them. I ran upstairs to warn McCabe. We still had time to escape through the farmland in back. I hesitated in front of her door, my arm raised, about to knock. I can't remember exactly what went through my mind. It was such a long time ago. Maybe I thought her wealth would protect her. I do remember turning around, and hiding in the cellar. From there, I saw McCabe being taken out of the house with her arms handcuffed behind her back. Her head was covered in blood. They had beaten her up brutally, as they always do when they first get you. They would torture her. One State Security henchman kicked her in the back. She fell face down on the snow. Then all three kicked her and stomped on her until they fell on their knees, breathless and exhausted. No sound came out of her. They remained there for a few seconds, kneeling around the majestic fallen figure as in adoration. Then they slowly dragged her to their car, leaving a red trail in the snow.

The house was searched many times over the next few weeks. They never found me. The closest they got was when one of them shone a light under the Judge's bed. I flattened myself inside a crack. What's that thing?" he said.

ABOUT THE AUTHOR

ANA SIMO is the author of a dozen plays, a short feature film, and countless articles. A New Yorker most of her life, she was born and raised in Cuba. Forced to leave the island during the political/homophobic witch-hunts of the late 1960s, she first immigrated to France, where she studied with Roland Barthes and participated in early women's and gay/lesbian rights groups. In New York next, she co-founded Medusa's Revenge theatre, the direct action group the Lesbian Avengers, the national cable program Dyke TV, and the groundbreaking *The Gully online magazine*, offering queer views on everything. *Heartland* is her first novel.

RESTLESS BOOKS is an independent, nonprofit publisher devoted to championing essential voices from around the world, whose stories speak to us across linguistic and cultural borders. We seek extraordinary international literature that feeds our restlessness: our hunger for new perspectives, passion for other cultures and languages, and eagerness to explore beyond the confines of the familiar. Our books—fiction, narrative nonfiction, journalism, memoirs, travel writing, and young people's literature—offer readers an expanded understanding of a changing world.

Visit us at www.restlessbooks.com.